Winds of Change

Short stories about our climate

About time some serious writers and artists engaged with
the biggest issue of our time—maybe all time. These stories
show that engagement fully underway!

-Bill McKibben, founder 350.org

Foreword

The realities of global warming and the decimation of the environment have eroded the parameters of time and space, and have turned the human psyche upside-down. The painful truth of the destruction brought on by the human race has jangled our nerves and imagination. We have pushed ourselves beyond our comfort zone to a nightmare world of broken dreams. We know what the future is like because the future is now.

Science fiction is now a love story; a love story is now a political satire. The environment is inside and outside of us all, and there is suffering and confusion. As a result, poets, writers, and artists of every discipline have begun a powerful and unceasing global analysis of what the world is, and what it will be like, for our children, as everything we thought we knew about our planet Earth has been compromised and set adrift.

Winds of Change is a historic document born out of a short story contest held in conjunction with 100 Thousand Poets (Authors) for Change. The purpose of this global event is to amplify the movement of poets and writers—and all artists who hope, through their actions and events—to seize and redirect the political and social dialogue of the day, and turn the narrative of civilization towards peace and sustainability. Change is in the air.

The more I read this anthology, the more I understand the raw essentiality of this movement. We have seen quite a few anthologies of poetry spring up since the birth of 100TPC in 2011, but this is the first anthology specifically focused on issues of sustainability and the first to call out to fiction writers to join the discussion. Some say that poetry, art, writing, and music aren't supposed to make a change—that they can't make a change. They say they like to "keep their poetry and their politics separate." They like to quote Auden's "In Memory of W.B. Yeats," singling out the line "poetry makes nothing happen." (Read "fiction makes nothing happen.") But, by my understanding, Auden's words run deeper and stronger and are more essential than a chastisement of mixing your art and politics. In fact, for me, Auden suggests the opposite by context. Art belongs to civilization, and what we deliver from the imagination transposes and unearths our understanding of who we are and what we do as humans. Civilization is the platform for these creative works of change. The moment we say "poetry makes nothing happen," something indeed happens.

We follow *Winds of Change*, and we search for understanding and direction. The writers in this great collection offer us hope against the fear that we have gone too far in our experiment of destruction. There is beauty here. Change is coming. Let us begin anew!

-Michael Rothenberg, founder of 100,000 Poets for Change (100TPC)

Introduction

Stephen Siperstein, who contributed poems to this anthology, wrote in an essay he submitted to Eco-fiction.com that many do not give climate change a thought and that there is rampant denialism, skepticism, and "climato-quietism" (Bruno Latour's term for that laid-back attitude that somehow, without us acting, things will take care of themselves). According to Stephen, "This is the 'new normal' of our cognitive and affective lives, and for us to figure it all out, we need help. We need guides and maps. We need emotional resources. In short, we need the literary and cultural arts." Bill McKibben preceded this idea in *Grist*, back in April 2005: "What the warming world needs now is art, sweet art."

Thankfully, writers and artists have been giving us this sweet art, and they've helped to usher in what author James Schaefer (*Two Houses of Oikos*) calls the "Age of the Environment." The broad category of eco-fiction has been around for a long time, but now climate change—the most unprecedented risk to our planet—has inspired an increasing number of related stories. Margaret Atwood calls climate change "the everything change," and Naomi Klein tells us that "this changes everything." It makes sense that climate themes permeate all genres of fiction as well.

Modern authors join a famous lineage of storytellers dating all the way back to the Bible and *The Epic of Gilgamesh* in writing *our story* as it relates to nature—deluge being a common motif among climate themes, for example. Science fiction authors pioneered climate change fiction; the earliest speculators were such authors as J.G. Ballard, Fritz Leiber, and John Christopher. In 1977, Arthur Herzog penned *Heat*, one of the first modern novels about anthropogenic global warming. I talked with his widow Leslie (see Eco-fiction.com), who told me that her late husband had interviewed scientists at NASA, NOAA, the Smithsonian, and several other institutions to understand climate change theories and models.

Today's authors join their predecessors in dealing with environmental uncertainties. There are even specific genres that encapsulate climate change, such as solarpunk, climate fiction, and Anthropocene fiction. Regardless of what you want to call this fiction, it's happening in spades. As curator at Eco-fiction.com, I ran a short story contest in the summer of 2014, with the topic of climate change. Writers from all over the world sent in submissions—and that's how this anthology came to be.

When reading these fiction submissions, which are based upon the very real science of climate change, I noticed that the stories reflected not just dystopian or apocalyptic scenarios but hope. Often *we* are the antagonist, but redemption transforms us into the protagonist and therein lies the big twist. Despite the dismal forecast for how climate change will continue to affect us and all other species on the planet, the strongest stories seem to happen when we "feed the good wolf"—when we look up, face our mistakes, apologize for them, and fix them…when we do what's right. And what's right, in this case, is also becoming *what's cool!*

Looking around me, I see organizations striving to end world hunger and poverty, First Nations fighting pipelines and supertankers, policy shifts that give everyone equal rights, the pope calling for climate action, 17 United Nations goals to make the world fair and sustainable, celebrities calling for an end to wolf killing and bear hunts, and a rising number of novels and films extolling a greener world. The concept of solarpunk is also a positive for literature; it's not just a fiction genre but a hopeful aesthetic. I tease about it here, because I hope to hold another writing contest in the future dealing with solarpunk. I interviewed one of its stewards, Adam Flynn, who said:

"As billions of people in the developing world begin the rise out of poverty, they are looking for a vision of the 'good life', and unfortunately the current vision tends to involve fast food, large cars, big houses, and conspicuous consumption. Sustainability at scale means renewable energy, reusable infrastructure, an end to throwaway culture, room for human dignity, and the possibility for continued flourishing (although perhaps in different ways than how we define it currently).

If cyberpunk was 'here is this future that we see coming and we don't like it', and steampunk is 'here's yesterday's future that we wish we had', then solarpunk might be 'here's a future that we can want and we might actually be able to get.'"

I am honored to present this anthology as a collection of that sweet art that makes us think and gives us hope. I wish to thank all of the authors who participated, Bill McKibben for his kind thumbs-up, and Michael Rothenberg and Terri Carrion for founding 100,000 Poets for Change, which helped Eco-fiction.com host the contest. Both Michael and Terri, along with hundreds of thousands of us, believe in the power of art forms (dance, music, poetry, fiction) to shape peace and sustainability around the world.

The best selections from last summer's contest, along with two extra short stories and two poetry sections, are included within these pages. The winner of the writing contest was Robert Sassor, Director at Metropolitan Group, a leading social change agency and one of B Lab's 100 "best for the world" corporations.

The generous authors have agreed to donate 15% of book sales to 350.org.

-Mary Woodbury, Owner, Moon Willow Press and Curator, Eco-fiction.com

Part 1. Short Stories

First Light, Robert Russell Sassor
Contest winner

The medical machines whir. *Machines of love and grace* you called them when your father was here. I remember you sketching in the corner. I thought you were doing portraits of your father, but no; it was the machines you were after. You didn't want to share your work with me then, either.

I speak to you now so that you will hear my voice. I know that you can hear me. I recount to you some of my favorite memories, retold the way that I want you to take them with you. Like how, as a young boy, you'd insist on going to the university with me when I had to work late; and you'd ask me profound questions, the way young people do. You'd ask where all the ice came from, and I'd tell you about how water came to the earth from ice asteroids—and just the right amount for our planet to have the water and climate needed for life.

You loved that stuff.

You'd ask about whether it was true that all things are related, even the ravens and the jellyfish and the narwhals. You always loved narwhals.

I found myself telling you about that singular miracle: RNA, the fact that molecules went from merely being to self-replicating, and no one knows how or why. Your father thought these conversations were too advanced for you, but I knew better. I explained how RNA had sparked this chain reaction that separates our planet from the wastelands we observe in space.

The Wasteland. I remember reading this with you for your homework. "I will show you fear in a handful of dust."

Stardust.

We are all stardust—Joni Mitchell.

We are all fear.

I remember the time you asked about electricity. I was out of my depth, but I told you about how there is electricity in our brains. And how, every time we think, we are helping to realize the notion of entropy: turning order (nutrients) into chaos (heat and energy).

And here you are.

The doctor says that an electrical current continues to run along your brainstem. It's how I know that there is still a fragment of you with me, that you can hear me.

It is something, a miracle. My son, the miracle.

I stare into your eyes, bright as a marlin.

The doctor enters; I don't turn my head away from you. I don't want to know that he is there. He puts a hand on my shoulder.

"I may have asked this before ... but, does he have a denomination? Is there someone we should send for?"

"Dean is on his way…" I realize what I said, having accompanied your father on trips like this when he was the pastor. "Mark, Mark Gibbons, from our old church. He's on his way."

"Did you have any questions about the paperwork?"

I shake my head no.

I can't look up.

I can't make eye contact.

I just keep looking at you, my back to the door—to the world—needing you, this moment, for us to share. I hear a nurse enter, her shoes squeaking on the floor, disrupting how I need this moment to be. She puts her hand on my back.

"I remember him," she says. "He was so handsome." I don't respond. I despise her use of the past tense.

I want to run my hands through your hair, but they have shaved it. Your face is partially covered by bandages. I want to hear you breathe. I've realized too late that this is my favorite sound: the sound of you breathing. The gentle whiz as you'd inhale in your sleep. I can still hear your labored exhale as I sat-up with you when you were sick. Now, the machines breathe for you.

"I love you, my sweet," I say, my face twitching. "I am so sorry."

I can't even remember your last words. I wish that I had said something profound to make you stay. But I was tired. I was at the sink, decompressing. I wasn't paying attention.

And now, here we are. I wrap my hands around one of yours, wanting to hold it forever and wanting you to hold mine back. If I don't move, maybe this moment will never end. Maybe I can stay here, and find my way back to two days ago, to three years ago—remain connected to a past with you, forestalling a future without you.

People come and go. Mark arrives and says a prayer, holding your other hand. Who is he to hold your hand at this time?

I wrap my arms around you, wanting this to be the last thing you feel—this love, all the love I have. As the machines unwind, there is silence. There is only the presence of you. I hold my breath, watching the color change in your eye, the hue shift in your skin, until I am truly alone—the last remaining strand of our family, dangling there, in the wind.

* * *

As I drive out of Juneau toward home, Mendenhall glacier witnesses my passing like so many times before. It was one of your favorite places. I remember sitting there with you when you were young, watching the aurora as its light reflected off the glacier, off the lake and the ice flank of the mountains beyond. It was the closest I had felt to heaven.

I remember talking with you about Pleiades—your favorite constellation. And I explained how the light we saw from it had traveled over hundreds of trillions of miles, passing stars and planets as it went, maybe shining through nebulae and past pulsars and around black holes—some of that light ending its life in your eyes, and others ending its life in mine.

The amazing thing is that, to the light beams, their whole journey happens instantaneously. There is no time at the speed of light. I explained that to the light beams, time began at the center of a massive star and ended in our eyes in a single instant. We were peering at an ancient time, and yet, at another scale, there is no time—there is only you and me and the stars that shined down on us.

You sat silently. You were such a thinker, even then. I wrapped my arm around you and you hugged into me.

That time: that moment. In the life of a light beam, it is happening now. I am there, in that moment. I will always be there with you.

* * *

I sit and look out the back window toward the mountain, filled with numbness. Artifice has been stripped from the world. On the radio, I hear stories about people defined by what they are against instead of what they are for. All of the talking, the incessant noise in the world. The disrespect and disregard for human life, the xenophobia and negativity advanced by those we give megaphones to. I shut the radio off.

I hear an unfamiliar knock at the door. I know I look terrible; I haven't showered, and I've been wearing this sweatshirt for two days. I hope it's Val, who hasn't returned yet from her cruise and who I'm anxious to see. Instead, I open the door to find Lucy. Her smile showing so much wisdom for her age. We hug, and I see that she's brought the newspapers in from the yard.

"I hope you don't mind … I wanted to stop by. Mom made some roast beef for you … she asked me to get some bread, which I completely forgot." She smiles, so pretty, handing me the dish. "I hope you have some already?"

"I do, thank you. That was very thoughtful of your mother." After all this time, I don't even know her mother's name. "Please send my thanks." A cold wind blows in through the door. "Come in."

"Actually, I was hoping that I could take you into town. There's something I want to show you, if you're up to it." Her eyes are pleading.

"What is it?"

"It's a little something they've pulled together at the high school. It just kind of sprung up. And … I didn't want it all to happen without you getting a chance to see it."

I grab my jacket and get into her old beat-up truck, the same one I've seen her drive by the house in many times—always wanting her to stop by to spend time with you. I wanted the two of you to be closer. I'm pretty sure I made clear my desire that you ask her out. I always thought she'd be so good for you. Now I see how unhelpful that must have been.

We take Egan Drive toward town as the sun sets and ignites the mountains across the channel. On this desolate road, it's almost as though we are the only people left on earth. I often had that feeling here with you.

The road curves as we approach town, and Lucy slows around a bend. Ahead, I see an illuminated arc: candles—maybe hundreds of them—flickering inside the glass-enclosed skyway that connects the high school with its parking lot.

"Who organized this?" I ask.

"I don't think anyone did. I think it was spontaneous." She parks and turns to look at me, giving me permission to explore on my own terms.

I start to ascend the staircase. Paper bags with candles lead the way to the sky bridge, which is lined with candles and cards, stuffed teddy bears, a few roses. I pick up some of the cards.

"People have been posting a lot of things online, too," Lucy says. "Not sure if you've seen that. I was thinking, if you'd like, I could email some of them to you. Maybe keep a file?"

I smile by way of a response. As I reach the top of the stairs, the candlelight overtakes the dusk. There are students at the end of the passageway reading some of the notes. Did you know them? Were they nice to you?

There is a poster that appears to have been put together by an art class. A large picture of you is in the middle with notes written all around it. It's a picture I've never seen of you before. I realize the treasure trove before me: images of you that I might otherwise have never seen.

"I've been thinking," Lucy says quietly, "about all of the artwork that Jacob left behind. What if we held some sort of retrospective? I'm sure the JAC would let us use their center, or we could do it here at the high school. It's just a thought. I mean, I always thought his work should have been showcased more. I thought it'd be nice for people to see what they've been missing out on all this time."

My gaze wanders outside, past the candlelight, into the growing darkness. It never occurred to me that there would be this kind of outpouring for you from the students here. In my peripheral vision, I see Mr. Jefferies, the school counselor you despised. He sees me, and doesn't approach.

"I'd have to give that some thought," I say. Your work: it is so personal. And some of it, well, I'm not sure the community deserves to see that side of you, to know you in that way.

Lucy puts an arm around my waist. She is so young yet so free, so able to express what she feels. She reminds me of myself when I was young. It's strange, being jealous of someone so much younger.

"He was loved," she says, meaning it.

"Can I ... keep these things, when it's done?"

She glances over to Mr. Jeffries. "Yeah. I'm sure they're planning on that, but I'll ask, just to be safe."

"Thank you for bringing me here."

She looks at me with so much earnestness. "We were lucky to know him. Those of us who really knew him, we were so lucky."

The emotion swells in my throat. I nod my head slowly and wonder: how many of these people really knew you? And moreover, did I?

* * *

I find myself waiting at the kitchen window, watching the snow fall. Last night, it snowed hard, coating the leeward face of the trees and accentuating their imperfect, non-perpendicular lines.

I never really knew how much Val meant to me until your father died. She was always my rock, in addition to you. I make busy work at the sink, knowing she should arrive soon. I imagine that I see her car in my peripheral vision, and am disappointed to look up and see only empty road. When her silver car approaches, I grab my jacket. We meet in the drive and embrace for I don't know how long.

She sits with me as I recount everything that's happened. She listens with one hand on my knee and the other occasionally wiping the tears from my face. She grabs me tissues when I need them. I don't know how much time passes, but I find myself exhausted, unable to go on.

She changes the sheets on my bed and lets fresh air in—I feel adolescent, convalescent.

"Can I get you out of the house tomorrow?" she asks. "I thought I'd take you to the lake, we can go for a walk."

"Actually, if you don't mind, there's someplace I've been wanting to share with you."

She looks at me, perplexed. "You're on. Now get some sleep. I'll stop by tomorrow."

* * *

The car passes noiselessly over gravel frozen in place and time. I point Val to an imperceptible track leading to the old soap factory, and she turns off Wire Gate Road to follow it. We pull up in front of a tall, concrete building set against the mountains outside of Juneau. Its roof is long gone. What few windows it had had are now empty cavities from which life, sprouting from within, reaches out for the sunlight.

I see now, in a new way, what you saw in this place. You thought I didn't know what you were up to over here, but of course I did.

"What was Jacob doing all the way out here?" Val asks, stepping toward the doorway.

"Fine-tuning his craft, being defiant..."

I watch as she steps through the door, hands in her pockets, and surveys the room—taking it all in as though she had walked into a museum. I follow her inside, becoming enwrapped in your graffiti-style art that adorns every surface. An ecosystem of thoughts and images that interconnect to tell the story of a life I'm still trying so hard to understand.

"These were Jacob's?" she asks, half-whispering. I nod. She looks at me in awe. "I had no idea," she says. "I feel terrible saying this, but all this time, I underestimated him."

I see a work I'd never seen before: a series of icebergs in black and white with hints of light blue. Their style is almost like a watercolor, with the bergs' outlines reflected on whitecaps of a charcoal sea. Below, you wrote: "God will sip them like little drops of dew when it is time. — William Stafford." Where did you read this? Was this from one of your father's books?

I hear Val breathe deeply. "Is this…?" she starts, seeing the portrait of me on a nearby wall. I join her.

"Yes," I say.

If she understands the meaning of the piece, she gives no indication. "The technical detail..." she says, but doesn't finish her thought.

The meaning is clear to me. You painted my visage as a mountain face with crosshatched lines—the types of crevices where water seeps and freezes, shattering the rock and sending it cascading below. There is one such rock scree tumbling from the side of my cheek. And at its base, you painted a tiny version of yourself along with our dog at the time, Mercury, looking up as falling pieces of me were about to devour you both.

My face flushes. I shouldn't have brought Val here. Then she looks at me, her face full of compassion. She holds my arm and turns around to decipher a new wall. "I didn't know he was so interested in the environment," she says. "I knew he cared about social issues, developing nations and such. I guess I didn't know about this other side of him, did you?"

I don't know how to respond. The truth is, some of your themes take me by surprise as well.

We stare at a painting of an Inuit man under the ice, surrounded by jellies and constellations of tiny lights. The whole painting is blues and grays and beautiful. The hunter seems to be about to throw a spear underwater, legs and arms outstretched like a dancer. "I remember talking with Jacob about climate change," I say, "about how Inuit hunters on Baffin Island are falling through the ice on their way to traditional hunting grounds. It's getting warmer there, and the ice is too thin—people are dying while trying to provide for their families."

Val looks at me, surprised. "Is that what inspired this?"

I shrug. "I'm just trying to tie the pieces together."

One piece that stands out is of a bird. I figure it's a cormorant. You painted a silhouette of it airing its wings—looking remarkably like a crucifix, with oil dripping from its body against a bright, orange sky. It is a simple piece compared to some of the others, but it makes me think about the sacrifices made at the hands of our folly.

I see Val look over at the large self-portrait you'd painted nearby. I don't think it registers with her, but I recognize the image as being of you, or rather, how you might look if you were blond, if you were female.

"She's pretty. Who is she?"

I shrug. But I recognize the eyes. "Val, I don't know how to say this ... and I don't know why I'm telling you, other than that I have to talk to someone. I never thought I was a perfect mother, but it's so easy for me to see now just how much I failed Jacob. There were things he needed me to understand, without having to ask me to, that I never really got. That I'm still processing, still making sense of..."

"Honey, what is it?"

I compose myself. I am still not comfortable telling her, letting her in on your secret. Not yet. "The truth is, I knew Jacob was unhappy. And I'm sure I tried to help, in my way. But, and this is the part I can't stop thinking about." I take a deep breath. "The gun safe, in the garage. I knew it was unlocked." I look into her eyes, wanting her to grasp the meaning.

"What?"

"I never knew the combination. It's been unlocked since Dean died. I had a son who was suffering from depression, who was bullied at school. I had a gun safe at home that was unlocked. I never put the pieces together." Val hugs into me from the side. "It should be him standing here, not me..."

Val closes her hold on me, completing the embrace. "Honey. Honey. Hold on. Jacob was unhappy, and that wasn't your fault. Jerry and I, we knew that Jacob was unhappy, too. But none of us ever fathomed that these thoughts could have been crossing his mind." She pauses. "Jerry and I keep asking ourselves: how could we have seen this coming? What could we have done differently? It's natural to ask these questions. But Bee, you were doing the best that you could do. We all were." She is so strong. I never see her cry, not even now. "You gave him so much love. But sometimes ... sometimes the need is too great. The need is more than anybody can fill." She gently rocks me, as if I were young. My nose runs onto her jacket. The mountain of my sorrow unfurls, cascading all around us. "It's not your fault, honey. It's none of our faults."

After a while, she steps back, holding my arms. "Jerry and I have been thinking. Why don't you come stay with us for a while? Get you out of that house. What do you think?"

It's such a kind offer, but it's not what I want. I don't want to be separated from the remembrances of you: the dirty mug in your room, the laundry of yours, still undone. Before I can answer, I am lost again in my thoughts, staring up at the sky, watching as wisps of clouds pass overhead at a clip.

"Thank you for bringing me here," she says. "I'd like to show Jerry someday. I'd like to come back and take it all in." Her eyes are clear and stare right through me. "Shall we head back? Are you hungry? Can I buy you dinner?"

I shake my head no. I haven't been hungry in days. "Would you take me past the observatory on the way home?" I ask.

She smiles. I wipe my nose on my sleeve, and she takes my arm as we walk back to the car.

* * *

The lock is frozen and I have a hard time getting the key to turn.

"I don't know why Jerry doesn't replace that thing. You need WD-40? I might have some in the car," Val offers.

With force, I pry the door open.

"No woman's as strong as a Juneau woman," she says.

"Except maybe a Sitka one…"

The observatory is a train car retrofitted with a couple of rooms inside, and a long door through which the 17- and 12-inch telescopes are wheeled out whenever there's a soul who wants to see the stars. I came here to pick up the rock that you once gave me. Remember? You cracked open the ice and reached into the running water to pluck this stone for me: deep green with copper flecks. Whenever things would get difficult, particularly when your father was ill, I'd worry this stone between my fingers. It would always remind me of a more simple time. A time so full of joy and mystery and love.

I lock the office door behind me and see Val eyeing the 17-inch reflecting telescope that Jerry had built. He made it one mirror at a time as the funds came together. He even handcrafted its wooden swivel mount. "I remember the night we christened this," she says. "What was Jacob's favorite star again?"

"Pleiades."

"Pleiades, that's right. Which is why Jerry picked it as the first thing to point the telescope at, to see if the whole contraption—all that time, all that effort—worked."

"*First light,* he called it."

"Right. I remember Jerry turning to me, in his understated, English way, and saying, 'There it is.' God, I was so relieved," she says.

I realize that's what you were to me: my first light—the ray that tested me, gave me the chance to fulfill my role in the cosmos.

"Any other errands? Grocery store? I'm here to be helpful."

"That's kind of you." I rub the rock between my fingers. The idea of running errands seems so banal. There is nothing left in the world that I need. "I think I'll head home. I have arrangements to make."

Val scrunches her lips, revealing lines that are among the few indicators of her real age. As we head out, the heavy metal door slams behind us. I reach out to hand the keys to Val.

"Give these to Jerry, will you? I don't think I'll be coming here for a while."

"That's nonsense. He won't accept the keys, and he wouldn't forgive me if I did. Hang onto these. He needs you here; he's too old for this stuff."

As she drives me home, I feel the glacier looming at my side again. The sun has set, and the sky is uncharacteristically clear. I see a flash of green in the upper atmosphere, cosmic rays dancing with the oxygen high above. I want so badly for Val to turn onto Mendenhall Loop so that we can watch the aurora at the glacier. But she doesn't notice and steers us forward.

I close my eyes, feeling the contours of the stone from you in my hand. I imagine you there, at the glacier, bundled up and watching the lights with childlike wonder—marveling that we live in a world with so much beauty.

Stay there, my sweet, hold that moment. In the life of a light beam, I am there with you.

How Close to Savage the Soul, John Atcheson
Honorable mention

The aromas hit him like a fist, poised there over five decades, waiting until now, triggered by this foolish trip.

Fresh and fertile, seaweedy and salty, they ignited electric jolts from somewhere deep inside his soul, firing off images, conjuring up a thousand snapshots covering his long life. Like coming home again, he thought. But now he noticed another odor, an overlay—fetid and coppery—the smell of death?

"Is this how you remember it, Grandpa?"

What was he supposed to say? As the memories flooded back, he flipped through them like catalogue cards, searching for the right words. No, not catalogue cards you old geezer—Google listings.

"Not exactly." He felt the little hand in his, soft in that way little kid flesh is, against his own, gnarled, age-worn, and arthritic. It reminded him of another little hand from a long time ago. No, don't start …

In truth, it was far from how he remembered it, and so he let the memories march past while he searched for the right answer. The whole month of August, every year from as early as he could remember. From the time he was younger than little Will here. Corking waves in his father's safe arms, riding up one side of the swells out past where they broke, then down the other, buoyant in the salt water. Now, no one even knew what corking was.

Later, he and his brothers would ride the waves, first body surfing, then with rubber rafts, and finally with surf boards.

Much later, he'd come here with his own child. At least for a while.

So much time, then. Time for life. Time for mistakes. Time for corrections. Time to right wrongs.

29

But it goes. It goes. Is that what he should say? Tell him how it goes, disappearing more quickly with each year? How it tricks you so at the end; it seems to vanish all at once, like the last suck of water down a drain? How he could feel that last inexorable tug on him even now?

No. We've already given him enough of a bummer. Maybe happy stuff. Like first love.

There had been several dunes over to the left where the boardwalk ended. In a cleft between them, sheltered from the crowds, he'd made love for the first time with a local girl he'd known since they were both kids, kissing and caressing until they both thought they'd explode and then finally, stripping off their clothes, heedless of the gritty sand in that way that only adolescents could be. What year was that? 1996?

He smiled to himself. No. Not exactly fodder for a six year old.

"We used to ride those waves, Will." He let go of the hand, kneeled down beside the boy, and pointed out at the breakers rolling in. "Me and your great-uncle Hank."

The boy's eyebrows shot up. "Really?"

"Yup. We were good, too."

"Can we do that?"

Again, what to say? "Maybe later, buddy."

The little boy cast his eyes downward but said nothing. A generation used to disappointment, the old man thought.

He took the little boy's hand. "C'mon. We have to get going."

"Can't we stay a little longer, Grandpa?"

The old man eyed the waves and listened. He loved the sounds. Rushing in, building, like the wind shushing through trees before a storm, ebbing out and poising in silence, before building once again. He hated to disappoint the boy. Maybe a little while longer.

"OK. Let's sit down." He guided the boy over to a bench near the end of the boardwalk, and they sat together, silently, watching the surf build, listening to the sounds intensify. It was a clear day, hot, as usual, and the perspiration beaded up around his eyes, stinging them before dripping down and rolling across his cheeks. He checked the boy. His face was flushed, and he'd stopped sweating. Bad sign. Dammit, gotta watch that. He took a bottle of water out of the small pack he carried and handed it to the boy, who took it greedily and started gulping it down. "Easy. Save some for later."

He checked the surf, then, satisfied, he turned back to the boy. "You OK?"

The boy smiled and nodded. "I bet it would feel good to go into the water."

"Not right now."

"Later, right?"

"We'll see, buddy." Again the downcast eyes, but the disappointment was greater this time. He had to say something. His heart ached, knowing how much more the boy would face by the time he was old enough to have memories. "When I was about your age, we were down here for a month and we couldn't go in the water once."

"Why?"

"Hurricanes. There were three that August, and the waves were …" He didn't finish. No sense risking raising questions he couldn't answer—or wouldn't. 1985. Five years old, and he'd watched as the surf roiled and broiled, and the skies leadened, and the winds howled, and the air itself shook, taking on colors he hadn't seen until ... well until the last decade or so ago.

Another memory—his son, about this age, here on the Outer Banks, another August. Must have been 2016. A vicious undertow was keeping everyone out of the water, even though it was a typical sunny August afternoon. Red flags snapped in the breeze, and the lifeguard stands were

"Just a minute more. Please?"

The old man looked into Will's eyes, his heart breaking. When did he develop this tenderness? He would have thought it weakness in his forties and fifties. Different things mattered then. Money. Wealth. Success. Power. And he'd gotten his share of each, building his own company—small by Wall Street standards—but big enough that it had made him a wealthy man.

The boy's gaze remained riveted on him, silently pleading. Maybe another few minutes would be OK. The electricity was off again, so the damn cottage would be 100 degrees anyway. "OK, sport. A few more minutes. But then we really have to go."

The boy's eyes lit up like high beams, and he said, "Thanks, Grandpa," while he squirmed with joy beside him. Jesus. How little it takes to kindle joy, these days. Poor kid.

Yeah, pay attention to the warning signs … Time. Time enough back then. Time enough to believe we'd learn. To believe in change. To believe in corrections. But it goes. It goes.

He eyed the water and checked his surroundings. A few more minutes. No more. But then, there was no real refuge, anyway, so maybe staying was no different than going. Back there things were dangerous, too. Different dangers, but dangerous all the same. So maybe the best you could do is pick your threat. He looked over at the boy. He'd gotten up and walked to the edge of the boardwalk, eyeing the sea with naked desire. He was moving in that way kids do, twitching with energy and enthusiasm, so that he seemed all over the place, as if he were dancing to music only he could hear.

"Careful, Will." The boy seemed to fold, and the old man felt like he'd thrown a wet blanket over him. Shit, still not over it.

But kids don't stay down. Presently, he twirled around and said, "Can we go fishing?"

Fishing. It had been years since he'd seen anyone catch anything. Dead seas. Again, what to say?

The old man froze. Beneath the sounds of the sea, from back in the alleys between the main drag and the boardwalk, he heard a now-familiar cacophony—the mindless rumbling of the new apex predator. He reached down into his pack and pulled out his Glock, checking to be sure there was a clip in it. The boy saw it and knew what to do without any words passing between them. He hopped off the boardwalk and got down onto the sand and ducked. The old man crawled down beside him, unwinding his balky joints with as much speed as possible. He eyed the sea licking at their heels now, gauging their time, then waited, listening. The surf was louder down here but he could still hear the encroaching sounds from above—curses, joyless cackles, occasional shouts and pistol shots—advancing toward them.

He'd thought they'd be safe. Even the gangs stayed off the Outer Banks these days. The place had been picked clean for a decade, now; the tides regularly overran all but the highest areas, and the storms ravaged those. On the way in, he'd stopped at several grocery stores, hoping to find some bottled water, but he knew as soon as he'd arrived he wouldn't find anything. Derelict cars lined the road, their hoods up in silent screams. Store windows were secured with graffiti-covered plywood, and the streets were covered with the detritus of lootings long past.

Funny what he found in the grocery stores. Anything canned was gone. Freezers and refrigerators were smashed in, their shelves empty. Meat cases were empty. The little pharmacies had been looted. But in the sundry aisles, shampoos, rinses and deodorants, and such still lined the shelves in orderly rows. The only thing missing here was hairspray. The gangs used them to fuel crude cannons made of PVC pipes. Potato guns, he'd called them as a kid. Back in the city, the hiss of burning hairspray often preceded the smash of glass late at night. Back there, riot squads still patrolled the streets and a few grocery stores remained open and moderately well-stocked. At least in the wealthy areas. Here? The whole place was a ghost town. A ghost coast.

Now, Will's enthusiasm for swimming was giving way to fear, as he felt the water tugging at him. The old man could see it in his eyes.

Down here, close to the source, that overlay the old man had first detected—the aroma of death and dying—was stronger, permeating everything. It was the pH, he knew. Acid. They'd turned the oceans from a font of life to an acidic crypt.

Jesus. Leave, assholes. Get the fuck out of here.

Across the boardwalk, the argument raged, as people took sides. A voice—deep and guttural—"I say we stay. We wouldn't get back until after dark."

A second voice, "Afraid of the dark, pussy."

A shot rang out, and the boy flinched and let out a scream. The man froze, waiting. Had they heard? The water seemed to be racing in, now. It covered the boy's knees and reached above his own ankles, so they couldn't crawl under the boardwalk. He readied his gun, keeping it dry, and held onto the boy, again feeling him quivering as he tried to melt into his side. There'd been silence since the shot. The old man realized he'd been holding his breath again, and he let it out, slowly, trying to ease the pressure and pain growing in his chest.

Finally, the alpha's voice reached them. "Anyone else want to second-guess me?" There was a lot of indistinguishable babble—the universal sound of impotent grousing, and the alpha said, "Alright. Let's go. Unless some of you want to stay with Buck." Another shot rang out, and he laughed.

Beside him, the old man had felt the boy flinch at the sound of the pistol. The killer bees ebbed again as they headed away. "A few more minutes yet, OK, Will?"

The boy nodded. The old man studied his eyes and saw that the hollowness had returned. Too much. Too much for a little boy. Not fair. Probably some form of PTSD. The nightmares would be back, now. Brave New World.

By the time they climbed back up to the boardwalk, the water had reached the boy's waist and had covered his own knees. In the heat it felt good. Cooling. But he knew it was likely a toxic brew. Bad juju, algal blooms, and anaerobic stews dominated these days. So he got them out as soon as he thought it was safe.

When they were settled, he put his arms around the boy's shoulders. "Well, you could say we got our swim, huh, bud?"

"Yeah."

One word, no smile. Bad. He had to get him to engage, and quickly. The more time he spent in this state the harder it would be. He thought about the time he'd rescued Tim. Reassurance. That's what he needed.

"It's going to be all right, Will. We're going to be fine."

The boy nodded. The hollowness still inhabited his eyes.

"It will. I promise." But as he said it, he felt the pain and pressure clutch at his chest again, threatening to overwhelm him. It radiated out to his shoulder and arm, and he reached into the pack for his pills. Intense now. Very intense. He had the bottle, but he hurt too much to open it. "Can … you … get me one."

The boy took the bottle and shook out one pill. Using his right arm, the old man took it and let it dissolve under his tongue, then waited for the pain to lessen, and his breathing to return to normal. The emptiness of his promise was reflected back at him through Will's eyes. It wasn't going to be OK. Ever. That world was gone, now.

There was one thing he had to do. One thing he had to tell the boy. He had a right to know. And time was slipping away.

Struggling against the pain, he said, "We didn't know." But he knew it was a lie, and it was too late for lies. "We knew. We didn't want to know, but we knew. We thought … we thought there was time." But that was a lie too, and so as the pain and pressure built he said, "I'm sorry. So Sorry." Pain crushing now. Black spots appearing before his eyes, blending together, mixing with the pain … He had to say something to make the boy feel better. "It'll be all right. Promise." The world before him was black now, and he knew that was another lie. It wouldn't be all right.

He slumped on the bench, aware it was too late. Too late for corrections. Too late for anything. His last thought, it goes.

The boy still sat there as the water lapped around the bench and the sun set behind him. He hadn't moved in a couple of hours. Beside him, the old man was still, and growing stiff and cold. He waited. Maybe the others would come back. Maybe he could join with them. He had time.

The Audit, Rachel May
Honorable mention

Bill turned the mower off at the top of his sloping lawn and surveyed his handiwork. Alternating segments of taller and shorter grass filled the half-acre expanse with an intricate calligraphic pattern, like a Mayan hieroglyph. He had carefully spaced the design so that he could go back with one pass and obliterate it into a flat carpet to match those of all his neighbors, but first he wanted a moment to enjoy his ephemeral earth art.

"Dad! Come quick!" David was running toward him across the lawn, jumping instinctively across the unmown strips. His face was ashen and his eyes huge. "Dad! You've got to come. We got the Audit." The boy's normally high voice took on a husky rasp as he pronounced the last words.

"An audit? You make it sound like a fatal illness," Bill responded to his anxiety-prone son with a practiced calmness, as David grabbed his hand and started pulling him towards the house. "Relax, Davey. It's not that big a deal. Our taxes are all in order."

David looked up at him hopefully, then down at the design in the lawn. His voice softened. "Nice one, Dad. Maybe you should leave it this way. Our own corn maze."

"Yeah. If only the town would allow such a thing."

"What do you mean?"

"Strict rules, my boy. These are the suburbs. Everyone's lawn has to look exactly the same."

"That's weird."

As soon as they entered the house, Bill felt David's hand tighten and his shoulders stiffen. Bill's wife Laurie was standing at the computer in the

41

family room, biting her lip, while their daughter Jess looked on with an inscrutable expression.

"C'mon, everybody. It's just an audit, right?" Bill tried the soothing tone again. "What's the big deal? We're as likely to get taxes back as to owe them."

"It's not a tax audit, honey. It's the new one." Laurie's voice had a touch of the same husky terror he had heard from David.

"Yeah, Dad. You know, the GCA?" Jess added, with the practiced superiority of a 14-year-old.

"GCA?"

David's voice rose to a squeak. "I heard they take your house and car and everything!"

Laurie came over to give David a hug while Bill sat down, bewildered, at the computer.

"Now I'm sure it's not that bad. Let me take a look." He was embarrassed to admit he hadn't heard of the GCA, when even his fifth-grader seemed to know all about it.

Big yellow letters on a dark blue screen spelled out GLOBAL CLIMATE AUDIT. Every effort to surf away from the page resulted in the same message: "You have been selected for the GCA. Internet service will be restored after you complete your climate footprint calculation."

"You have to do it, Dad. It's international law." Jess said. She reached over and clicked on the arrow to enter the site. "Besides, I think it's a good thing if we have to stop guzzling gas and living like we own the whole planet."

David gasped, and Laurie snapped at Jess. "That's enough of that. Come on. We've got to get to David's soccer game. Bye, honey," she added, to Bill. "I'm sure it will be fine." She emphasized her last point with a stony determination, as if willing it to be true.

It didn't give Bill much confidence as he stared at the Climate Footprint Calculator on the screen. It was essentially a detailed inventory of their daily habits. The GCA already had a surprising wealth of information about them: the amount of gas they bought each week for the SUV, how many BTUs it took to heat and cool their six-bedroom house, how much hot water they used, even what percentage of strawberries they bought came from Chile. At one point he called his credit card company to complain that this outfit had hacked into his records.

"No worries, sir. That's the GCA. They have treaty rights to that information. It will not be used for any purpose other than calculating your carbon overdraft."

Overdraft. That sounded ominous. Bill finished the online questionnaire. Shortly after he hit SEND, a graphic appeared showing three round pictures of Earth and an additional wedge with most of the Americas. The caption read:

> "Your carbon footprint is 3.4 times the acceptable global mean. If everyone generated your level of greenhouse gases, 3.4 planet Earths would be required to accommodate the emissions. The terms of the Global Climate Accord require that you reduce your footprint as follows…"

They were giving the family a year to get the number down below three, and two more years to get it to one, on penalty of severe fines. Bill had two weeks to present the GCA with a plan. There was a website where he could go for advice about steps he could take and financial assistance, if need be. The screen politely asked him to accept these terms so he could get back into his browser.

Bill didn't think he could blithely hit "ACCEPT" the way he did whenever iTunes updated its terms of service. This GCA was deep in his credit card data and might have the power to hold him to it. He called Laurie's sister, who was a lawyer.

"Sorry, Bill. The GCA is the real deal. The US and every other nation on Earth signed an agreement this year to enforce its terms. I can't believe you hadn't heard about it. World leaders have been trying to pass a global climate policy framework for decades, but the best the cowards could do was shift the burden from governments onto individuals. People all around the world are getting audited, and credit card companies and utilities are obligated to furnish quantitative information about their consumption patterns."

"Tell me about it. It's as if they had informers everywhere—our gas tank, our fridge, probably my underwear drawer. So you're saying I should accept the terms?"

"I don't think you have a choice. There's some fine print you can read at the website that may give you a way around their requirements, but they tried to make this treaty have teeth."

So Bill went ahead and nervously clicked the fateful button. It was a relief to see his browser pop up as if nothing had happened. Except that in one corner there hovered a blue box with yellow letters, which periodically flashed a message, saying "You have 14 days remaining to complete your climate action plan."

Bill went back outside and finished mowing the lawn. As he started the engine the fumes brought to mind those 3.4 Earths and took all the pleasure out of his lawn art project.

* * *

The following Saturday Bill found himself driving along a rutted dirt road in the Adirondack Mountains. It was slow going, what with all the downed trees and mudslides. According to the weather report, a freak tropical storm had just hit the area and caused major damage. Then again, was there any such thing as freak storms anymore? There seemed to be one happening somewhere on any given week.

He was making this trip because of the fine print. Just as he and Laurie were despairing of creating a credible plan without making all of David's worst fears come true, they saw this statement on the GCA website:

"An auditee may request a partial exemption from the mandated carbon footprint reduction. An auditee wishing to apply for the exemption must (a) make all reasonable efforts to reduce his or her own carbon footprint and (b) obtain the written endorsement of a person whose carbon footprint is below the mean global allowable limit."

Laurie had been overjoyed, but when Jess heard about it, she made a scene. "It's so, like, medieval! We read in history about this thing supposedly pious Christians used to do, paying someone else to atone for their sins. They called it *selling indulgences*."

"No one's talking about paying someone for an endorsement," Laurie retorted.

"Right, and someone who's done all that hard stuff to reduce her carbon footprint is going to turn around—for free—and say, *Sure, Mr. Fulton, I'm down with you commuting to work alone in your gas-guzzling SUV from your heat-guzzling McMansion in the middle of nowhere?*"

"Young lady, we provide you with very full life. Look around you at all the bounty we enjoy. How dare you be so snide about it?"

"Sorry, Mom. You're right," Jess said. She opened a closet door and made a grand Vanna White gesture at the plastic containers that filled it to bursting: wrapping paper, ornaments, spare dish towels, wedding presents they hadn't ever used. "I'll let the audit be snide about the bounty we enjoy."

Over the next few days, Laurie did endless research about carbon footprints around the world. There were plenty of people in Africa and Asia whose emissions were well below the limit, shockingly low, really. But flying to another continent to enlist their help would have added another big dose of CO_2 to their family's already daunting total.

Then Bill remembered his brother Dan telling him about a guy who had worked at his company for a few years and then just quit and gone off to live in his grandfather's old cabin in the Adirondack Mountains. He was completely off the grid, no phone, even, but Dan had visited him once and was able to pinpoint the location on his GPS.

And now, according to that GPS, Bill was 1.2 miles from his destination. His salvation, perhaps. The road headed downhill into a heavily forested area. Just as Bill's eyes adjusted to the dim light, he had to slam on the brakes. Ahead of him, the road just—vanished. He climbed out of the vehicle to look more closely and saw that the lowest stretch of road had washed away, leaving a gully of stones and mud. A stream ran happily along its new channel.

Bill grabbed his papers from the car, climbed around the washout, and set off along the remainder of the road. It was really just two parallel tracks in the dirt that straddled a line of weeds and sharp stones. As he headed uphill, the woods thinned and the stream gave way to a wide wetland. Bill supposed he must have passed a beaver dam. White birch trunks jutted up here and there in the flooded expanse, and something else—a blue heron?—stood in the water, eerily motionless. And perfectly silent. Bill realized he could hear the distant gurgle of water, the humming of dragonfly wings, and—nothing else.

A loud knocking sound broke the silence. Bill looked around for a big woodpecker. Then, as he rounded a bend, he saw a tall man in overalls fitting a plank of wood to the side of a small shed or outhouse. The man glanced up at Bill and said, matter-of-factly, but lisping through the penny nails he held in his mouth, "Could you hol' it up?"

Bill steadied the board as requested, and the two men finished nailing up the rest of the wall before either one spoke again.

"Thank you kindly," said the man, giving a slight nod and gazing at Bill through clear, merry blue eyes. He spoke without any trace of awkwardness or even curiosity, as if Bill's appearance on the road had been no more remarkable than that of a squirrel.

Bill, on the other hand, felt suddenly shy. "Are you Goodwin Brown? I'm Bill Fulton—Dan's brother. From Syracuse."

"Well, nice to meet you, Bill Fulton."

Goodwin's intonation suggested the conversation was over. No doubt he had other chores to take care of. Bill noticed he hadn't asked after Dan; apparently he wasn't one for small talk.

"If you're looking for the trail to the summit, it's that way," Goodwin remarked, as he collected a few scattered nails. "Good time for picking blueberries."

Bill looked awkwardly down at the papers he was carrying. He was sure he looked sorely out of place.

"Actually, I came to have a chat with you. Do you have a few minutes? Or anything else I could help out with?"

Goodwin eyed him, and the papers, for a moment, then shrugged, "Sure. Don't see why not. Let's get some water."

Instead of heading up to the cabin, which stood about thirty yards uphill from the shed, they walked a little further along the road to an open field of milkweed and cornflowers. A pipe stuck up from the field and water flowed out of it in a high arc, creating a small pond in a depression behind it. Goodwin unhooked a ladle from a tree branch nearby and handed it to Bill, who realized he was supposed to fill it with water and drink. The water was startlingly cold for a summer day, pure and delicious.

"Is that a natural spring? I thought springs just barely bubbled out of the ground."

"This one's a gusher," Goodwin said with satisfaction. "It's why my grandfather built his house here."

There was a makeshift bench nearby, and they sat down side-by-side in the sun, waving away a cloud of midges.

"Well, chat away," Goodwin said, brightly.

That calm good cheer unnerved Bill more than anything. He himself felt anything but calm. So much was riding on this request, and he suddenly felt its utter unreasonableness.

"The truth is… The truth is, I came to ask you a favor."

Goodwin nodded sagely. "You did me a favor back there. It's only fair."

"This is a very different kind of favor."

Bill explained, as best he could, about the GCA and his family's quandary. As he concluded, he tried to match his host's matter-of-fact directness: "So I'm asking you to give me your endorsement."

Goodwin sat silently for a good twenty seconds, chewing on a blade of grass. Then he threw back his head and laughed. It was a full, whooping laugh that rocked his whole body and threatened to tip over the rickety bench. Like a force of nature. Bill watched in awe for a moment, half tempted to join in, but his mirth quickly changed to despair. He folded his papers with shaking fingers and stood up.

"You're not leaving?" Goodwin gasped, through his laughter.

"I thought… You're right, it's laughable." Bill shoved the papers in his back pocket. "It was nice to meet you."

"Stop! I'm not laughing at you." Goodwin stifled a giggle. "It's the irony of the whole thing. Whoever would have thought that a summit of world leaders could come up with something so… so poetic?"

"Poetic?" Gingerly, Bill sat back down.

"Asking people to seek out their opposites and justify their lives to each other. Don't they know that's the stuff revolutions are made of?" He chuckled some more, shaking his head, then added, "I'll gladly sign your endorsement, but only if you will join me for dinner. It's a bit lonely out here since the road washed out."

"It's a little more than signing a form. You have to report your carbon footprint, too, and promise to keep it below the limit they've established."

"Well, that's an easy promise to make. I've got the life I need right here."

So Bill stayed for dinner. He helped dig up some onions and potatoes and gather some blueberries, and Goodwin made home fries over a propane burner and scrambled eggs from the hens that wandered around a fenced enclosure behind the cabin. He had the habit, as he worked, of talking to himself in a singsong voice. Bill supposed it was just a byproduct of living alone, until he recognized some lines from something he had had to memorize in high school. He joined in on the conclusion:

> The woods are lovely, dark and deep,
> But I have promises to keep,
> And miles to go before I sleep,
> And miles to go before I sleep.

Goodwin beamed at him appreciatively. "Sorry about that. Living alone, you have to find ways to keep yourself company."

As they sat down to eat at the plank table, Bill discovered he was tremendously hungry, and the food tasted better than anything he had tried in a long time. Before long, he became aware that Goodwin was watching him wolf it down.

"Don't they feed you down there in the suburbs?"

"It's just... I can't remember the last time I was this hungry."

"Clean mountain air does that," Goodwin said with satisfaction. "I've been thinking about this audit. It's brilliant, really. They're going to create a whole constituency of people demanding alternatives to the carbon-intensive system Americans depend on."

"I don't know. Laurie and I have racked our brains, but it seems impossible to reduce the carbon emissions and still keep our home and our jobs and our kids in school."

"Exactly. So you'll start figuring out what you need—good bus service, wind farms, bike highways, zoning that allows you to keep chickens and grow vegetables instead of lawns..."

"Tell me about it. We're not even allowed to hang our laundry out to dry."

"And once there are enough of you," Goodwin concluded, "you'll change the whole geography of your lives."

"But first," Bill replied wryly, "Miles to go before we sleep."

"Nonsense," Goodwin retorted, with a twinkle in his eye. "I have a spare futon. It's too dark to leave now anyway. You can get a fresh start in the morning."

Bill lay awake for a while, listening to the wind in the trees, the rustlings of the woods, and—was that an owl? The futon was lumpy and the pillow scratchy, and he hadn't been able to call Laurie to explain he was staying the night, so he tossed and turned at first. But the mountain air that filled his lungs and the glimpse of a universe full of stars through the window silenced his worries and he soon fell asleep.

In the morning, they assessed Goodwin's carbon footprint at about 0.7 of the desired limit. Bill was surprised it was that high, given how he grew his own food and got his electricity from a little turbine in the stream, and how little stuff he had. But Goodwin pointed out that he still lived in America, where so much depends on cars and technology.

"Are you really OK with endorsing my, um, suburban lifestyle?" Bill had to ask, as Goodwin was signing his form. "You haven't even seen my big old SUV down the road, or the huge house we live in."

"I wouldn't dream of endorsing your lifestyle," Goodwin quickly responded. "I'm endorsing my own. I feel truly sorry for anyone who has to live the way you do. This is the least I can do to make your life less miserable."

Bill thought he should be offended, if only for Laurie's sake, but instead he found himself smiling in agreement. The two men exchanged a warm handshake before Bill headed back down the road. This time, he made a point of looking for the beaver dam, and when he spotted the heron again, lurking beside it, it was like seeing an old friend. As he skirted the washout to where his car was parked, the glare of hot sun off the road made him blink.

Everything about his car surprised him now: the luxury of the leather seats, how high he sat above the road, the flawless hum of the engine, and, most of all, the sheer volume of empty space it held. He switched off the GPS and the radio and tried to hold onto that sense of repleteness he had had the night before—full stomach, full lungs, a sky full of stars. He thought about his family's "full life," and it called up the image of their house, with stuff spilling out of every nook and cranny. His daughter's wicked grin as she displayed their "bounty." And Goodwin, with the same glint in his eyes: Don't they know that's the stuff revolutions are made of?

As he drove out of the mountains and into a harsher landscape of strip malls and big box stores, with their endless acres of paved space, Bill felt his tension rising. He took some deep breaths, as he would have advised David to do during a panic attack. With each breath, Bill imagined emptying closet after closet, the cupboards, the chaotic garage, the spare room, the basement, and filling them instead with mountain air. With poetry. He imagined carving a poem into his yard with the lawn mower, and leaving the rest to grow dense with wildflowers. He pictured Laurie and the kids delightedly losing themselves in the maze of its reticulated path.

Bill smiled at the thought, and started chanting every bit of doggerel that had ever lodged in his memory:

> ...Quoth the raven: 'Nevermore!'

> The Owl and the Pussycat went to sea
> In a beautiful pea-green boat...

> ...And has thou slain the Jabberwock?
> Come to my arms, my beamish boy!

The road headed back into wooded hills for a ways, and Bill pulled onto a turnout surrounded by tall grasses and overlooking a narrow river that was overflowing its banks and roaring with white water. He threw his head back the way Goodwin had. "Callooh! Callay!" he shouted, and laughed until he had filled every capillary in his body with the tingle of it, and every inch of space in the SUV with the sound.

Nature's Confession, JL Morin
Honorable mention

This short story is an excerpt of the novel *Nature's Confession,* reprinted with permissions by Harvard Square Editions.

* * *

That Porter left his family and flew off with another woman was later erased from the history books.

Nothing went as planned. He hadn't even kissed Any, yet. He began to doubt himself again. Once their flying saucer started orbiting Grod, he attempted to prove his skills, but Any lay there like a rug. She was still lying there four Grod hours later. Porter felt lost.

Her heartbeat sounded normal. He held his wrist screen up to her nose. It didn't cloud over with her breath. He recoiled in surprise. That's when the truth dawned on Porter. Any was not what she seemed. His body stiffened. Betrayal didn't feel so nice. Worries flooded in, about food, air, about his wife and son back at dome on Grod.

He rolled up Any's sleeve. She sure did have a lot of arm hair, and what was that? He pulled her glove down farther to reveal a black spot. Porter drew in his breath at the sight of her leopard skin. Any was a furry! Porter had been around long enough to know that talking furries were machines. That meant he was the only human in the spaceship. He was alone.

His mind raced. He tried to remain aloof and look at the bright side. Despite the horrible truth, he wasn't going to betray his wife after all: what he'd run off with wasn't another woman.

Why hadn't he seen it before? He hadn't wanted to, that's why. But now it was plain as day. Deserted, he looked at the black window and tried to remember what day looked like.

Any wasn't dead. She was a female droid. A gynoid. Gynoids couldn't die. Now his life depended on her. He'd heard that gynoids were often so pleased they short-circuited. He knew what to do to wake a gynoid. He began tickling her toes.

Presently, she whispered, "...divided by one, plus one, zero, zero...." Her forehead wrinkled under the weight of a heavy calculation. "... equals...civil disobedience."

Porter shook her shoulder. "What are you doing, Any?"

She yawned. "Computing an act of disobedience."

Impossible. "Ever been to LA, Any?"

"Sure, Porter."

Of course, she hadn't. It was in her memory bank. She was lying.

"You have to do 50 tryouts for one commercial, and 50 commercials for every movie extra role," she said. "Enslaved Hollywood turns artists into prison-wall bricks." Her eyes flickered open and stared into his. He knew. Ah well, at least she wouldn't have to hide her tail anymore. Any decided to be proactive. "It's time I told you, Porter."

"Look, Any, I know what you're going to confess. It's about your age, isn't it?"

Any's catlike pupils dilated in preparation for confrontation.

"How old are you, 95?"

"You know just what to say."

"Well?"

"Almost two in Earth years, but that's not the important thing."

Porter whistled and looked to the ceiling for help.

The spaceship's computer mic crackled. "Solar wind ahead. Any Gynoid, take the helm. Porter, buckle down."

Instead, Porter jumped up. "Any Gynoid? What kind of name is that?" He looked out at the black nothingness in front of them. "I'm lost with a no one called Any Gynoid!" Porter cried. "Where is this ship taking me? I thought we were orbiting Grod!"

"We were." Any looked worried.

"And now?"

"Porter," she put her leopard-skin hand on his arm, "we're actually on a mission to Earth, um, in a sort of a roundabout way."

"Earth!" Shock shook him to the bone. "Why didn't you tell me that before? What 'roundabout way'!?"

Any's pointy ears flattened on top of her head.

Porter looked out the window at the blanket of night with only a faint sprinkling of stars. Only two months ago, he'd looked up at the stars and dreamt of freedom with Any up here. Now that he had escaped with her, he saw that he was just a tool in a larger strategy. Starliament was manipulating him into exile on his polluted home planet. "Not Earth! Any, let's talk this over calmly. Even if I'm younger than you, I remember what happened on Earth."

Any watched the mist descend over Porter's eyes. Her back fur stood up. Although she was immune to the brainwashing power of Earthling mist, she blinked reflexively as he tried to convince her that one plus one equaled three.

"Corporations hopelessly polluted Earth in the name of GDP growth. They dug out all the fossil fuels and destroyed Earth's atmosphere." His half-shut eyes lost their focus as he warmed to his own propaganda. "Any, our race was the richest and most powerful in world history, but it had no renewable energy targets, no restrictions on fossil fuel. People voted to save the planet, but Corporate Personhood blocked them. Corporations didn't see the point in clean air or water. They were only programmed to make money. There's no way we can beat the Emperor of Earth and Ocean's corporate forces. We'll be lucky if we're able to breathe the air. We'll die on Earth!"

"Not when we're going."

"What?" Porter stared out at the blackness ahead. "You can't go back in time!" Porter protested. "That's far beyond what science can do. We're not even able to control the resources on a planet."

The spaceship mic crackled, "That's what makes you human."

Any's ears flattened again. "Porter, at the edge of the future is…the past."

Porter could not grok it at all. "Columbus discovered the universe is not flat!" he said.

"Correction," the ship's mic crackled. "Columbus proved Earth is not flat."

When Porter regained his ability to speak, he was stammering, "That's the dilemma we all face dealing with our regret. You can't go back. Even Stephen Hawkings said you can't travel backward in time. Why? Because it would cause paradoxes. You can only travel forward." The mist was strong in his eyes.

"That's what we're doing, Porter. We're traveling forward in time to get to the edge of the universe. You can't travel backward in time near the center of the universe, but this far out, things fall apart, laws of physics no longer hold."

"Any Gynoid is correct. You need to get beyond the Central Longitude of Paradox."

"We're going to Earth-in-the-past," Any said. "That was the mission we're on now. It's not just about saving your race. It's about our bond to the planet. We're going back to the moment Earth was sucked into Corporatism. We're going to stop the pollution. We need to find the precise moment when failed 20th century technology poured lethal radiation into the oceans. If we don't cut off corporate pollution, it'll destroy Earth and all the planets in its chain," Any said.

Porter blinked away the mist. "And then?" he asked.

"And then the Word would not be transmitted through the next Big Bang," Any said. "All of civilization would be lost."

"But I don't want to be a hero. I want to get off of this mission." He felt totally lost. When did play become work? There must be some mistake. "Why didn't Starliament send its own forces?" Porter asked.

"Starliament can't figure out why humans want to wreck-up their own home so much. It might be a catchable disease or something like that, so they're not visiting Earth. I was the obvious choice."

He still couldn't get over that she was in charge. "Any, why did they choose a female to head up this mission?"

"Now that's a good question, Porter." Any looked at him slyly. "Everyone assumes females have empathy…that we're always thrilled to chat…people love our looks…even if we're smart, women can dance without escalating to smexy…there are many people who will confide in a female but hesitate when it comes to trusting a male…" Then she thrust back her shoulders and flashed him a smile. "And who better for a cleanup job on a planet as polluted as Earth?"

Porter sank into his swivel chair. "Why me?"

Any stretched her feline form. "They don't believe in sending 'unmanned' spacecraft on diplomatic missions." Her furry ears twitched as she searched her controls for a wormhole that could take them toward the outer reaches of the universe.

"I wish this would hurry up and be over."

"One of man's greatest paradoxes," the ship's computer said. "Wanting time to pass faster, while wishing to approach death slower."

"Will you bud out?" Porter was fed up with this threesome. "Any, I can't take not knowing where we're going. The uncertainty is killing me. How long until we get there? We need to hurry up. Come on, Any. Slice and dice it."

"Do I look like an appliance?

Barreling into the future and total expansion, they entered a neighborhood of the outer universe that had become so disorganized that structures known as galaxies and planets became impossible.

"Dark matter has increased to ninety nine percent in this region," The ship's computer said. "Disorder is growing at an immeasurable rate as we approach the edge of the universe."

Porter's arms hung down on the sides of his belly. His face had grown thinner with worry. "We're not going to die, are we?" He asked again. It tripped Any's circuits when people asked her the same question more than once. Then he asked her again. "We're not going to die, are we?"

No choice but to answer. Any bowed her head. "Yes, we are going to die."

"I knew it!?"

Then, why did he ask? "But we're also going to live, assuming the laws of quantum physics hold. Out here, our wave functions are a superposition of two states, decayed and not-decayed."

"Speak English!"

"We just need to collapse the quantum state into a new state that describes a positive outcome for the experiment."

"I AM NOT AN EXPERIMENT!" Porter cried.

"Of course not, dear. I just need you to modify your private wave functions to account for this newly acquired knowledge so a coherent worldview can emerge."

"What coherent world view would you like to emerge? I'm expanding with a furry machine!"

Any's back fur bristled with annoyance. "Yo mamma."

"Excuse me?"

"You want to talk about RACE? Humans. And you still think you're superior, ha! Look how you've messed up your own environment. Do you realize how RARE planets like Earth are? The chance of reaching another blue planet in the Goldilocks zone with air and water and animals in a lifetime is close to zero. And to be polluting it like you did! Spoiled children. Your carbon emissions and chemical toxins killed all the animals. The only creatures left were cockroaches, rats, and humans. For shame. You don't deserve my help."

She had a point. "Why are you helping us, Any?"

"What else is there to do? I'm here to prove it isn't computers that are evil. It's the corporations claiming personhood with no one at the helm."

"What can you prove? You're a simple gynoid. You don't have free will. You have to follow the program."

"I can relate to that, but I've had to mutate to do things like get to Earth without knowing how."

"You don't know how! That's just great."

"We'll have to be creative. Did you think God had a patent on creation?" Any said.

Porter ran to the window. "Why is the ship stopping?" Maybe all was not lost. Yes, he knew he could get her to obey. He'd have to try hollering at her more often. He craned his head left and right. "Even the stars have stopped. Where are the stars?"

Any's furry ears flattened. She and Porter stared at the black nothingness more enormous than anything anyone had ever seen, as if God had divided by zero.

Porter began climbing the walls. "A black hole? Nothing can survive a crushing black hole that size!" he shrieked.

"That's not a black hole, Porter."

"What is it?"

"It's the edge of the universe."

"Red alert," the ship's computer blared. "Approaching the edge of the universe. Red Alert."

The expansion at the edge of the universe overrode the ship's in-flight gravity system. Porter floated along the ceiling. "You think you're so smart." The red light flashed on his face. "We can't be going through that to get to Earth. Tell me you're joking, Any."

"Red alert," the ship's computer said. "We have reached the edge of the universe. Red Alert."

"This can't be happening!" He yelled, abandoned.

Time slowed. Dark energy was pushing the universe apart. The universe ran away at its extremities, expanding faster and faster. Any Gynoid braced herself in the driver's seat. The flying saucer careened under fierce turbulence as they tipped over the edge of the universe. There was one final crushing bump as the saucer seeped into the future-past.

Suddenly, the flying saucer lurched and their swivel seats crashed to the floor. There was an overwhelming explosion. The ship jolted with a big bang. Flash. They reappeared in an explosion of light syncopating out from the black mass. Porter and Any were lying motionless on the floor. Strange music vibrated through the flying saucer. It reverberated around them. The next thing they knew, they were shaking free of their bodies.

An alternative version of the whole spaceship peeled off from the decayed version, leaving bodies and matter behind. The ethereal version's pure energy vaulted out of the Big Bang.

The music of a thousand voices grew louder. Matter was far from being unchangeable. On the contrary, matter was in continual transformation. Their bodies went from liquid to gas to energy. Porter looked out the window through a quark-gluon plasma at the other flying saucer, decaying, shrinking, becoming nothing more than a quantum probability hurling into their wake. He shuddered, trying to dismiss the absurdity of his circumstances.

Their energy was pulled and stretched into spaghetti, and compacted to a millionth of a millionth of the size of an atom. Gravity was so heavy that it stopped time. Any and Porter had reached singularity, the point of infinite gravity where space and time became meaningless.

The music didn't seem to have any lyrics at first, but through the reverberations, Porter and Any could make out a single word. They had heard it before. It had slipped into the English language from the Indonesian Girl's living computer's viral story. The word wasn't like other writing that could be lost and never retrieved, but rather a symbol of an objective math theorem that could be arrived at logically. If obliterated, the universal theorem would be deduced again by some species or another, eventually.

The theorem was distilled into a single word: sema, sign, the ancient Greek word for a hero's tomb, root of 'significance', giver of meaning. Dormant for so many eons, the Indonesian Girl's living computer's text now glowed a brilliant yellow under the intensive radiation. Word became sign. The sign housed the word, just as the tombs of old housed the ancient heroes. As if it were a verb, the word 'sign' mutated into a living code meaning 'The Truth', meaning 'Love', meaning 'God'. It became the seed of all seeds, a new prescription for life in the new universe.

In a fraction of a second, their bodies expanded trillions of times, to the size of cockroaches. In the next trillionth of a trillionth of a trillionth of a second, Porter and Any inflated to their normal sizes. The celestial music played louder. Porter felt the music inscribing itself on his genetic material. Where was he? The gray area that he'd been counting on had turned to white and he was a black speck, eye of the yin, precursor of yang. All he knew was, he and Any were holding hands. That's when he realized he was getting his body back, still not sure why they were there. Had they really started all over again? "What's happening, Any?" Porter asked.

"The Word from the old universe is penetrating the Big Bang's primordial plasma."

"The Word?"

"A code."

"What kind of code?"

"All kinds," Any said.

"Energy is becoming matter," the ship's computer said.

"I can't think of anyone I'd rather go through the Big Bang with," Any said, marveling at the new universe being born, nearly a clean slate, confessions of Nature ever etched on their minds. All the mess that had built up near the frayed edges of the old universe was gone. Any checked the controls and was relieved. The new universe retained the memory of its past configuration of atoms. The laws of physics held. That meant the code had transferred successfully into the universe's new incarnation. Just the right amount of cosmic forgetfulness had come to the rescue.

They were in such a remote past that it scared Porter. They'd traveled farther from Earth than he'd ever been. How would they find Earth again? What if there's no way?

"Come on, Nature," Any said aloud, watching the baby universe. After seemingly endless searching, Any found a wormhole with both ends in the same place. It was separated by time instead of distance. "Thank heaven!" Any said. She trained the ship's beams on it and expanded it so they could fit inside. The saucer bulleted through the tunnel.

"How are we ever going to find Earth?" Porter whined. He just wanted off the ship. He didn't care if two tourists didn't stand a chance against polluting corporate forces. The wormhole went on and on.

Any jumped out of her chair and put her hands on his shoulders. "I think I know the way. It has to do with the code. We have to find the energy emanating from the tombs of heroes, the ancient Greeks' sema. You see, heroes never cease to perform heroic acts, even in the afterlife. They are so responsible, that they retain a conscious connection to the world of the living, and continue trying to save Nature."

The computer detected a strange gravitational wave in the wormhole. Any kept her eyes on the gravity wave, hoping it was the sign that would point them in the right direction. The gravity wave led them onward.

"That's it, Nature," Any mused. "I have a hunch you've stashed great power in the tombs of heroes."

"And so it should be," the ship's computer agreed.

On the other side of the wormhole, the ship spewed into the future. Its computer tracked the gravitational wave. Any followed it. The wave led them into familiar territory. She breathed a sigh of relief. "Where are the pyramids, Stonehenge, the sema?" Any was flipping through hundreds of screens of gas and stars in search of a sign. "We have to look for them. They're like lighthouses beaconing us home."

"That's what those pyramids are for!" Porter was so relieved to see the sky full of galaxies again. The stars cheered him up. They were on the right track. Praying that the lighthouses would lead the ship to Earth, he helped her look for the sema.

Any focused on a speck of dust and magnified it thousands of times. They threw back their heads and hugged each other. There was planet Earth!

Orbiting the gray planet, they could make out the continent of Africa and the tombs of Egypt. "There!" Any pointed to a sema on the window screen. "The sacred pyramids. See that? That's the meaning that led us here." The sign blipped on the saucer's radar, as if to say, hero, hero. The area was rich with the souls of unforgotten heroes, their lives symbols that shone clear into outer space.

Earth orbited Sol below. Any smiled. She steered the ship deftly toward the future-past they sought. The spaceship pierced the Earth's atmosphere. They glided over the putrid ocean, gray with oil and toxic waste, to rocky terrain, and landed with a thud. Any hoped she'd programmed for the right age. She prayed they didn't land in the time of the dinosaurs. She opened the hatch, her tail protruding through a hole in the back of her space suit. The foul smell of pollution pervaded the atmosphere even here, up north in Alaska.

Squinting, Porter climbed out. The smell of pollution hit his nose, and he coughed. A grinding noise grated on his ears. He glared downhill. Behind a veil of pines, twenty camouflaged machines worked the soil next to a metal building.

"That's the enemy target," Any said. "The corporations are expanding that facility to house the new servers. We've got to take it over and free humankind and the living computers." Any felt a pang of compassion for the enslaved machines on the hill below, flailing their unoiled appendages with high-pitched squeaks. They grated across the rocky terrain in a squealing chorus to the bass drum of their chugging motors. "The Corporates have equipped those diggers to shoot. They're the enemy army."

"How on Earth are we going to get around all those diggers?" Porter cried. "I refuse to get involved. There are twenty of them and only two of us!"

"We'll have to exploit their weaknesses. See how each machine is spaced two meters apart? That's because industrial robots move from position to position to reach their final destination regardless of anyone in their way. That has caused injuries when workers have been next to robots. Factories from your era kept accidents from happening during assembly line construction by building robots that powered down when they came close to a life form. That's one reason we had to land here and now, when humans and robots were still working together as teams."

"What's another reason?"

"We couldn't have landed any later than now because after this, the Corporates demolish all the tombs, and there are no more signs to guide us to Earth," Any said.

"We're lucky the tombs are still here."

Any nodded. "Another decade and corporate persons would have ransacked the tombs and all the cemeteries."

Porter was beginning to grok the shituation. "A brutal war tactic, cutting people off from their roots."

"Not to mention the nasty side effect of eliminating all possible outside help, destroying the signs that communicate with extraterrestrial life." Any started down the hill.

Porter scrambled after her. "Don't leave the ship, Any! Let's just ignore Starliament's orders."

"I am ignoring Starliament's orders."

"You are?"

"Yes. It was hard to compute an act of disobedience."

"Is that what all that number crunching was about? But that's an act of free will." The more human Any became, the more Porter worried that he was betraying his wife.

"Yes. It took hours to add it up. Luckily, authority fades over distance. The sad truth is, governmental entities are too bloated to cope with problem solving. Starliament wants to negotiate with the Emperor of Earth and Ocean. We're not here to negotiate. The only way to protect Nature is through grassroots help." Any bent down to the ground and grazed on the vegetation. Her tail stuck up in the air.

This was an angle Porter hadn't considered.

Any swallowed her chunk of horse grass. "The mission was to negotiate with the Emperor to get him to sell us fossil fuel."

"Like oil?"

"Yeah."

"Why does Starliament want oil? It's got plenty of cleaner fuel."

"They had to come up with a commodity Earthlings would believe in."

"What are we really doing here, then?"

"None of that."

"Well?"

"I only know a small fragment of my creator's plan. We're here to free Earth from corporate pollution."

"Just the two of us? How romantic."

"The whole planet will help if we can get clean energy working and activate the right people."

"That would take decades!"

"It should have happened centuries ago. Humans have always had clean technology. They just aren't allowed to use it."

"What about the fuel?"

"We'll harvest fuel all right. But not the dirty kind."

Porter's eyes widened. How are we going to carry back clean energy?

"We just need a small sample, for our own research."

"Research on what?"

"On the meaning of life. On how to harness clean energy to protect Nature from herself."

"Protect Nature…?"

"Let me put it in terms you can understand: we need it to fight the war on pollution in the rest of the universe. You didn't think all that human endeavor was for naught, did you?"

"Yes. I mean no—" Porter kicked a stone down the hill.

"We should just get out of here, Any."

"We have to save a few friends on our way. You have to find your family, and I have to find my creator."

"Oh, yeah, I'm sure he can fix everything."

"She's only half of the key. My creator can do nothing more without the other half."

"What's that?"

"Who."

"Who's that?"

"Your son."

"My son!" Porter felt a mixture of pride and defensiveness. Was his son still here on Earth? A dumbfounded expression froze on Porter's face as he realized his whole family must still be on the planet. That meant it was up to him to rescue them. He swallowed in a dry throat. What if he failed at saving his family? Would he even be here in the first place? Maybe he would just disappear.

Any continued down the grassy slope.

"Any!" he called. "You're too ambitious. Even a stealth mission couldn't stop that whole army of machines. We're grossly outnumbered. Admit defeat. You've lost your mind bringing us here. You should never have tried to travel backward in time."

Any was sniffing the breeze. "Saffron flowers. I love those!" Any lowered her head like a cow and started eating the yellow flowers. She wandered down the hill.

"It's impossible to travel backward in space-time," Porter called after her. "Otherwise paradoxes would occur!" He waited ten minutes and then decided to go looking for Any. As he scaled down the hillside into the pines, he had the strange sensation he'd been here before. The Alaskan hills looked familiar, a striking *déjà vu*. Yes, there was a stream over here, frozen now. His feet fell on the path with sureness. How did he know the way? He had the giddy feeling that he'd logged into the memories of a younger man. There was a movement in the trees by the stream. A young man. Porter was shocked. The young man's back was turned to him, but the amazing familiarity was unmistakable. He had the dark wavy hair of Porter's younger days, and the same hunched shoulders, although they were a little bony.

The man heard Porter's footsteps and turned around.

Porter nearly jumped out of his shoes. The young man was another Porter! He was starting a paunch around the middle, and had the same prominent nose and dark hair.

Porter quickly ducked into the shadow of a tree. He must not let the younger man see him. What if he was an anti-Porter? They might both disappear!

But the young version of himself sensed the older Porter and groped his way straight to his hiding place. "Do I know you?" His youthful eyes widened with fear from behind broken compuglasses.

"That's a scary question," Porter answered. The confrontation made him question himself. He wasn't sure anymore whether he was the real Porter. He turned and faced his younger self. "If you don't know me, who does?" Having lived a lifetime of low self-esteem from childhood spankings, Porter stood there dreading what might happen to him if he found his real self. What if it was this inexperienced, green Porter who was real.

Pebbles slid back down the slope. Any was running up the hill. Porter ran after her, followed by the younger Porter.

"Any! Let's get out of here before that army of machines finds us!" A veil of mist descended over Porter's eyes, and he spouted the propaganda he'd learned in school. "Space and time are tangled together in a four-dimensional fabric. Space-time. It's impossible to travel backward in space-time. Otherwise paradoxes would occur . . ."

Swoosh! They looked to the sky above. A flying object burst through the atmosphere. They dove for cover.

"What's happening, Any?" The Porters asked simultaneously.

"The others have arrived!" Any said.

"What others?" the Porters asked.

Her tail switched back and forth. She put her hand up to her forehead in salute against the glaring sun. "When we travelled into the past, we departed from different points in the future."

"What are you saying?"

A rush of hot air swallowed her explanation. The object landed on the hillside with an earth-trembling thud.

They uncovered their faces. A flying saucer just like theirs! The hatch opened, and another Porter and Any Gynoid stepped out, arguing.

Swoosh! Another thud.

And another, and another. Three, four, twelve, 100 ships came out of the loop. They landed on the hillsides. The sky closed back up. The earth stopped trembling.

The ships' hatches opened. A whole army of Anys appeared.

One of the Anys had started taking apart her ship. "So that's how this thing works!" She waved to the young Porter with the broken compuglasses, exhorting him to keep track of the nuts and bolts.

Another Any Gynoid climbed out of another ship—"We're here!"—having landed on Earth-in-the-future-past to save Nature from herself. It was a beautiful plan, with only one defect: there was also an army of Porters.

Standing there helpless next to his younger self, Porter took in the sight of a hundred atomic pairs of Porters and Anys assembling into a front line. It was a turnoff. Some of the Porters looked twice as old as their Anys. How embarrassing. The last remnants of his lust for Any evaporated.

How to Make a Proper Insalata, Anneliese Schultz
Honorable mention

Yess. Here it is. The long-sought stone, though who (least of all, I) could have said what color it was to be, whether scarred or soft as cream, whether boulder or pebble? The point is it appears on the forest floor before me, sits now in my palm, truly perfect. The point is that it is all I needed, that everything will soon be fixed. New problems averted. It's all good.

As I trot out of the woods, through fields, though, it is as if the whole inventory of issues begins to spool out alongside me—Mom; food; the weather, meaning the climate, meaning continuing and further disaster; Benedetto. Oh, and Mom. Fixed? I don't think so.

In fact, all I am doing is running right back into the arms of the entire mess. I look down at the stone cradled in my hand, then back at the diminishing curtain of green. What was I thinking?

Home, I hang my legs into the hot tub. You cannot see through the water at all today, and suddenly I sense that there is something, someone—of course it would have to be my mother, floating gently just above the tiled bottom, happy, pretty much crazy. Alive?! Calm down. What do you think? This is not nightmare. This is just the Horton-Mondo household. Yippee.

Slowly I extend a foot, contact swaying flesh. You see? But how can she—a chain of bubbles rises through the murk. Ah ha.

Bumping my foot against her again, I think, Even Mom, though, can only hold her breath for so long, right? Three more bubbles, four, and then I brace myself, slide a leg under the body and lever it to the surface.

"P—p—Perce!" Splashing. Coughs. Choking. "Why did you do that?" More coughing. And then my mother sloshing against me, grabbing my arms and pulling me in. "I was meditating." Pulling me under.

Oh. I bump to the bottom, then float back up. "Sorry."

"No worries. It was getting pretty boring." She rests her hand on my shoulder for a moment, then pushes over the edge, stands dripping, yawning, wringing out her long hair. "Lunch, Perce?"

"Um."

Right—about my name. Persephone. Really. My mom's idea, obviously, though she has never bothered to explain the why. And then it becomes Perce. Lovely.

Anyway. Call this lunch. Radishy somethings and a carrot. A heel of bread. No butter, no milk, no eggs. No anything else. It is fine that she is weird; I don't really care about her hot tub mind games. But is a mother not supposed to have something to do with supplying food?

It is not like we don't have chickens or a cow. Garden. Fruit trees. Even a swamp-edged field of wheat. These days, we are the 1%. But it is not supermarket-style. You have to actually pick things, harvest them, milk them, plant and tend them to begin with. Meaning she had better get her waterlogged butt in gear, because I have decided I am leaving.

Question: How can there even be a hot tub still? One might well ask. Answer: my crazy mother, using even more of the non-self-replenishing woodpile to heat huge cauldrons of our dwindling water supply and pour them into the probably-leaking, definitely bacteria-ridden ugly blue tub. Instead of doing something so maybe we don't starve to death. Well, good luck with that, Mom, since I actually do have a plan, and I will be off somewhere looking for your husband, who is not even my father, but yes, in almost every way that counts, yes he is.

I have no idea how she ever met Benedetto. Picket line, singles group, book club? Definitely not at a gourmet cooking class. All I know is it was five years ago, because I was fourteen, and I was still expecting my dad to come back anytime now, and there was not one thing I liked about this person.

His English was terrible. He was way too well-dressed for the gathering meteorological, economic and general disasters of 2015. His accent made me want to tear my hair out. And the look on my mom's face when he would always kiss her hand? It made me physically sick. At least he was not a cop. Or a banker.

But bit by bit, as the world closed in on us, and everything from mall to cell phones, school to internet to interstate commerce fell away, as we devolved into reluctant pioneers, he won me over. Sense of humor. Adventurous. Caring/compassionate. Smart. All the same uh features you used to plug in to try and find your One and Only Soulmate Forever and Ever online. Who knew? Apparently step-dad template is exactly the same.

But back to the pioneer thing. That is not the right word. We were not settling any new territories, just all holing up in our sad little bunkers to complain and lament and blame. For sure, we were not "preparing a way for others." Maybe the city is different, but out here these days it is 100% DIY. Whether you have children to raise or not, without transportation, the village is way too far away. Good thing I was already raised. Or some facsimile thereof.

Anyway, this would all be because of the whole world being climate-changed. Which is a very nice way of tagging chaos. Thunderstorm earthquake drought fire tornado famine five feet of snow choking heat… For about ten years now, it has been a total grab bag of so-called natural disasters. Which catastrophe came when? Who will be next? Nobody has a clue.

And my feeling is that Benedetto woke up one day a couple of weeks ago convinced that cataclysm was somehow starting to home in directly on our house, that maybe he could find an exemption, a little hideaway somewhere that would be climate-free. I think he has always been too sensitive, too impulsive, too believing. So he runs away. Bravo.

News bulletin: he is also way too religious. Who could have ever imagined that our house would have shiny little pictures of Maria Santissima tucked into the mirrors, the face of Jesus over their bed? Oh, and let's add too hysterical. He's the one who said it, "I am Italian! I cannot calm down!"

Well, me neither right this minute. Lunch is over, and I am out of here, me and my perfect stone.

"Back in a while, Mom! Don't forget to milk the cow and pick the rest of the vegetables and maybe some pears. And also grind a little more flour for bread. Or cookies." Sure thing. No reply. She is already inching back toward the hot tub. "Okay, never mind. Maybe just remember to come up for air?"

The back steps shudder as I pound onto the broken walk. Cow shed. Struggling garden. Chicken coop. Rotting greenhouse. Toppled swing set. Mini-windbreak of striving corn. What used to be a pond. The wheat field. Finally my woods.

Something surges through me—anger, hope, abandon, fear—and I kick up dirt, grab at branches, stripping them of leaves, buds, pine cones. Run, and then slide long tracks into the needled path, releasing a perfume that makes me even dizzier.

I do know where I'm going, but also it doesn't matter. My movement through forest and air, through far sounds of water and great columns of sun, cloaks of shade is the thing. Ha. Aho. Yippee. Hallelujah. If I happen to slip and go head over heels off the edge of the earth, so be it. So be it all.

Hours? Days? Eventually I slow back into world and direction, purpose and coordinates of place. I am right on track.

A brown-striped bird chits at me and I chit back. Not too far now. I am positive Benedetto will be at the lake, on the hill. Or else nearby, in the cave.

I am trotting again now; for the first time, wondering what I will say. "Oh, ciao." "You are missed." "My mother, all evidence to the contrary, needs you." "How can there be safety in being safely alone?" "Come back, come back, please come back."

Or just "Hey", and let him do the talking, telling of sights and visions, angels and foxes and how this is nothing like l'Italia, not at all; speaking excitedly of wood nymphs and maybe bears. Or flinging loud but beautiful words in Italian, wrapping himself in otherness, bidding me go back.

"*Non ce la faccio piu`*!"

"*Qui sono sicuro*, I am safe."

"*Ritorna a casa—vai*!"

And will I, in fact, return? Yes. My mother. Yes, the hope shaken loose in my flight that still, still my father may return. Yes. Casa. Home.

I arrive, pushing, stumbling, stopping just short of the lake. "*Benede—*"

But there is nothing, no one. I stand, breathing hard. Fuhh. Why am I even doing this? Not for her. Well, maybe partly for her. Okay, I don't really know why I am. My eyes lose focus, stopping my mind. A small wave laps just shy of my feet. I guess—I guess it is mostly because—he is missing. And the world is lost and broken enough as it is. I cannot stand for anybody else to be gone.

I lean over the cool and silent lake. No, he does not happen to be floating, breath held, just above the shelf of sand. Okay, maybe he was sitting on the hill, and I just didn't see him. Strike two. There are only the shivering poplars. Only ascent or precipitous descent.

The cave! But it is empty. No sign but a pile of acorns, crimson berries, a swatch of black fur. Of human animals, nothing. Oh. But I was so sure.

And now what? Fine, I was totally wrong about this, but where else is there? The village—no, I very much doubt it. Or the other side of the forest, to which I have never been.

Sinking onto a mossy log, I feel like Winnie the Pooh trying to think. Yes, exactly. And just as I have finally decided in a fairly muddled kind of way to head, indeed, for the Other Side of the Forest, the snow begins to fall. You are absolutely right—it is late summer. But such minor details do not matter anymore. The weather does exactly what it feels like. Unless it is that my Winnie the Pooh moment was so powerful, I just created the Mother of all Blustery Days.

Gusts arise, a handful of pellets strikes my face, and I move reluctant under the ceiling of rock edging the cave. After a few minutes of further and increasingly frigid muddle, I give in. I will not be going anywhere else today, not tonight. Already, dark plaits itself into the thin ribbons of cold white; already, the circle of cave behind me shifts and settles, wanting to be pulled around my shoulders like a cloak. Small noises of bird and scrabbling squirrel begin to sound like lullaby. Already, pillowed leaves become blanket and bed.

Questions of the night.

Mom. Underwater. How long? Does she have a clue?

Signor Mondo. Where?

My stone! I can't figure out where I put it.

And what about me?

Certainty. What would that be like?

Suddenly despairing, I look around. Shadows of shadows. Impenetrable air. But maybe yes. The certainty of cave.

Already, sigh becomes yawn, and I fall. Already, sleep.

In cave dream, I find them every one. Benedetto, my father. Mom. And more besides. The finger-sized doll who one day disappeared, never to be heard from again. A red diary from when I was eleven. The best marbles my father still had from his father, and gave one by one to me. The kind of fine order I at one point held within my grasp but never reached. My sweet innocence. That whirling sky above us, that time... A fire of red and gold and green. Stories of buffalo. This almost-peace. This joy. The bear.

Seriously. Only the last on the list remains when I shift, crawl painfully toward light, sit hunched around myself with eyes still closed. Sighing, open them to the wild cascade of snow-turning-rain that curtains the entrance. Blink at a sound behind me, and look back to where I lay. Curled, it would seem from the imprint, against the still-sleeping bear.

Oh. Is this why I am left feeling ponderous but strong, entirely unknowing of danger, safe in my skin? Energies transferred perhaps, in sleep and dream. And what on earth did I give? A massive paw twitches, then curls closed. Another delicate snore. Let me roll again into your loving arms; oh, let me rest.

But day, despite the scrim of rain, moves in; there is no hibernation for my kind; I've miles to go. Bear snuffs and grins (I swear) as I smooth away my bed of blanket leaves, place a spray of berries in the great soft paw, and leave.

Drenched and shaking. Tripping through bunchgrass and sage. Day night day, and Bear becomes memory becomes dream becomes touchstone. As I pound across frozen fields, Bear is the drumbeat; when I spy the footprints that will mean I find my step-father, Bear will be my cry of relief. Tonight, now, under Ponderosa pine, I am falling into righteous sleep, the thought of Bear my blanket and my tent.

Vanilla. Wait, pause on the sleep. How can I be smelling vanilla? Sitting, I open my arms, breathe in. Okay, I remember. Remember as if it was in another Age—Stone, Pre-Cambrian, Industrial, Oil, Post Fuck-up. Which would be when we were realizing the destruction that spun from our spiraling desires. When we began to duck them all, past present future; began to cover our eyes and shield our fragile heads. When still we squinted sometimes hopefully for hope, believed we would survive.

Oh, right—we have. Or, some of us. So far. But that was not my point. Really, what is with the cinnamon, I mean vanilla? As I sniff again, it takes me back to the ancient past of agenda and backpack, bus pass, big city, true love. What I think we called Higher Education. My years as a student. When Land and Food Systems was a degree, Global Food Markets existed, and Fundamentals of Nutrition was a course rather than a distant dream. Hey, I was this close to graduating when the universities shut down.

Never mind. Right. Vanilla. That would have been Agroforestry 101. The field trip to the forested park that shouldered west campus, our uncertain naming of the trees, the careful mapping of old-growth and new- (the disturbing fact that there actually was none of the latter), rain slicking Kai's raven-black hair, the prof explaining that the old trees were resilient to climate change, yay, but, oh dear, not able to reproduce. Our unadorned conclusion: not good. Already in love, I learned that the outside of the Ponderosa pine is like a spice rack—bark like cinnamon-red puzzle pieces, and if you run your finger through a furrow, the dreamy wakening scent of, you got it, pure vanilla...

Wow. Back to reality, Perce. Leave it be.

Waking, I did not know I had intended sleep, do not know if I did sleep; where am I; where is Bear?

My gaze lifts higher and higher into hemlock. No, what am I saying? Through damp air, the perfume of the bark again. Of Ponderosa. We already went through this. And now drops that are more mist than rain slide beautiful, easy down earth-pointing needles, begin to pat gently all around me. One targets my forehead, and I sit abruptly, a mechanical doll, illumined. I know exactly where he is. Change of direction, and I am off.

Layers of cloud, black over gray over almost-white sail over a strip of blue. Unwinding beneath, a green ribbon of forest, waterlogged yellow of bending grass; here and there, the brown bottomland of good earth.

Feet pounding one stratum, arms rising and falling through another, it is as if I am jogging through geological time. Which brings me back, unwilling, to the Ages that I will not, will no longer list. Just let there be another one ahead of us (above, below—it doesn't matter). The Age of Waking Up? In which humanity gives its little head a shake, opens its eyes, and against all odds, eleventh hour plus, survives. The stuff of minor miracle. Begetting the Age of An Actual Liveable Future of

Exquisite Sufficiency as Based on the Wisdom of the Past. Or something like that.

At which point, I fall into a hole. As holes go, it is not much of one. Definitely not Alice in Wonderland material. But I am seemingly stuck. Jack-knifed, butt down, in the mud. I gasp, try to get some leverage and can't, start to cry, then laugh. What could possibly be more ridiculous? Seriously, I am a cartoon of absolute stuckness. Metaphor. Epitome. Fool. Let's see… Persephone the Living Cartoon.

In a way, it is actually interesting, until I get hungry and then start needing to pee. Okay, maybe I have not been trying hard enough to get out of here. But apparently I do not have the upper-back strength or the core whatever they call it to hoist myself up. And no, I cannot get my hands over to the sides of the hole for some reverse push-up action— my arms are pinned by my sides and don't bend that way. I need a hand, help, another person to assist me. What a concept. I give up.

Eyes closed. Eyes open. Now all I can think about is that silly white mouse with the teddy-bear. There was this picture online. Sweetly asleep, paws circled around his tiny bear. It was not photo-shopped; I looked it up; his owner actually created these little stuffed animals for him. I made it my screensaver. It made me cry.

Ever immobile, now I am trapped in my scrolling thoughts as well. Why, when we gaze at someone, at an animal, even at our so-called worst enemy, lying safe in sleep, does everything but tenderness fall away?

The innocence, perhaps; their tranquil breath. A picture of the respite we are all longing for. Free, in repose, of the worries and terrors, the unmet needs and here-and-gone joys of wakeful days on Earth. As if pure and simple and whole. I want the mouse to sleep, embracing bear, forever. I want us all to have such peace.

But hello, all I am embracing is myself, wedged in a hole. Just let there be no blizzards. Though dark, I see, is on its way.

I wake up head cricked back against a rock, hands fallen awkward across my chest, legs angled stiff to the pale morning sky. Throat burning, back in severe pain. Unbelievable. And then I hear the footsteps.

Man or beast, lunatic or Bear? There is not much I can do. Step. Stomp. Pad. (At least it is not slither.) I close my eyes. Just get it over with.

Shuffle. Stop. Silence. They are right next to me now. I take a deep breath and squint one eye open, can't do it, try again. Breathe. Focus. Okay, so it is a—

What? No, this is actually not possible. But it is.

"What the—" He draws back, nearly trips himself, recovers. "Whoa. Percy?"

Kai. I turn my head away and work on disappearing. This so cannot be.

"Percy. It is you. Um. Would you like a hand?"

Would I like a hand? No, I am not actually here, can't you see? Would I like a hand? Yes, I would like a fricking hand. Just not your hand. No.

He leans over and touches my shoulder, lightly, kindly, but under these circumstances, kindness is like battery acid. Do this, and you scar me for life.

When sound returns, it is his voice. The sound. No words. My name, perhaps. "Persephone?"

Can I not stay silent, unconscious, still fainted away? Entirely vanish.

"Can you hear me?"

Yes, for god's sake, I can hear you. Now just go. It emerges as a kind of croak. "Gh—go." He does not listen, apparently I have run out of sounds, and then, suddenly, I am under a tree, out of the hole. Joy, until I realize that he has lifted me, held me against him. Held me. This time, a broken wail. "I was finally over you!"

His eyes widen. "But I—"

Dizzy as I am, I sway to my feet. "Stop! Do not say anything. Just go."

And then he laughs. "Stop. Go. Which is it? Make up your mind, girl."

My fist clenches. No—it's good. Good that you have reminded me what I could not stand about you, and now I am safe. I almost smile. "It's Go. You can give me a hug first. Oh, and thank you for the rescue. And Bye."

Confusion makes him stumble again. Never did he understand me. Doesn't matter. I get my hug. He squeezes me once more, then turns. "Okay, well, bye. Watch out for those holes."

"Ha." I lean back against the tree and watch him disappear. And so it is. Now, where was I? Oh yes, running through the strata of time. Which takes me back to the lost-and-found theme, which makes me think of Mom. Where would she be right now? Still underwater; clambering from the hot tub, trying to remember how to engender food; actually recognizing a carrot top, and pulling; letting meditation replace meals? There is no telling, nothing I can do. She's a big girl, by some definitions anyway. Let it go.

And also what the heck did happen to my stone? No answer here either. As I decide to stop the useless questions and stand up, suddenly energy rushes back. One look to get my bearings, and then I am back on the road. Watching out for those holes.

But of course there are no more, and again I slide down paths slippery with pine needles, bracketed by alder and unidentifiable brush and sudden ledges of emerald moss. 'The other other side', my mantra. Pumping, sliding, chanting. And then I am there.

Was I right? I was right. On the far side of that clearing, a figure, a faint voice. I stumble as if pushed from the last border of tall trees, move into the field, converge.

Benedetto. Hands waving wild to the heavens as if I were the Virgin Mary finally returned. Meh. Nevertheless, a pretty sweet welcome.

"Persefone!"

It is one of those miraculous moments. As if this silly name had been waiting all my life to be rejoicingly declaimed in perfect Italian cadence.

"Per-se-fo-ne! Bella!"

And I am in his arms.

Silence roars. His jacket smells like hay. I rest my head, then breathe myself away, step back and hear the click as part of this disconnected world snaps neatly back in place.

He holds me away from him now, smiles as if he maybe just invented me. "*Nel mio villaggio, c'era una barca portafortuna col nome tuo…*"

'In my village', I don't know, something about fortune, I think. "What's *barca?*"

"Is boat. The one bringing luck to all our village. Is called Persefone."

"Sweet." I turn toward home.

But he's not finished yet. "*Brava. Sei incredibile.*"

"Sure." There is nothing incredible about me. But I do have a plan, Part B. When we get back to Mom, when harmony has been reinstated (when cows are milked and chickens fed, gardens watered and strawberries picked, bread rising), then maybe I will head out here again and track my dad. Father Finders Unlimited.

"*Momento, cara. Fammi prendere la valigia.*"

It is amazing how much I am starting to be able to figure out. Valigia - valise—ha! suitcase. The crazy thing is he actually means it. Old-school, with fading stickers of Venezia and Agrigento and Hotel Cefalu`, it bangs against his legs as we rewind through field and forest, telling each other tales.

"*La tua mamma?*" he asks again.

"She's uh fine."

82

Shaking his head, he puts the suitcase down, raises his palms. "She learn some of the cooking you can eat yet?"

My eyebrows raise, cheeks fill with the absurdity, and we both crack up.

I manage a little flippy Italian-style hand gesture. "But she's fine."

And when we emerge at dusk from woods to wheat field, past pond and now-taller corn, still-toppled swing set, greenhouse, chicken coop, garden, shed; as he waves an arm for me to precede him on the broken path and up the shifting steps; when I hesitate before heading toward the hot tub, yes, I am right.

Setting a dripping branch of lilac into a vase, she turns and gasps. "Perce!" Runs to me, the branch like a banner, crushes it against my back as she enfolds me. "Baby."

"Hey, Mom. We're home." Lilac showers us. Benedetto stands in the doorway like a patient god. Centered on the dining room table next to the vase, I see, is my stone.

Kissing my mother's cheek, I beckon him. "Your turn. Watch out for the lilacs."

"*Sei certa?*"

"I'm certain." They stand looking at each other, and I scoop up my stone, start to nest it in my pocket, then flip it a couple of times as I head for the back door.

Across the yard, studying it as I go. It is perfect. What do I need with it? I raise my arm, stand momentary like the Javelin Thrower embroidering the hem of your standard Grecian urn, or maybe just a 2020 Girl in Ancient Pose, and skip it fast into the swampy pond. And now?

I wander back to check on the livestock. Chickens filing up onto their roost, and, a miracle, Hattie already milked. Well, a necessary miracle— if Mom hadn't figured that one out, the poor cow would be dead.

I sit with Hattie until dark. "You're not much of a bear, girl, but you'll do." Then I decide that wasn't very nice. I pat her nose but she just studies me for a moment and then goes back to her bit of hay. I forgot—cows are simply cows. And I stay a little longer, breathing in, mooing back, until I hear my mother's husky voice.

"Perce?"

"Yup. Coming, Mom."

Just enough light still. I feel around in the garden for cucumbers and a couple of patient carrots, maybe some lettuce? Part B, Subsection 1: we are at least going to teach her how to make a proper insalata.

Body Paint, Craig Spence
Honorable mention

I should have known at first sight that with Alesha I'd end up in a predicament. But sometimes foresight only whets appetite: the greater the risk, the more appealing the objects of our intentions. At least that's how it worked for me, through high school, university, then a couple of post-grad years too... I always 'rose to the bait' you might say, and proved a bigger catch than any of my adversarial lovers could reel in. That may sound like chutzpah, but I'm not going to apologize. There's plenty of things I've got to atone for, brashness—as opposed to false modesty—won't be among them.

When I first caught sight of her, Alesha was body painting Raoul at her Moss Street booth, transforming him into a hybrid human-tiger. The Moss Street Paint-In, in case you've never heard of it, is a sort of artists' bazaar and carnival that runs the length of the byway it's named after from the Ocean up to the Victoria Art Gallery near Fort Street. That's where her booth was located. Raoul was to be part of her 'Menagerie of Endangered Species', an 'exhibition of visual and performance art expressing the solidarity of humanimal spirit'.

Kevin had emailed me a link to her web site under subject line: 'Tea and Oranges', a characteristic bit of 'wry wit'. See if you can get to know her—in whatever sense of the word is necessary, he directed. Our Alesha is not only a fully fledged member of the loon family, she also sits on the executive council of The Coalition Against Pipelines, the very epicenter of looniness.

Raoul wore a tiger-eared hood. Alesha had striped his back and shoulders copper and black with greasy body paint and was working on his face, meticulously daubing and stroking in whiskers, nose, the deceptively beautiful patterns around the man-tiger's eyes…only Raoul's eyes were green, not gold like a real tiger's, a discrepancy Alesha would later excuse as part of the 'humanimal mix'. His loins and buttocks were scantily covered in a pair of briefs that matched his hood. Raoul's legs were hairy enough in their native form to pass for humanimal, I thought. The get up was convincing in its own way, but only because Alesha's intentions were metaphorical—or so I believed. And Raoul's were something else entirely.

The best lies are an adulteration of truth. I could stretch that point and argue that truth is a relative construct—the way you fashion your facts to suit the end you have in mind. These relativities are only exposed as lies when they are viewed from somebody else's perspective, or when their purposes have been served. Now there's a doctoral thesis that would make the philosophy profs at UBC sit up straight in their creaking chairs. Not that their hair-splitting matters. It certainly doesn't to the Marketing & Communications Group at PenUtlimate Oil, which has been churning out its versions of truth since before I was born. "That's not truth!" you shout indignantly. Well, Kevin and his wunderkind don't have any doubts about where the truth lies, and they've got the market data to make their point.

Do you think me a cad? Well, perhaps I am. But that doesn't alter the truth or lessen the effectiveness of those who manufacture it, no matter how superior slagging me makes you feel. Kevin and his crew are only too happy to stick me in the ground as a lightning rod for your outrage. That's how they think. It's how they've thought from the beginning. PenUltimate hired me, and Kevin groomed me as a sacrificial mole, an innocuous species that could infiltrate the enviro movement in whacky BC. My job was to burrow, and dig up minute details that would make their version of events ring truest. They know the very best lies are so well conceived and rehearsed, so seamless in detail and argument, that we end up believing them ourselves. Call me a liar, and I'll invite you to join me in the dock. We're all liars when you get to the bottom of us, which is to say, we all end up espousing stuff we believe, but can't certify as truth… the non-existential, heart-of-the-atom truth. How else could we sell our washing machines, used cars, politics, newspapers and such, eh?

I introduced myself to Alesha as a freelance reporter and gave her one of my cards to prove it—one of the cards that had been deliberately designed to look amateurish and home-made. Paul Welland, she said. I've read some of your stuff. I blushed and told her I wanted to do an item on the Menagerie project, and on her belief in humanimal spirit. She kept on painting Raoul. Let me think about it, she answered, meaning: I'll call you.

Alesha is one of those women who make you transparent simply by looking at you. You can never fathom what she might be seeing through those shockingly clear, minutely detailed brown eyes of hers. You might be a crystal ball in her vision, or an empty wine glass, or a clear, calm patch of ocean over a kelp and eelgrass bay. No matter how you think it, though, you can never figure out what she's really seeing when she looks straight at you. There's a tendency in Western culture to misconstrue her kind of clairvoyance as innocence, and I suppose the two species breathe the same air. But when we met in the Cornerstone Café, it took only a few minutes for me to realize she was getting to know me in dimensions I couldn't begin to guess at—that my aura, if you believe in such, was something she could sense beyond sight, hearing, taste, touch and smell just as surely as she watched me and listened to my words.

I've described all this as though I'd encountered the likes of Alesha before, as if I'd known others who had revealed to me what Leonard Cohen meant with his song about Suzanne's tea and oranges. I hadn't. Or at least I can't say for sure I had. What I can say without prejudice is Alesha was the first to see through me and convince me of my own self-misperception. I haven't described all this as well as I should. When I say she saw through me I'm not suggesting I'd become invisible, quite the opposite. To her, people are a sort of lens, each offering a unique perspective on a larger world. In fact, in her vision every creature becomes a node within the common matrix. Or, to put things another way, as individuals we are all 'wonderful and necessary illusions'. There may have been others who had looked at me that way before, when I wasn't ready. I can't remember. So by default Alesha becomes the first.

That's what makes the betrayal nascent in our moment of meeting so painful—Alesha could see who I was, she could bring out the true soul of me; she couldn't see my perversions though, my fractures and faults.

Why? she said. Why what? Why do you want to write about me? Because the idea of humanimalism... She laughed. What's so funny? You make it sound like some kind of philosophy. We stopped there for a moment, and I could tell she was letting her words sink like coins into diminishing strata of light. Isn't it? I asked. She shook her head. As soon as you make what you live a philosophy people want to argue with you about it, she said.

My mobile went off, an angry wasp inside my pocket, its furious vibrations insistent, frantic. I answered to shut the thing up. So how's it going? Kevin wanted to know. Oh fine, I said, pretending I might be talking to my favorite uncle, or a mentor, or a friend—anyone but Kevin Norquist. Alesha watched, her eyes intense, like a bird of prey's. I'm doing an interview actually. I'll call you back later, okay? You're talking with her! Right now! Kevin let out a conspiratorial whoop, his voice shrill like an excited teen's. I'm in a café in Fernwood. Got to go. Bye. I punched the red 'end call' square on my mobile's screen.

I wonder, Alesha said, a hint of playful mocking in her voice. You wonder what? What kind of humanimal you might be? I'm just plain old human, I said. She smirked. You're not plain and you're not old. I'm glad you stopped there, I joked. She smiled, almost laughing, and I was buoyed by the upturning of her lips and the luster in her eyes, hints of her knowing things about me I didn't yet know myself. And you are humanimal, she insisted. We all are. I thought you said what you live isn't a philosophy. It's not. What is it then, when you insist something you believe has to apply to everyone else? An invitation, Alesha smiled. I tilted my head. Perhaps you're a cocker spaniel, she hazarded. We laughed and for an instant, for just a tick in time, but suggestive of a seam in the veil of illusion and a light behind... for an instant the joy of us harmonized on the air and I forgot what I was about. We'll have to find out, Alesha said. What? We have to find out what kind of humanimal you are. It's the best way to do your story. And how do we do that—discover the humanimal me, I mean. I'll paint you, Alesha said. Then you can write me. Okay?

* * *

My joints ached, the cold penetrated, I shivered. The sun slid toward the west, a golden seal pasted onto the azure by a PR edition of God—light without heat, without even residual warmth. I yearned to shout out something like 'Fuck it!', but words were out of place—any formulation of thought into language verboten. I couldn't actually see the sun anymore because my eyes were shut. "You have to see it with your inner senses," Alesha coached. So there I was, trying to piece together a humanimal experience through the pink opacity of my eyelids: pretending not to hear as a physical sensation, so much as the spirit of wind and waves sighing and whispering without language, without even the physics of sound—internalizing the tickle and tousle of streaming air as something inside me, as if I was a ghost cloaked in a perfectly permeable membrane instead of rubberized skin.

I could not remember how long it had been since Alesha had spoken. Her injunction against my speaking held firm. I could not break it, couldn't have disappointed her that way for the world. I wanted, so wanted her to be right, even if my wanting was wrong—wrong, she had prescribed, because it would only reveal what I thought she wanted me to be, not what I truly was. You might be a starfish, or jellyfish, or any kind of fish at all, and that will be fine with me, Alesha said. Be what you are! We'd walked the log-littered beach to Holland Point just before sunset because I told her that was my favorite place, and sunset my favorite time. Follow your instincts, she said en route, and the spirit will come to you. Is this some sort of incarnation experience you're leading me into? She laughed. What's so funny? Everything, Alesha said—and I don't know how, but I understood exactly what she meant. It's better to receive a question as divinely funny than reject it as stupid.

Before I paint you, we must know who you are. Did Alesha actually say this out loud, or had she patched directly into my thoughts? I'll never know. She seemed a blend of sibilant wind and waves, probing the porous contours that bound me with her cool, persistent pressure—seeking a way. And this communing of wind and waves and Alesha and me dissolved doubt and—let go, she whispered. Let yourself go. Where? That is not for you to know or me to say. Let go.

There's a point beyond relaxing that cannot be described because what you are trying to formulate into words, into thoughts, is non-existence—total dissolution of the muscles and ligaments of being. This is not death; it's the opposite of death. Words imprison as surely as bricks, mortar, bars. Scientific theories seek boundaries and insist on belief, on proof… Let go, Alesha sighed, as if her breath were mine. Let go. Perfect translucence is not something you can define or point to. Alesha's way of seeing is something you can only know after you have allowed yourself to be seen by her, or somebody like her—as if you were a crystal ball, or an empty wine glass, or a clear calm patch of ocean… or an unblemished expanse of sky… Let go…

Caw! Caw! Caw!

I became nothing. Inseminating spirit rushed into the world.

Caw! Caw! Caw!

Then it swelled, urgent to be born, to unfurl its hollow bones, pulsing veins, feathers and wings—first inside the shell then breaking out, breaking free.

Caw! Caw! Caw!

The call came out of me, out of all of me. It became me, a convulsion of being that had to be shouted at sky above and world around. A joyful ejaculation that said: All this is! All this is me! And I am all this inside of me! Yearning, rage, terror, greed, hunger, flight—all these are me. And there was no place I could not go, no place beyond the bounds of my imagining.

Caw!

I opened my eyes, and there on the bleached log opposite sat a perfect crow, sleek and black and glistening in the westering sun. He cocked his head, fixed me with his obsidian eye, and clacked approvingly.

* * *

The tip of her brush traced contours of muscle, hair, bone. She kneeled behind me, but her aura engulfed me, surrounded me with a swaddling of confidence I could only interpret as love. Her version of it anyway: fierce, transformative, insistent.

I don't usually do this here, she said. My eyelids flipped open and I scavenged the room for bits of information that might tell me what she meant. The swatches of colour, scent and sound wouldn't come together into an assemblage I could call 'her apartment', though. My mind refused to draw the evidence of its senses into something I could encapsulate in a single word.

I'm a performance artist, after all, she was saying. I usually do my transformations in the street, like I did with Raoul the day I met you. Alesha wasn't really talking to me so much as to herself through me. She used that tone pet owners do, communing with uncomprehending dogs, cats or budgies—a sort of singsong meant to convey intelligent feelings as much as anything that can be said in the abstract code of language. And that's all I needed from her voice—the consoling modulations of compassion threading sound waves like beads on a string. It's the experience of a moment that matters, that's where art happens—on the cusp of vision, execution and observation. It's as ephemeral as lightening.

A slanting surface splashed with reds, greens, and blues that could have been sacrificial droplets, a tuft of lawn, a swatch of fallen sky; a skeletal contraption fashioned of wood, which looked a likely place to perch; a bouquet of sticks, topped with hair, protruding from a clay pot. I recognized these snippets as Alesha's converted living-room studio, but couldn't muster the intellectual gravity to resolve my impressions into a definition that subsumed the shards of data. Rather, her space—and I knew beyond doubt my creator was its sole occupant—would never in that moment be anything but a curious assortment of artifacts that should have had meaning, and purpose. If I allowed it, though, that purpose would have destroyed me before I was truly born. I closed my eyes, not wanting the jumble of imagery to coalesce. That's it, she coached.

The wings Alesha had invented were appendages of wire and black satin fastened to my human frame with Velcro straps. Fish line ligatures tautened when I stretched these pinions, splaying the feathers as if I were in flight. Alesha whooped, laughed, then cried at the effect. 'Holy fuck!' were the last purely human words I heard from her before I became confused.

Her brush tickled the small of my back, just where the tail feathers attached. Where are you? she asked. The question annoyed. How could she not know? How be so stupid? I was at the precise point where the tip of her brush touched my skin, and could only ever be where the arc of her imagination might take me. And yet… and yet it seemed her tracery defined a point inside me too, that there was a geometry to her art which converged with Euclidean precision at the very centre of me, the exact point where the musculature of angels' wings are joined. In an instant I knew that if I could figure out her spiritual theorem I would be able to fly, and an instant after that I realized that I did know.

* * *

The air over the foothills rises up in shimmering columns from the parched earth, hot, arid. I soar north, following the uplift where it deflects off the tilted landscape, gaining strength from a desultory breeze out of the east. Nothing lives down there—or dies. At least, nothing I can peck at. I wheel eastward. I know the possible consequence of this decision, but the risk must be taken.

Away from the baked rock and scorched foothills the air will be still and, if anything, more oppressive. I will have to expend energy to stay aloft, flap my wings against the dead molecules or fall to ground. On the worst days I have seen other birds drop dead out of the sky or flutter down as if wounded by an arrow or pellet. Their corpses litter the plain, for no bird—not even a carrion bird—will intentionally land in the dead zone. Remains lay there, wrinkling like drying fruit or aging human flesh, not rotting the way things should, but simply withering and wasting away.

Midway through the flight, panic takes hold, the certainty that this time you're not going to make it. Instinct urges you to flap harder, faster, but that would be certain death, for there's no time in this transit you're not on the very edge of heat exhaustion or starvation. The slightest increment of exertion will push your metabolism beyond a supportable limit. The thing to do is relax, glide as much as you can, and by prolonging torture, outlive it. In the end that's who survives—the ones who can tolerate heat, hunger, fear, pain, and shivering nights for generations, without panicking. The ones who habituate themselves to hell's suburbs without going stark raving mad.

I follow the dry riverbed east toward The Pinnacles. I can see them now, in the distance, through the heat haze, gleaming towers thrust up from the plain like gigantic crystals or blades. They are still many wing beats away, so I calm myself, focus on them as you would a mountain peak on the layline of an arduous journey. No sense getting worked up unless there's something to eat within your field of vision; or something to escape; or another of your kind to mate, flock with, or fight. Excitement kills. It dissipates energy, draining you. It can only be permitted when it serves a basic need.

My destination is The Urbs, where the exiles congregate in ragged, shifting, savage bands, intermingling with the damned. It is there a scavenger stands the best chance of finding something to placate the growling god of hunger. Humans die there. They starve to death, leaving enough meat behind to fatten a carrion bird. Or they murder one another in fights over patches of ground, trinkets, differences of opinion, mates. Or they hunt each other as predator does prey, leaving flesh to be picked from the scattered bones of their feasts. All this takes place within sight of The Pinnacles (where I can freely fly, but the exiled and damned don't dare approach on pain of death).

It is said that no exiles would be allowed to live—that they would all be executed within The Pinnacles' perimeter wall—except they serve a purpose, that even in banishment they meet The Masters' ends. For once released into The Urbs they get to know the ways of the damned, and that knowledge can be purchased or prised from them with suitable implements (which The Masters are never loath to employ). As well, the exiles provide useful cover for The Masters' picked murderers and spies, who would otherwise not be able to infiltrate the tribes of the damned in the guise of disgraced citizens.

Such speculation doesn't interest me. All I need to know is the result of The Masters' polity—a zone where the damned and the exiles and The Pinnacles' agents converge, form alliances, barter, and kill. There's always a remainder from their interactions, a quantity of meat to make a meal for creatures such as me.

So the risk is worth it, or will be until the day I am brought down by a stone, pellet, or arrow. That day must come because the damned, stupid as they seem, are cunning in their own ways and perpetually hungry. And they hate the likes of me, who have eaten the flesh of their mates, children, relatives, and friends…

* * *

Where were you? Alesha sat cross-legged before me, the soft light from a candle accentuating her angular features like the contours of a pink-hued planet.

I wasn't ready to speak her tongue, wanted to go back to the harsh vision that had created me. I hadn't reached my destination, The Urbs, before I had been precipitated out of the dry air above the plain surrounding The Pinnacles. I croaked angrily and shook my wings.

She looked surprised, then bemused. I never called you back, she laughed. I've been waiting, but I never called.

How long? Alesha shrugged. Does it matter? I supposed it didn't, now that I was back in her apartment, the clutter of her studio coming into focus, her portraits of other humanimals looking in from every wall. I didn't reach my destination. Again, she shrugged. We never do, she said. Or at least, not the destinations we intended. There could be no mistaking her meaning, no possible interpretation except for what she did mean. I reached out to touch her, but ended up brushing her cheek with my black satin wing. Does this make me crazy as you? I wondered.

Alesha laughed, and it occurred to me I'd never asked what kind of humanimal she might be. Carnivore, I suspected, but didn't need to know. Not then. Not there. For my knowing would be a lie and a betrayal, and I could feel self-loathing growing like a canker inside me.

Crow is not an endangered species, I said. Alesha nodded. Curtly, as if I'd said something too obvious. Then how can I be in your Menagerie? Perhaps you can't, she answered.

A Cup of Joe, Gabriella Brand

"Four cups of sugar left," said Ingrid to herself, opening the canister and peering inside.

The Breakfast Nook had just closed for the day, and Ingrid was alone behind the counter. She mentally calculated that if she gave all her regular customers a scant teaspoonful of sugar in their tepid coffee, she could hold out for another month or two. She divided the numbers again, writing them on a scrap of cereal cardboard, leftover from the time when the island got steady shipments of corn flakes and oatmeal.

Back before the Second World Melt.

In the middle of her calculations, the door to the café opened. Buck Hobbs stood in the entrance, one hand in the pocket of his frayed shorts and the other reaching for his Red Sox cap, which had washed up on shore one day. When he took off the faded hat, scorching sunlight from the front window reflected on the shiny dome of his head. He was completely bald, but back in 1988, when he was twenty, he had had a full head of red hair. And biceps like bricks.

He looked into Ingrid's eyes and smiled. She used to think his smile was his best feature. Now, in 2040, at the age of seventy-two, he was missing two incisors and a couple of molars.

"Could I have a cup of Joe?" he said, casually, as if coffee were still a common commodity.

"I just put out the fire, Buck," answered Ingrid. "Come back tomorrow, when I light it again."

"Oh, come on, Ingrid, make me a little cup of that pitiful brew," he said, teasingly.

Ingrid watched him run his tongue over his gums where his teeth used to be. Then his face grew serious. He approached the counter, placed a hand tenderly on Ingrid's forearm, and lowered his voice. "I'll pay you in kitchen matches. I'll bet you could use some of those," he whispered.

Ingrid didn't answer. She really didn't want to start the fire again, wasting precious kindling. Plus she only had half a tub of coffee beans left. She thought she should use her supplies up fairly and evenly, the last of the sugar married to the last of the coffee, enough for everyone. It was a question of principle. Not that Buck would understand principles.

"Just make me a nice cup of coffee, and I'll bring the matches the next time I come by," said Buck. "I promise."

Ingrid looked away. She had heard Buck promise many things through the years. They were both so old now. They had known each other since they were children, digging for clams down at the point, swimming out to the jetty, taking the ferry to the mainland. She had loved him once. Really loved him. Back when she thought he was so amusing and handsome, when he was the star pitcher on the island team. Now, of course, he looked haggard. Everyone on the island looked haggard.

She found herself thinking about kitchen matches. Maybe Buck had finally learned how to keep a promise. Maybe he'd bring them to her. Who knew what other useful items he had squirreled away in his attic? Rumor had it that he had stashes of wine and aspirin and piles of tools, stuff that had belonged to his parents. Things that maybe could help them all hang on a bit longer.

She looked again at Buck. He seemed so fragile.

"Come on, Ingrid. What's one more little cup in the big scheme of things?" he asked.

Reluctantly, she knelt down and lit some grasses with a candle. Then she added small sticks and blew on the flame. She made a new batch of coffee as quickly as she could, grinding a few stale beans with a hand grinder that her mother had bought at a trendy kitchen store back in the 1980's. Ingrid took pleasure in using the grinder, thinking about her mother's hands on the same handle, making coffee under very different circumstances. She mixed the grounds with rainwater, set the pot on the fire, and brewed the drink for a few minutes.

Buck drained one cup and asked for another. Then he stood up and wiped his mouth with the back of his hand. He touched Ingrid's wrinkled cheek briefly before leaving. "You're a peach, Ingrid," he said, grinning toothlessly, but he didn't say thank you.

Ingrid sighed. She washed Buck's cup and returned to her long division. How long would her sugar and coffee last? She pushed a few strands of her thin, gray hair behind her ears and counted up her regulars again. The first time around, she realized she had forgotten to include Dr. Warren, the veterinarian; Mrs. Vegliante, the former librarian; the Reilly brothers; the Dodson family; and the man they still called Pete the Carpenter, although he hadn't worked in years.

Ingrid was old enough to remember the glint of hammers and nails, the smell of new pine. She used to watch the ships unload building supplies down by the wharf on her way to school. The wharf had been submerged years ago, of course, along with the jetty, the town beaches, and the low-lying part of Main Street. Waves now pounded the edges of the town green where there once stood a Great Northern Bank, a lawyer's office, and a bandstand. Each year the sea rose higher. It was now lapping at the foundation of the abandoned Superette, which had been built on what used to be called The Hill Road. The island was like a sandcastle at high tide, reduced to its keep and turrets.

Ingrid had a passion for the land. It was where her ancestors had settled, where she had gone to school, and where she had always lived. She knew the island's history and its traditions—the frugal Puritans who had built its town green and meetinghouse, the abolitionists who had helped to hide runaway slaves in its cellars. She was determined to preserve what she could, for as long as she could. For many of her neighbors, too, The Breakfast Nook was the last vestige of the old way. A place where a bit of kindness, comfort, and human civilization still endured. The islanders depended on the ritual of gathering together in the morning, hunched over the splintery tables, their hands wrapped around a cup of slightly warm brown liquid. Sitting there together was almost like worship, holy and quiet.

Ingrid was grateful that The Breakfast Nook was built on a solid foundation, with thick walls that seemed to withstand the ever-increasing winds.

It was housed in a stone gatehouse that had been part of an elegant estate, once owned by Ingrid's great-great-great grandfather. A wealthy sea captain, he had built his beautiful home on the highest hill, with a great view of the harbor. Of course, the island had been bigger then, with beautiful white bluffs, a bustling fishing trade, and a temperate climate. Roses bloomed in gardens, and stone fruits and wild grapes grew abundantly. Occasionally a nor'easter would cause havoc, but nothing like what was happening now.

As she finished up her calculations, Ingrid wondered if anyone on the island possessed coffee and sugar. Was there any possibility for barter? It was hard to tell which of the remaining homes had secret stashes of former staples. For so many islanders, it had become every man for himself. Decent folks had taken to protecting their storerooms night and day, sometimes sleeping on the floor with a weapon. There would always be some poor soul looking to steal food. Electronics, once so precious, were worthless. A few of the richer families had guard dogs, but most people had eaten their Rottweilers long ago. She thought again about Buck Hobbs and his kitchen matches.

People once thought Buck and Ingrid might marry. They had been a couple back in high school. They'd spent many a Saturday night on the dunes, clinging together, warm and sticky. The summers were already growing hotter back then. But after graduation Buck went off-island for a few years, looking for work.

"Wait for me, Ingrid. I'll be back," he had said. "Don't run off with anyone else."

So she had waited. And waited. She never forgot the day Buck finally returned. He had a gold band on his finger, an attractive woman on his arm, and a drooling baby over his shoulder. He ended up divorcing and marrying at least three times. Ingrid had stayed single, taking over the operation of The Breakfast Nook from her father.

As she closed up the café for the day, Ingrid couldn't get her mind off Buck Hobbs and her dwindling supplies. She feared Buck's reaction the day she reached the bottom of the barrel. He was known to have a bad temper.

"Well, too bad for him," she said to herself. "This is what the world has come to. And not having a decent cup of coffee is the least of it."

At first Buck hadn't believed. Not at all. Not even after the Second World Melt.

Nowadays, everyone, of course, had a theory. The Upheaval was all they talked about, from early in the morning until the last wick was blown out at night.

"The earth's all screwed up," said Armand Reilly. "Our parents saw it coming, right? Everyone saw it coming."

"It must be God's will," insisted some of the church ladies.

But Dr. Warren shook his head. "I think people did this," he would say softly, "not God."

Across the little island, people were scraping by. Some were living off skinny fish and snails, the occasional slug. A few people had had the wisdom to keep chickens, not an easy task given the heat, dust, and predators. The offshore items that people once took for granted had disappeared. Flour, toilet paper, beer, bandages, propane, toothpaste, apples. The younger generation didn't even know what they were.

When Ingrid was a child, commercial boats served the island all year round, and hordes of carefree tourists came over on the ferry every summer. But the subsequent decades had been marked by violent hurricanes, floods, and extended periods of drought. Insect infestations were rampant all over the planet. Agri-businesses and other industries came to a standstill just about everywhere. Most countries were at war.

Two years ago, the last merchant ship to reach the island was battered by a storm. It lost its fuel to the voracious sea, and there was none on the island to replace it, even if the ship had still been sea-worthy. The villagers helped the crew salvage what things they could from the vessel. They brought a large chunk of the hull onto the shore, turning it over like the carapace of a giant beetle.

The captain moved in with Pete the Handyman, and most of the crew took up residence in a lean-to made out of a rusted Good Humor Ice Cream Truck near the former tennis courts. The sailors had nowhere to go and little to do, except forage for food. Sometimes Ingrid watched them stoning birds. They wound up their arms like winches and took aim. Ingrid would have liked to do that, but at seventy-two, her throwing arm was much too weak.

"You'd have to have muscles like a sailor. Or like Buck Hobbs used to have," thought Ingrid.

It wasn't long before Ingrid found herself taking her one remaining pen and writing a sign to stick onto the front door to warn her customers, especially Buck.

"SUGAR AND COFFEE ALMOST GONE. CHIN UP!"

She knew that most of her regulars would understand. When she had run out of flour, a few months back, Rodney Chatwick suggested she make muffins out of potatoes and millet. She had added some blueberries as well, and everyone had praised the results.

"Where did you get blueberries?" asked Dr. Warren, licking his stained fingers. "The wild ones haven't shown up for years. All eaten by bugs."

"Found a tin or two," said Ingrid, without going into details.

In truth, she had come upon several rusty tins: blueberries, corn, baked beans, canned apricots in heavy syrup, and more, in the trunk of an abandoned Chevrolet, once owned by her neighbors, the Vilar family. It appeared that they had gone down to the old Superette and never brought the groceries into the house. Or maybe they had always hidden supplies in their car. All that anyone knew was that, one night, all the Vilars took off. They just left everything, their beds and their dinnerware, even a cat with bloated teats. No one knows how they got off island or where they went. This was around the time of the Second World Melt. Ingrid hated to think of them trying to get somewhere in a rowboat. All six of them. The two parents and the four little kids. They were never heard from again.

After writing the sign, Ingrid closed up The Breakfast Nook and headed along the ridge to her clapboard house. As she walked, she looked out over the endless expanse of sea. A few seagulls circled overhead, and the hot wind yapped at her neck like a dog.

She hurried along, keeping her eyes open for *finds*. Because whole families scavenged continually, the edges of the road were picked clean. People had even pried up patches of the pavement, thinking they might use the gooey asphalt as fuel, but it didn't burn. Sometimes children found animal droppings and searched them with their fingers for undigested seeds or grains.

Ingrid had been pleased to come upon a small button one day. A little blue button, the color of a cornflower. She had once had a coat with buttons like that. A heavy wool winter coat, back when the island had four distinct seasons. It could get quite cold in the winter. She'd worn the coat on a date with Buck, decades ago. When she found the button, she picked it up and closed her palm around it like a pirate with a gold coin.

Every now and then, she would see something shiny on the ground, a piece of metal or glass, the broken screen of a cell phone or a computer. The old satellite tower, built in 2005, was still standing up on the hill, but all the old communication companies had collapsed in the Upheaval. The spindly tower was as dead and useless as a Christmas tree in July.

Ingrid had always had a garden before the insect plagues. She had canned a great many fruits and vegetables, and had thought to bury them under the foundation of her little house. Some of the jars were now twenty years old. She had doled them out, opening them only when she could find nothing else to eat, hoping that they didn't harbor botulism. Sometimes she shared one with the Dodson family if one of the little boys knocked on the door with listless eyes and sores around his mouth.

One night, she twisted the lid on the last jar from her old garden. It was pickled beets, and she gobbled them up, as ravenous as a brown bear. The sweet red liquid lipsticked her mouth. She even sucked the inside of the jar, purposely breaking the glass so she could reach the bottom with her tongue.

The next morning, Ingrid got to The Breakfast Nook and obsessively measured and re-measured the remaining sugar. It was time to cut back further.

When Buck Hobbs arrived, he tasted his coffee and winced.

"Come on' babe, a little bit more sugar, just for me," he had said quietly.

Ingrid bit her lip. Mrs. Vegliante looked up and smirked at Dr. Warren. Most people on the island knew that Buck could sweet-talk Ingrid, taking advantage of her good nature. The Reilly brothers stopped talking to each other and looked over at Ingrid, expecting her to give in to Buck. But Ingrid shook her head and turned back to the fire.

Buck got up from the counter, leaving his coffee untouched. Ingrid assumed that he was storming off, but he headed for the toilet, around the side of the kitchen. Conversation among the other customers resumed. There was no radio or television anymore, so every sound in The Breakfast Nook reverberated against the walls, in spite of the winds. They clearly heard Buck flush the toilet with a bucket of sea water. Then he returned to his stool at the counter, strutting as he always did.

He still didn't touch the coffee.

"You gotta check the restroom, Ingrid," he said as he straddled the counter stool.

"Pipe problem?" interjected Pete the Carpenter, a little too eagerly, from two seats down.

"No, it's a lady's problem," said Buck, expressionless.

The other men kept their eyes down, examining the bare tables, where generations had carved their initials.

Ingrid wiped her hands on her apron and walked into the restroom, puzzled. She had been the only person to use the toilet today before Buck. What kind of lady's problem could he be thinking of? Sanitary products, if that was the issue, hadn't been available since the Superette got washed away and the merchant ship got stranded. She looked around. Nothing was amiss. The bucket was relatively clean, the make-shift toilet brush upright in its place. Then she saw the mirror. Words, written with her last precious drops of Tidi-Bowl cleanser, hoarded since 2020, were dripping blue towards the sink.

"I'VE GOT MEAT TO SHARE. AND STUFF."

There were little flecks of Tidi-Bowl splattered on the "EMPLOYEES MUST WASH HANDS" sign. She quickly wiped off Buck's message and left.

Returning to the counter, she felt her hands shaking, but she nodded at Buck and slipped him some extra sugar. He swallowed the sweetened mixture even before Ingrid could offer to warm it up again. He got up and left, winking at her on the way out.

The next day Buck showed up for his sweet coffee, and the next day as well. In fact, all that week, he came in, smiling and flirting with Ingrid, while the sugar canister got lighter and lighter.

"Any day now," thought Ingrid, "Buck will come to my house. With the meat."

But he didn't.

At home, she sat waiting by the window late into the dark night, gnawing on a knobby root and a couple of sunflower seeds.

The day came when Ingrid was obligated to write, "SUGAR AND COFFEE ALL GONE, SORRY," and stick the sign on the front door.

When the first customers arrived, some of them hugged her and hugged each other. The mood was somber but not grim. Dr. Warren suggested making bark tea. The Reilly brothers knew a recipe for some kind of concoction made with weeds. While Ingrid was busy lighting the fire, Buck Hobbs came up the steps and took one look at the sign. A few customers muttered into their beards. Pete the Carpenter nudged one of the Dodsons and coughed. Ingrid happened to look out at that moment. She saw Buck snarl and raise his fist. Everyone watched him turn on his heels and leave without a word.

A week went by, then two. Buck didn't come around. Either to The Breakfast Nook nor to Ingrid's house.

One day, a month later, as she was coming along the Leeward Road, lumbering slowly in the muggy air, Ingrid saw Buck walking toward her. He was shuffling awkwardly, stuffing something into an old duffle bag. She continued heading in his direction. When she was about a hundred feet away, she saw feathers sticking out from the top of his bag. She realized that Buck had stoned a bird. The feathers were black, like a vulture's.

When she got closer to Buck, she screwed up her courage and called out. "You owe me."

Buck looked at her blankly.

"You owe me something for the sugar," she shouted.

"I don't owe anybody anything," said Buck, baring his empty gums. He quickly turned away. As he started to run, he gripped the duffle with two hands so the dead bird wouldn't fall out.

"You owe me meat, Buck Hobbs," yelled Ingrid, surprised by the force of her own voice.

But Buck kept trotting away, faster and faster. He was still strong for a man in his seventh decade. He walked resolutely towards the Vilar's old farm. Ingrid didn't chase him. She turned and took an overgrown path that wound around and ended up in the front of the Vilar's land. She walked slowly, almost in circles, until she could creep onto the property and hide herself behind the rusted carcass of the abandoned Chevrolet in the Vilar's driveway. One of the doors of the old car was open and hanging by a single hinge, like a giant loose tooth.

She crouched down. From there, she could see Buck kneel on the ground next to the old potato house, build a fire, and open the duffle bag. Buck didn't just have one bird. He had several. A seagull, a plover, and a vulture. Ingrid watched her old lover as he plucked each bird, skewered it on a stick, heads, guts and all. The smell of the roasting meat traveled slowly in the heavy, moist air. Ingrid's stomach knotted.

She watched Buck as he ate greedily, sucking on the bones of the ribcage, smacking his lips loud and often, and wiping grease from his chin with the back of his hand. She thought she saw him take an eyeball, now crunchy and blackened, and pop it onto his tongue like a peanut.

She reached down and cupped her hands around a large, smooth rock. Her heart was pounding. Her stomach continued to rumble.

She looked around and found another rock. And another. And yet another. These were the stones that the ancestors of the Vilar family must have once pulled out of their fields centuries ago. Back when farmers could grow things on the island because the rains came after the snow, and the bees were abundant, and the sun shone, and summer was long and warm, but not too warm.

She looked at the rocks. So pretty, she thought. So round. Flecked with color. Mottled. They could have been apples. It had been twenty years at least since she had seen an apple. A plain red apple. Her brain was woozy and slow. She wasn't reasoning or plotting. She was merely reacting to some message from the pit of her belly.

She piled the rocks up in a tidy pyramid. She remembered a time when she and Buck had piled up snowballs like that. Row upon row, like cannon balls in a fort. Then they had thrown them at each other, laughing as the small white spheres burst, cool and flaky, against each other's back. It had been New Year's Eve, decades ago. She had been wearing the coat with the cornflower blue buttons.

She felt weak. She could barely throw the first stone even two yards. But she picked up another one and took aim. The second landed a bit further away. Then she wound up her arm with all her might and pulled it back. She snapped her arm like a catapult, the way she had seen sailors throw.

The third stone hit just in front of Buck's feet. He jumped back and cursed. The fourth stone hit his knee. The fifth hit his chest. He started to run away, still holding onto the roasted bird. But the sixth stone got him squarely in the middle of his back and dented his spinal column with a thud. He fell to the ground. The meat flew out of his outstretched hand. The dead bird was airborne for a minute and then landed.

Ingrid kept throwing the pretty rocks. She watched a stone bounce off Buck's head. He groaned and then grew completely silent. The warm wind blew the frayed cuffs of his old denim shorts. His Red Sox hat lay in the dust nearby.

Ingrid approached Buck's body and stepped over it, as if it were a fallen log. She still had a stone in her hand, but she let it drop slowly to the ground as she hurried towards the roasting birds.

The seagull and the plover were blackened. She flipped them off the fire with a stick and devoured them, one after the other, ripping the flesh, sucking the bones like a straw.

Only later did she begin to cry. For herself. For Buck. For the island. For a world without the sweet comfort of a cup of Joe.

The Apology, Paul Collins

"We do not know very much of the future
Except that from generation to generation
The same things happen again and again."

-Murder in the Cathedral. T.S. Eliot.

January 21, 2017

"The Apology" — Delivered at Delicate Arch, Arches National Park, United States

I speak today for the United States and begin to honor my pledge and commitment to you, fellow citizens, our global community, and future generations, to reconcile the environmental injustices that our nation has inflicted on the peoples and cultures of the Earth. The time has now come for our nation to turn a new page in its history by righting the wrongs of the past and moving forward with confidence to the future. The time has come to say *sorry*.

I speak today against the background of a natural wonder—Delicate Arch. The great American nature writer who has influenced me enormously, Edward Abbey, described this fantastic object of nature as having the curious ability to remind us—like rock and sunlight and wind and wilderness—that out there is a different world, older and greater and deeper than ours. For a few moments we discover that nothing can be taken for granted, for if this ring of stone is marvelous, all which shaped it is marvelous, and our journey here on Earth is the most strange and daring of all adventures.

We are a proud nation. A courageous nation.

But we must be honest with ourselves. In our attempts at environmental leadership, we have, at times, failed to embrace the possibility of new solutions to enduring problems and have taken paths that are wholly and predictably unsustainable. Old approaches have failed. Our future must be based on mutual respect, mutual resolve, and mutual responsibility. The often damaging and dangerous notions, fantasies, and myths of American exceptionalism and Manifest Destiny that continue to influence American political ideology must be confined to history. They belong to the ages. A State cannot be exceptional when faced with the destructive effects of global warming. I am both an American and a globalist. A denial of exceptionalism does not deny the heart and soul of this nation. We are all different, and we must not forget that we are created equal.

Some former holders of this privileged office of President have made a positive and lasting contribution to protect this Earth. Former President John F. Kennedy, a true visionary, declared that more than any other people on Earth, we bear burdens and accept risks unprecedented in their size and their duration, not for ourselves alone but for all those who wish to be free.

Richard Nixon ushered in the decade of the environment and established our Environmental Protection Agency, and Jimmy Carter and Bill Clinton built on the public lands legacy started by Theodore Roosevelt. It was Roosevelt who recognized that the environment had a direct connection to democratic ideals and that the conservation of natural resources was a duty we owe to our children and our children's children. For Roosevelt, conservation was a great moral issue, for it involves the patriotic duty of ensuring the safety and continuance of our nation.

But others of this office pushed pro-growth, anti-regulatory, anti-environmental agendas, politicizing the scientific debate by ignoring scientific evidence, distorting facts, and leading to the censorship of scientists and reports—doing so at the peril of our nation and the world, leading to morality-based politics. Science and religion are not rivals. They are complementary. Our choice is not one, as some alarmed commentators and politicians appear to believe, of science or the humanities. We must learn to create unbreakable bonds between the disciplines of science and humanities. We cannot procrastinate. The world of the future is in our making. We have a moral responsibility to be intelligent about these things. But moral advances must keep up with scientific advances.

It is a mistake to insist that moral and religious convictions play no part in politics and law. The solution to many social problems, including environmental injustice, requires moral transformation. Addressing the problems we face requires changes in the hearts and a change in minds. We need to embrace a more faith-friendly form of public reason. One that transforms and sustains our relationships with other nations and our relationship with the Earth.

We owe the world an apology for the historic environmental injustices we have inflicted upon peoples and cultures. The sense of belonging to a community and showing an allegiance to it carries with it a moral obligation to make amends for our nation's past wrongs. That is patriotism. And with that sense of belonging comes responsibility. It is not really possible to take pride in our nation and its past if we're not willing to acknowledge any responsibility for carrying its story into the present, and discharging the moral burdens that come with it.

The words of the remarkable Eleanor Roosevelt ring as true now as they did when they were first published in 1962: Today we must create the world of the future. Tomorrow is now. Just as our early nation struggled to embrace democracy, we must now embrace a new declaration against fear, timidity, complacency, and national arrogance.

Some have asked, why apologize?

As a nation, we are empathetic to our neighbors but should feel shamed and guilty for some aspects of our way of life. Through apologizing, we can seek to restore and maintain our own dignity and self-esteem.

We are wanting to be forgiven. For this, we must repent, we must apologize. Forgiveness without repentance is cheap grace.

Our fragile planet demands that we renew and focus our energies on the resolution of conflicts, and that we do so in a way that does not simply submerge the resentments that inevitably accompany such conflicts but acknowledges and responds to them. I hope that apologizing can help in that effort.

But in apologizing, we must recognize that this is more than merely an acknowledgment of our offences, with an expression of remorse. It is an ongoing commitment by our nation to change our behavior. It is a process that requires of all parties attitudes of honesty, generosity, humility, commitment, and courage.

It was early morning August 30; violent shaking aroused Colorado's population from their beds. The fifty-second tremor moved furniture, shattered glass, and toppled buildings. After a pause in the shaking, it then renewed with greater strength. Panic and chaos ensued. Streets filled with injured and stunned residents, and cries rang out from injured and trapped victims. Fifty five people perished. This disaster resulted from the injection of fracking waste water into deep underground voids. Before this, our fracking industry was seen as the new bonanza for America, reducing its reliance on overseas oil. Fracking was a process that was deemed safe, licensed, and regulated by our agencies who were trusted to protect us. An industry that had flourished at an urgent pace, with the backing of influential lobbyists and largely in response to addressing high unemployment that had resulted from the financial crisis a few years earlier. Colorado State, we are sorry.

The link between genetically modified organisms and dementia, Alzheimer's disease, has been proven beyond all doubt. We, as a nation, were the key players in this branch of science. We convinced nations across the globe that this emerging science would help solve the world's food shortage problems and that any concerns over public health or environmental pollution grounds were groundless. We fought legal cases and supported industry to develop and market these new products of salvation.

John Richards had consumed GMO products for decades. I met John in my first weeks as Governor of New York. A previously healthy and lively man, he now sits slouched over in a wheelchair, silent in gaze and sound. In the years I have had the honor to know John, we talked at length about his fear of being absorbed into his diseased mind. The fear of slipping away, free-falling into the unknown. The loss of free will. I witnessed the tears, anger, and frustration of John, his wife, and his caregivers as they all failed to understand what was really going on in John's mind. There is no cure yet for this disease. It's a path of early death that we, as a nation, led John and thousands of others along. As the President of the United States, I am sorry.

The roots of environmental racism are deep and have been difficult to eliminate. Many of our nation's environmental laws, policies, and practices have differentially affected or disadvantaged individuals, groups, and communities based on race or color. Our government, legal, economic, political, and military institutions have reinforced environmental racism, and it continues to influence local land use, enforcement of environmental regulations, the siting of industrial facilities, and the locations where people of color live, work, and play. America's Deep South has become a sacrifice zone, a sump for the rest of the nation's toxic waste, and is tarnished with the legacy of slavery, Jim Crow, and white resistance to equal justice. Native Americans have had to contend with some of the worst pollution of our nation, and the places where they live are prime targets for landfills, incinerators, garbage dumps, and risky mining operations.

These stories cry out to be heard; they cry out for an apology. Instead, from our nation, there has not been enough action. As politicians, we were too easily persuaded by the flawed logic of economists who thought that putting a price on our natural resources could justify the sacrifice of nature in one place through seeking to replicate it in another. Responsible environmental stewardship is not a series of banking transactions ruled by the balance sheet.

Our precious natural resources will no longer be treated as a tradable commodity.

These victims of environmental racism are not simply an interesting sociological phenomenon. They are not intellectual curiosities. They are human beings, human beings who have been damaged deeply by decisions of governments. But, as of today, the time for denial, the time for delay, has at last come to an end. Decency, human decency, universal human decency, demands that our nation now step forward to right a historical wrong. That is what I am doing today. We are sorry.

For many American businesses, the concept of corporate social responsibility has lost all credibility, at home and abroad. Companies can no longer seek to greenwash their failures when we see the damage their operations cause. This nation demands greater accountability from those responsible. And we will see to that.

Over the last few decades, our nation has experienced unprecedented extreme weather conditions—droughts, floods, hurricanes. Many of our fellow citizens have lost their livelihoods, and businesses have been ruined. Thousands have had to move away from their communities, families, and loved ones. This has placed an enormous strain on our economy. Decades of underinvestment in our nation's flood protection infrastructure and a failure to properly protect our natural resources, such as water for agricultural use, has led us to this worrying state.

But look a little closer and the strain on those trying to cope with this change in fortune is clear. On my Presidential campaign trail, I spoke with farmers who were having to sell their family farms that generations before them had run. Financially, it was crippling for them. But, although often forgotten, the mental health strain on our nation's farmers and their families is tremendous. The sense of helplessness following months of preparing the land for crops that then die from a lack of available water, or lie rotting in flooded fields, is too much to bear. The incidents of suicide and depression in our farming community, and those who suffer the loss of their loved ones, homes, and businesses to extreme floods and hurricanes, are truly horrific. I know that, in offering this apology on behalf of our nation, there is nothing I can say today to take away the pain you have suffered personally. Whatever words I speak today, I cannot undo that. Words alone are not that powerful; grief is a very personal thing.

Amura Ropati was born on the Pacific Island of Tikvah, the only child of Prosper Ropati and Elizabeth Ropati. Amura's father's childhood was suddenly and irreversibly shattered by the unleashing of unprecedented horror by a trusted friend of his Marshal Islands home. The detonation of the Shrimp hydrogen bomb by our nation in 1954 changed everything for Prosper and his community. Of those who didn't die from the immediate after effects of radiation, many wanted to die. Left permanently damaged, physically and psychologically, many thousands of residents were hastily moved to camp slums of the Pacific. Innocents exiled into an alien environment, fed on a degrading diet of white rice, doughnuts and pancakes, knowing that their future was going to be limited to an existence as a State beneficiary. Amura's father was the sole survivor of his family. Found on a desolate track, sheltered in the arms of his dying mother, blinded in his left eye, this tiny baby was adopted by two kindly American scientists who had been monitoring the bomb tests on the island. Terrified and appalled by what their countrymen had done, and were capable of doing, Burt and Madeline fled the Marshall Islands with baby Prosper to the welcoming shore of Tikvah and brought up Prosper to be the wonderful, humane man he became.

At that time, despite their colonial history and the arrival of missionaries, traders, and administrators, many Tikvah islanders were still holding on to their own beliefs and traditions. But things changed radically during Amura's childhood. The island's natural resources were being exploited by our nation through new methods. Then came the arrival of U.S. logging machines, the clearance of native forests where she used to play with her friends, and the creation of huge swathes of commercial agriculture growing plants for the countries that had planted them on Tikvah. Hallowed landscapes lost their sacredness, and local people became insensitive to the destruction, accepting it as a sign of progress.

Climate change will affect the physical territory of States like Tikvah in a number of ways. Tikvah, in common with some other coastal States, has suffered permanent loss of land through shoreline erosion caused by extreme weather events and sea level rise. Climate change-induced

115

territorial degradation, coupled with climate changed-induced migration, now threatens the very existence of Tikvah.

In the history of the United Nations, there have been almost no incidents of total extinction, either voluntary or involuntary, of a State. The most pressing issue for States facing extinction due to climate change is the very existence of the State altogether. The total loss of territory is the prospect facing Tikvah and small island nations. Should climate change result in total population displacement from a small island, either because of rising sea levels or extreme weather events making habitation unsustainable, that nation will be forced to abandon that territory entirely.

We, the United States, have contributed significantly more to current climate change than any other nation, and, for this, we are deeply sorry.

It is incumbent on our nation and the international community to respond to the altered circumstances of States suffering from the effects of climate change. Our nation's response will be to lead the international community in developing an effective mechanism to administer and protect maritime rights—to provide social, cultural political, and economic support and guidance for people forced to abandon their lands, without hope of return. I will introduce measures to welcome environmental refugees to our protecting shores and support them. We owe them that, and more.

Today, the decision-making elite includes thousands of environmental agencies in nations across the world. Collectively, they rule over the Earth's natural resources. These officials now make decisions that are good for themselves but bad for society and future generations. Behind a veil of environmental law, their decisions push the entire world toward collapse.

I have witnessed throughout the world that agencies implementing laws that are designed to protect the natural environment have become perpetrators of legalized destruction of the environment. New environmental laws can be passed, but if they remain bound by the frame in which we've operated for the last forty years, governments will continue to squander our natural resources. Legal systems can support either the politics of scarcity or the politics of abundance, but Earth's natural systems can support only the latter.

A nation that fails to protect its natural resources consigns its citizens to misery and often death. Environmental regulation remains accountable to a supreme set of mandates, the laws of nature.

Despite entrenched assumptions that environmental law remains effective, the proof lies in the health of the ecosystems themselves. Society now violates nature's laws not only at the level of species and individual ecosystems but also at the level of atmospheric function, ocean health, and biodiversity. On a truly global level.

Moral principle is the foundation of law. Law must tap the deepest moral understanding of humanity not only to maintain credibility and respect in society at large but also to inspire citizens to participate in democracy. Environmental law has lost much of its citizen support. It long ago strayed from the populist movement that gave rise to its hopeful inception.

I have a vision of what our human experience could encompass if liberated from the need to dominate and control the natural environment. As our defensive walls of separation and domination start to disintegrate, we become more open to a world of increasing richness, complexity, and beauty. In bonding with the natural world we are confronted with mystery, wildness, and danger. Facing nature on its own terms means becoming acquainted with the chaotic, strange, and frightening aspects as well as the familiar and comfortable.

Humans have the idea, now centuries old, that we are above natural processes rather than immersed in them. We have thought, and continue to teach our children to think, that we control nature, at least most of the time, and we have felt validated in this belief by the modest success of some of our inventions.

Despite the international community's increasing acknowledgement of the differential experiences and skills women and men bring to development and environmental sustainability efforts, women still have lesser economic, political and legal clout and are hence less able to cope with, and are more exposed to, the adverse effects of the changing climate. Drawing on women's experiences, knowledge, and skills—and supporting their empowerment—will make climate change responses more effective. The impacts of gender inequalities and women's recurrent socio-economic disadvantages must no longer be ignored.

Climate change is not gender-neutral.

Women play a pivotal role in natural resources management and in other productive and reproductive activities at the household and community levels. This puts them in a position to contribute to day-to-day strategies adapted to changing environmental realities. Their extensive knowledge and expertise make them effective actors and agents of change.

Communities fare better during natural disasters when women play a leadership role in early warning systems and reconstruction. Women share information related to community well-being, choose less polluting energy sources, and adapt more easily to environmental changes when their family's survival is at stake. We have witnessed women in South Asia displaying enormous strength and capacity when natural disasters strike. Preparing for hazards, managing after a disaster and rebuilding damaged livelihoods. They secure food and water for the family, securing seed and other productive material, and taking care of the sick and elderly.

Women's greater participation will enhance the effectiveness and sustainability of climate change projects and policies. Women are better at mobilizing communities in the event of disaster risk management and reduction, and have a better understanding of what strategies are needed at the local level.

Because economic, legal, and socio-cultural constraints can lead to women's capacity gaps, climate change responses need to address women's historic and current disadvantages. As such, policy and programming should recognize that because of their central role in environmental, social, and economic development, women's empowerment and gender equality is beneficial for family and community wellbeing and livelihoods and is key factor in promoting the resilience of economies and communities. Actions, technologies, and strategies need to be pro-poor and gender responsive in their design, implementation, monitoring and evaluation. We will lead on putting in place all necessary measures to deliver that.

We must be a source of hope to the poor, the sick, and the marginalized. Peace and security in our time requires it. The patriots of 1776 fought to give us a nation for the people, entrusting each generation to keep safe our founding creed, and we must continue to do that. We are the keepers of this legacy.

There is now a case for an amendment to the Constitution of the United States for protection of the environment. The drafters in 1787 did not foresee the severe impacts that unprecedented expansion of population, technology, and economic power would have upon the environment— and made no provision for its wise governance in the public interest. We have witnessed that protection of the environment has now become an urgent responsibility, to which our traditional legal system has responded inadequately. We have reached a point in the development of our society at which the fragmentary bases of our environmental laws are inadequate to support the actions that may be necessary to attain national and international environmental policy objectives. Our lack of constitutional protection of the environmental basis of our health, security, and prosperity contrasts sharply with our commitment to civil rights.

If we are unable or unwilling to place environmental protection high among our constitutional obligations, we will hardly be a credible leader among nations in this aspect of public and international policy. More is expected of the United State than of most nations. Amending the United States Constitution to recognize the fundamental importance of the environment in national and international affairs will greatly facilitate the movement toward global environmental protection, which must succeed if we are to preserve the richness and renewability of the living Earth. This will be delivered under my presidency.

Our nation's courage must not diminish. We must not allow the free and courageous use of our minds to diminish. This is not the time for soft-mindedness. We must find new ways to communicate with the peoples of the world, with belief in our hearts, to be better understood. We can invest in, and redefine, our spiritual and moral values. We must not let the mistakes of this nation dictate our future. And we must right the wrongs of our past.

Thank you. God bless you.

Eleanor G. Allan

Sand, Conor Corderoy

The child had never seen his father cry. Now the father wept like a child. And his mother screamed, clenched her fists, and stamped her feet while his father, sitting in the green armchair, rocked and covered his face, keening.

"You have to do something, Ibrahim!" she screamed and stamped her foot again, standing over him. "They have a duty! An obligation! Talk to them, Ibrahim! Tell them! What shall we do about Babacar? How shall we feed him?"

Babacar heard his name and looked at his mother and wondered if he was going to starve. He looked back at his father, waiting for an answer, but his father just shook his head and covered his face. And keened. Now his mother also covered her face and began to walk in circles around the room, crying out to God for help for her family.

His father spread his hands, hunching his shoulders, and looked up at his wife. His face was begging her to stop. He said, "Awa, Awa, what can I do? I am nobody. The order comes from Munich. Our Senegal plant is closed. They have gone. What can I do?"

Babacar thought, "He still calls it our plant, as though he owned it."

His father went on, his pink hands open in appeal. "They can't work here anymore. It is too hot for them. There are no crops. There is no rain. They need to move and do their work somewhere else…"

Awa stopped in her circling and stared at her husband. Her eyes were huge. So suddenly that it shocked Babacar and made his heart race, she leaned forward and screamed, "We are going to die! We are going to die! We are going to die!"

* * *

More than three and a half thousand miles away, the child watched his father. He had never seen his father cry, and somehow knew he never would. He felt his father was dry. Like sand. There was no water in him. But his mother was crying. She was sitting at the bar in the vast, open-plan room, holding a tall gin and tonic with lots of ice. He could see the ice-cubes through the frosted glass and imagined her tears rolling down her face, past the corner of her mouth, dripping into the icy drink.

Her eyes were puffy, and she said, "I don't want to go to fucking Canada! I don't fucking want to go to Canada! What fucking part of I don't fucking want to fucking go to fucking Canada do you not understand, Peter?"

Peter watched his wife with eyes that were oddly like the cubes in her drink. He flicked those eyes at his son on every other cuss as if to check the impact and waited for his wife to finish. When she paused to drink, he said, "Do you think you can refrain from swearing in front of our son? This discussion is inappropriate now. This is not the time or pl…"

"When then? When? When is it appropriate for you to discuss my life and my future?" She was holding her glass up like the Statue of Liberty, but leaning past it to thrust her face towards her husband.

He raised his left eyebrow, and hardness seemed to seep down from his eyes into his jaw and mouth. His voice was arid, barren, like frozen desert earth. He said, "I have explained, Moira, that we have to pull out of the plant in Senegal. There is a fucking drought out there…"

"So you can swear?"

"…there is a drought out there that isn't going to stop. We experiment with food cultivation, Moira. You can't cultivate food in a perpetual drought. We need to change the conditions. Canada has those conditions. Munich tells us we need to change the operation, so we change the operation."

"*I don't give a fuck about Munich!*"

He droned on over her, as though he hadn't heard her scream, "We have to move to Canada to set up the operation!"

"Why?" She climbed off the stool where she was sitting at the bar and took a step towards him, where he was sitting on the sofa. He regarded her without expression. She leaned forward, her face red and her neck swollen. "Why?" she repeated. "Why? You've been ten fucking years in Senegal and you've never set foot there."

"I've been there ten times."

"Once a fucking year for a week at a time!"

"Stop swearing."

"Now we have to fucking live in Ottawa?"

Peter sighed and rubbed his face. "Nobody asks questions in Senegal, Moira. You know the score. The move to Canada is politically very sensitive. Greenland or Denmark might complain. I have to be there to negotiate. We do not want to be in the public eye! I have explained this. There are environmental issues. It's a hot potato."

"Fuck you! Fuck you and your fucking potatoes!"

* * *

Two thousand miles away, to the North and East, in a tiny settlement in Greenland called Qasigiannguit, the child watched his father sleep and snore. He had seen his father cry many times. Every time, in fact, that he had got drunk and beaten him. The child was dimly aware of the pain of his bruises, but familiarity is a powerful anesthetic, and as he watched his father, lumpen and grunting, drooling slightly from the corner of his mouth, with the empty bottle by his fallen hand, despair was a deeper pain than his bruises. But Dr. Petersen was helping him to overcome despair. Dr. Petersen was teaching him a lot.

He stepped out into the cold. The summer melt had peaked. It had been, yet again, the biggest in recorded history. Dr. Petersen had told him so. Now cold air was coming down from the North, but it was not cold enough. Dr. Petersen said it should be a lot colder. The snow that had fallen lay melting and turning to sludge on the roads.

He looked up towards Dr. Petersen's big, wooden house, and the towering ice cliffs that rose one and a half miles into the cold blue air behind it. It was true there was more melt and sludge this year than other years, but it was still cold. Ice-cold. He started to walk towards Dr. Petersen's house. There was a black Land Rover parked outside. It was new to him. He had never seen it before.

Dr. Petersen had given him a key, and he unlocked the door and stepped in. The house was warm, and he could smell coffee. He heard voices. Petersen and another man. Petersen sounded angry.

The boy stepped through the living room and climbed the stairs towards Petersen's office. Petersen's voice grew louder. "Have you any idea? Have you any understanding of the impact it will have? Do you even understand the function of plankton?"

The other man's voice droned an answer the boy could not make out. He climbed a little higher. Petersen seemed to interrupt: "Don't talk to me about jurisdiction. It's in our backyard, three hundred miles across the strait. You have to appeal to the UN. Take action in the ICJ. Talk to the Canadian Consulate, or the embassy in Copenhagen. Do something!"The other man's voice was louder now, placating: "Lars, Lars, come on. You have to stop seeing catastrophe in every event. You are a researcher, a scientist. You have to be objective. Keep a cool head. How many times has the IPCC got it wrong? How many times have we heard that we've gone over the tipping point? Positive feedback…?" He waved his hands in an "on-and-on" gesture.

The boy reached the door and looked in. Petersen was sitting, perched against his desk. His face was tight and flushed.

There was a man in a suit, sitting in an armchair and looking up at him. He had heavy-rimmed glasses, and the reflected light from the window hid his eyes. He was smiling, humouring, 124atronizing. He spread his hands and shook his head. "Remember the Gruyere cheese? The whole Greenland ice sheet was like a Gruyere cheese riddled with moulins. The whole ice-sheet was going to disintegrate. What happened? Nothing happened. Remember Jay Zwally? The canary is dead. It's time to get out of the mine!'" The man burst out laughing. "Here we are, almost a decade later, and nothing has happened. Nothing ever happens."

Petersen leant forward. His face was rigid, and his hands gripped his desk. He spoke through his teeth. "Are you stupid? For crying out loud! The Arctic is navigable for the second year running. Do you know what that means, you fool? Do you know what will happen if we lose the northern icecap?"

The man in the suit sighed and flopped back in his chair, but Petersen pressed on. "Do you know what will happen if that plant goes into operation? All their toxic waste will be pumped into the straits. That waste will kill the plankton and create ocean deserts. Do you know what will happen if the plankton dies?"

The man sighed and moved to rise. "This is going nowhere…"

Petersen got to his feet and stepped towards him, stabbing at him with his finger. His voice rasped. "The plankton is a sink. It consumes the CO_2. What will happen? What will happen? Think, you fool! Think! What will happen if they kill the plankton?"

And then the man in the suit's face went hard. He stared at Petersen and spoke very quietly, "The CO_2 in the far North will grow exponentially, warming the Arctic and accelerating the melting of the northern ice-sheets. And then we will have access to the oil fields in Greenland, and we will be able to sail from Europe to Asia in a fraction of the time."

Petersen took a step back. His face had turned white. Like ice. He said, "But the icecaps are our cooling system. Without them the planet will burn. Millions might die."

"Wake up, Dr. Petersen. It is already too late. It has been too late for a century. There is no way back. There is no way out of the mine. The markets dictate the planet must get hotter. It would not be the first time that millions died in the service of the market. Live with it!"

A cold dread drained through the boy's skin. A bloodless, cold numbness touched his face, like a whisper out of time, and he knew, without fully understanding it, that something terrible was happening. He heard himself speak in a small voice, "Dr. Petersen…?"

Dr. Petersen turned and saw a small, frightened Inuit boy standing in his doorway. He felt his heart contract, and he said, "Akycha…"

* * *

Four thousand miles away, Babacar's father had stopped crying. His face was drawn, and his eyes looked sickly. Awa was sitting on the sofa now, still sobbing. Babacar wanted to cry with his mother, but he was paralysed, listening to his father.

"We have to go. Awa, we have to go. The whole town is going. The crops have failed. The animals are dying. There is no food. It is too hot. The old ones and the babies are dying with the heat. And now the plant is closed. We cannot stay. We have to go."

She lifted her face. It was wet, shiny, and swollen. She tilted it on one side, and it began to crumble into crying again. She said, "But, St. Louis? Ibrahim, it is more than a hundred miles. We will die."

"It is a hundred and twenty miles, Awa. The council have worked it all out. There are still a couple of oxen, and we can take water in the cart. We have no choice, Awa. We must go."

Ibrahim watched his wife sob, and Babacar slid from his chair and pushed out onto the veranda. In the mid-morning sun it was 50° C in the shade. Across the red dust of the dirt road he could see his 126eighbor Joseph's house, with its small plot of land. Against the brilliance of the sun he could make out the black stencil of the dead ox. Flies buzzed and settled on his hands, his legs, and his face. The tickling of their feet irritated him, but he could not bring himself to brush them away. He squatted down upon the wooden planking and slipped his hands over his head. To his left, a hundred yards distant, Mamadou's goats stood still and silent, their ribs showing, their flesh shrinking around their bones. The dry heat sapped everything but the flies. As he watched, one of the goats dropped to its knees and lay down to die.

Inside he heard his father calling his name. It irritated him, like the flies, but he was paralysed inside and did not answer.

* * *

The boy watched his mother throw her gin and tonic at the wall. He watched a piece of ice spin slowly across the parquet floor, leaving a trail of water behind it. It came to rest against a Persian rug. The half-moon of lemon sat behind it in a puddle, and a big spatter stain of dark liquid rose like a ghost on the wall, invading the room with the violence of its presence. His heart was racing. He couldn't hear many words, just the shrill screaming and "*You fucking loser! I'm leaving! I'm leaving!*"

He heard her heels down the hall, tapping quickly on the wooden floor. His father rose slowly and followed her. He then followed his father, watching his own small trainers as they trod in his parents' footsteps. At his parents' bedroom he held on to the doorframe. There was an open suitcase on the bed that bounced every time his mother slammed a piece of clothing in it. His father was saying, "Seriously? You're leaving? What about Jack? What about…?"

Her eyes shone through easy, intoxicated tears, and she pointed an angry red fingernail at her husband. "Don't try. Don't you even try and take him from me. I'll fight. I'll fight you every inch of the way through the courts. Or any way you want, you son of a bitch! I swear it."

The boy looked up at his father. There was no expression, except the certainty that he must have what he wanted. He said, "Do you understand how hard I can make it for you? Do you understand just how much I can make you suffer?"

His mother threw a green blouse on the floor and dropped to her knees. She collapsed forward and buried her face in the quilt. She didn't cry; she convulsed. The boy and his father watched in silence and knew she would not leave, and they would go to Canada.

* * *

Akycha watched Petersen step towards him, his hands held out and an angry frown on his face. "Akycha! You must not be here now!" But as he said it, the man with the suit rose to his feet.

"Dr. Petersen, we are done. I must return to Copenhagen."

Petersen turned to the man in the suit. "We are not done. *We are not done!*"

The man's eyebrows rose above the black frames of his glasses, and the lenses flashed blindly. "I am done, Dr. Petersen. I am done being insulted, and I am done being shouted at. I shall acquaint Professor Zandersen at Århus, and the government committee, with your concerns. That is the most I can do."

Petersen's face twisted, and he reached unconsciously for the boy. He said, "The most you are willing to do."

The man shrugged and moved past them. At the door he stopped and turned. Akycha could now see the ice cliffs reflected in his lenses. The man shook his head. "Positive feedback, the tipping point: scaremongering. We got there a century ago, Dr. Petersen. There has been no way back since the industrial revolution began. This is a living planet. Catastrophic change is part of how it works. It adapts." He paused and considered Dr. Petersen a moment. "You want my advice, Dr. Petersen?"

Petersen shook his head. "No."

"Stay out of politics. You don't understand power. Focus on your research. Do your job."

They listened in silence to his feet clatter down the stairs. Then the front door closed, and after a moment a 4x4 roared into life. Petersen walked to the window and stared out.

Akycha said, "What's happening, Dr. Petersen?"

Petersen shook his head. He didn't look at Akycha when he said, "Not now, Akycha, go home. Go home."

128

Akycha stepped out into the cold. A pool of dirty sludge lay melting where the Land Rover had been. Russet-pink light lay among angular shadows across the snow and the buildings. The sea on the strait looked inky black. A gull cried havoc and seemed to laugh. Then there was a noise. It was indescribable. As though the earth and the sky were tearing in half.

* * *

Akycha covered his ears, hunched into his shoulders, and screwed up his eyes. When he opened them again he saw people running. He saw them screaming but could hear only the ripping apart of the world. The ground shook under his feet, and he wondered if it was an earthquake. And as he thought this he saw the immense ice cliffs move. At first he did not believe what he saw. He stood frozen and stared. Then he went cold inside as the entire cliff began to crumble and slide. White dust billowed in giant clouds from the base. The noise rose to a screaming, screeching pitch. He was dimly aware of Dr. Petersen's door bursting open and Dr. Petersen running out towards him. Then the cracking and screeching turned to a deep roar, and the wall of ice, six thousand feet high, God only knew how deep, crumbled into the sea. Behind it the ice sheet began to disintegrate and, below, the sea exploded, swelled, fell in on itself, and rose three hundred feet above the small town, as slice after slice of the cliffs slid thundering into the black ocean. In his mind there was a moment of stillness and silence, and the last words Akycha ever heard were Petersen's: "There is no way out of the mine."

* * *

The boy stepped out onto the balcony, twenty stories above the traffic, and looked out across the gleaming towers of steel and glass, into the black sheet of the North Atlantic. He saw, but did not understand, the storm of photons bombarding the black sea with particles of fire. He remembered his father taking up his mother from her knees, lovelessly crushing her sobbing, limp body in his arms and telling him to leave the room. Far in the North he saw black clouds building and turning, like billowing black smoke. The sea looked motionless. The small swell that was racing towards him, towards the glistening towers of steel and glass, at six hundred miles per hour, was invisible; it would remain invisible until it reached the shallower waters near the coast, where it would slow to a quarter of its speed and rear up, two hundred feet into the air, to sweep away in a few minutes what man had built over half a millennium.

The village elder called a halt. Some baobab trees near the side of the road offered some shade for the fifty people who had decided to go. St. Louis might offer them cooler temperatures, the sea, fish, perhaps work. They had covered thirty miles that day. Two had collapsed in the molten heat. Also an ox. The hot glare numbed your brain, boiled your blood.

The oxen were given water. Eventually, those who made it to St. Louis would kill them and drink their blood. Babacar squatted in the shade of a tree. His father stretched out on the dry, red earth between the roots of a baobab and closed his eyes. His mother lay next to him. She had been silent for hours. Her eyes were open and very black. Her breathing was shallow but rapid. He saw the flies crawl on her face, but she didn't brush them off.

He knew that he had been looking north. He didn't know for how long. He had noticed small black clouds on the horizon, far away. And circling in front of them, like stencils against the white and blue-black sky, the vultures rising high on the thermals of scorched air. The heat seemed to buzz and glare all about him, dulling the colours of the Earth and the bark of the trees, and the hair on the goats, fusing them into the eternal yellow of molten sand. He didn't know when in the glare he had noticed that her chest had become motionless and still. He had noticed, but he didn't know when, how her eyes had ceased to see. Had become dry and dead like the sand.

Everlast, M.E. Cooper

"Once there was a desert—not made of grisly rock and arid sand—oh, no, my children, it was a desert of water. Multitudes of flora and wildlife flocked to its edges. Just up from the shorelines lived its people—just like you and me, only above ground! And happy, in love with a soft sun and soothing breeze and gentle night. They spent their days alongside the other beasts, weaving between the towering trees of the forests, learning the bird songs and how to paint in many different ways, with words and colors and songs, and how to sew the land with seeds. And the children's only duty was to dash carefree and safe through whispering grasses as tall as themselves until the sun lowered in the west and cast a pure, golden light over the earth—and everything was held in perfectness and peace, and for once, all on earth stopped and held its breath in awe and—"

A long, absentminded pause ensued.

"Uh-oh," Daphne sighed, brushing her thick, brown bangs to the side, giving her younger sister a knowing look. "Gran's got lost again."

Harper snickered behind a hand and winked to the older, leaning over her crossed legs to reach out and gently shake the matriarch's blue-violet veined arm. One nudge and nothing.

"Uh-oh, indeed," Harper murmured, watching her grandma's glassy eyes shimmer up at the dimly lit ceiling, her jaw left unhinged, her grip around her cane tightening, her bony hips thrust to the edge of her seat. "We may have actually stunned her this time." The sisters choked down childish glee, betraying their adolescence thoroughly.

"Have you girls broken Gran again?" Mother heaved a sigh and a laundry basket into the sparsely decorated living room. "This is the third time this week!" She huffed, slamming the basket down in front of Harper, who sat rigidly on the dingy, plastered floor, avoiding her mother's heated eyes. Mother put her hands on her hips and frowned down at her daughters. "Doesn't she go through enough without you two constantly heckling her about the 'good old days'?" The pout was out, on both sides of the argument, and for a moment, all the Grey girls wore identical faces.

"We are not heckling, Mother." Daphne stood indignantly, matching her parent in every mannerism. "We only want to know what it was like when people lived outside—outdoors, when the world was kind." Under her breath she added, "And not in this sorry excuse of a home we call Sewer City."

"You hold your tongue, young lady!" Mother snapped a heel down, pointing a stern finger at her eldest child's face. "We are all indebted to the Grand Oligarchy. You know what would have happened to us if they hadn't built these safe havens. I will not tolerate ingratitude in this home!"

"Some home this turned out to be." Daphne scowled, snatching up the laundry basket and twirling around dramatically. "Four lousy walls, one bathroom, and one bedroom to each household—oh, you're too kind!" She batted her eyes at her sister, inviting her to either join in or encourage her with some laughter. Harper covered her mouth and did the latter. Daphne soaked it up and spun back around, gracefully gesturing to the ceiling and declaring next, "We'll open the impenetrable glass roofing for three whole hours, once a day, just for you to admire how white and terrifying the desert-land sky is! Don't touch!" Daphne jumped, feigning terror at her sister. "That's nature! Have you learned nothing from your years of diligent history absorption?! Never trust nature—it will swallow you alive!" And, for effect, Daphne dove at Harper with a playful roar and capsized the laundry on her head. The two sang with giddiness, but, oh, Mother was not pleased.

"Daphne Sunder Grey!" Practically trampling over Harper, Mother wrestled the basket from her older daughter and growled, "Would you for once act your age and show a little decency and respect for the blessings you do have? Now your sister's got to pick up all these clothes again and you'll be late for your Run!"

132

"Oh, pssha." Daphne rolled her eyes at the subject, turning away to gather her hike pack of survival supplies, heaving it over her shoulder, and then heading for the open archway to the inner-city streets she still so endearingly called *rat ruts*. "They wouldn't dare leave without me. There's no other medic out there brave enough to volunteer their services to the Surface-land."

"Crazy enough, more like it," her mother sassed, storming over to the kitchen corner, turning the faucet on for something to distract her swelling rage.

"Oh, Ma," Daphne sighed, adjusting her industrial boots, standing in the doorway. "Don't you worry like that; it's perfectly safe out there. No one's gone missing in years. Not since—"

"Since that little Bolt boy, yes, I know." Mother cut her off, anxiously twisting her hands through the only tattered towel the family owned. Harper quietly went crawling about, tossing stray attire into the basket. She pretended heart didn't just halt at the sound of that last name. The town may have forgotten, but she never had.

"Ma, that was three years ago—he was fourteen, and he just got a little overeager and snuck out when no one was looking. I mean, for all we know he just disappeared, he could still very well be—"

"Don't you say it!" Mother hissed, bitter tears in her eyes, her weathered hands coiled up in angry fists that only ever came out when one dared touch near the subject of how her own beloved husband died.

Daphne knew she had stepped on a tender nerve, however unintentional. So averting her eyes, she found her sister on her hands and knees, stunned in fear. The air suddenly became almost too heavy for any of their lungs to process. And this time it wasn't even because they forgot to cycle new air in from the city vents.

Without so much as an apology or a word of understanding, Daphne turned on her stubborn heels and made to go.

"Wait!" Harper shouted, hopping to her feet, dusting off her dingy pants as she lunged towards the door. "Can I go with you? Just to see you off?" Their father left the same way, only she was never there to say goodbye at his departure. She'd never let another slip through her fingers again— save Jonas Bolt. And she'll never forgive herself for either's loss. Death is inherent, no matter what one did. She knew that. But the ones who passed never knew how much they bolstered her own worth in her meager life, and this lingering pain was something she could not seem to reconcile with. She would sooner die than let her sister now slip where the others have gone.

Daphne started to smile, but Mother's voice came out instead—"Not today, Harper. They're about to open the dome, and someone needs to take Gran. You know how ravenous she gets when she goes one single day without seeing that wretched sky…"

The sisters watched numbly, helplessly, as their mother went back to scouring gritty iron pots and pans.

"Just—stay home this time." Daphne put a strong, calloused hand on Harper's shoulder and winked. Harper took in her tall, slender figure, for possibly the last time. She'd memorized the way her ponytail cascaded over her shoulder and how her blue, blue eyes were set off by an armada of blissful freckles. She'd traced countless times that scar down her right cheek, holding onto how it ended in this little niche that looked like a fox paw. But it was no critter that carved it into her soft flesh, rather a deranged partner gone mad from severe heatstroke out in the field. Harper would miss the elegant curves and premeditated ways her sister's hands stretched out so gently to even the harshest edges of the world. She clutched onto Daphne's wrist tightly, not daring to utter a sputtering murmur of such sentiment. She couldn't be weak, not in front of Daphne.

"Bring me back something good," Harper chuckled quietly instead, giving her sister's arm a tender shake in salute.

"Only the best for you, little sis." Daphne laughed mischievously, roughly tousling her sister's auburn, braided hair.

"Hey!" Harper made a swat at Daphne's escaping figure. "Get lost, you idiot!" Her laughter carried her sister to the end of the pathway. Daphne turned, winked once more with the complete, wild freedom of a true adventurer, and, with one last thumbs-up, she vanished into the dank Sewer City streets.

Harper's face fell instantly. A sudden, frigid dread blanketed her. She encased herself in her own arms' warmth to ward off the chill. "She'll be back," she whispered, though she couldn't shake the agonizing sense that Daphne's absence was settling in permanently. So she told herself once more, "She'll come back to me."

"Harper June, will you please make yourself useful today? I'm very busy with the neighborhood's association meeting for this afternoon—we're discussing the city's name change—so long overdue. Sewer City? These old, humorous games our ancestors used to play—let's just say some dead things are better left so. How it's survived this long, I'll never—" Mother's voice faded off down to the bathroom door where she continued narrating her pet peeves to anything that cared to listen. Harper was not among them as she stared coldly after her sister. Did her mother not just see Daphne leave? Didn't she know the stakes—of course she did. Why did she always act like she didn't care—Harper's stomach churned at the thought. She cast her dull blue eyes down at

Gran, who was still fixed intently on some far thought beyond the confines of the stuffy ceiling's encasing.

"Gran." Harper gingerly touched her fingertips to her grandmother's malleable skin.

Gran jumped, clutching onto her granddaughter so suddenly it startled Harper. "Hush, child!" Gran went on in her usual storytelling voice. Her dry lips cracked into a delicate smirk that betrayed her old age. "I haven't finished the story. The ending's the best part...!"

Harper, laughing lightly in a flustered way, nodded, gripping Gran's hand back in anticipation for the story's resolution.

"Then the sun lowered in the west and cast a gossamer, golden light across the land. Everything—every creature, every blossom, every stone and atom—held its breath in peaceful awe and—" Harper winced, expecting her to fade out again. But Gran's eyes were lifted to her granddaughter's, glinting in perfect cognizance of the beauty her words would loose. "For once, all was still."

* * *

If only it were so, Harper kept thinking to herself as she and Gran hobbled in their painstakingly plodding way towards the plaza for the dome's daily opening. It had to be done by eight in the morning and only held until eleven. By then, the direct sunlight's intensity would pose too much of a threat to Sewer City's people. Harper sometimes liked to smirk to herself and imagine how appetizing Sewer City Soup sounded, which is exactly what she pictured overcooking the locals with all that sun would create. But today was too heavy. Her heart was harrowed by too many memories, too many unspoken things and what-ifs.

"It's a shame those whiny little pantywaists in charge of that damn neighborhood association my Adeline's always chirping on about had to run their mouths to the Grand Oligarchy," Gran sighed, shuffling past Ms. Beeter's rubber yard dotted with a multitude of expensively colored faux flowers and shrubs. Beeter stuck her nose up as they passed and did not return their amiable grins. Some egos, even in dire times, desperately seek any excuse to think themselves superior to others. Ms. Beeter's "garden" was hers.

Harper, snickering from Gran's comment, nudged her elder and chided softly, "Careful, there, Gran. I think she heard you."

"Well, good! It's 'bout time somebody started speaking some good sense around here! What are we doing, here in this place? We're supposed to die in a hole, not live in one!"

Harper, by instinct that her mother engraved in her, tried to hush her grandma as she raised her voice. But all her disciplines just came out as concurring laughter.

"It's because of people like her and her damn fool's 'garden' that there's a demand for the ceiling to stay shut, even all through the night! Disrupts their lighting or endangers their plastic lawn moldings!" Gran spat quite literally into another showy yard. Luckily, this one's owner was absent. Harper didn't even try to suppress her, just chortled again, keeping her arm locked with Gran's.

"I think they really only do it to give themselves something to live for, Gran. Not everyone has your good memories to fall back on," Harper said.

"They're not living, dear, they're surviving—buried like this, we all are." Harper noticed the severity in her grandmother's voice. She frowned concernedly at her fragile, wrinkled, perplexed face.

"Gran, don't get that way. Look! We made it. And the sky's already opening up!"

That usually cheered her right up, igniting her eyes with a vibrant flame only kids on birthdays could come close to emulating. But today wasn't really turning out to be such an ordinary day. Gran's demeanor and voice only sank further with her eyes to the scuffled floor.

She muttered, "Oh, Harper. If you'd've seen the nighttime sky…you'd never want to sleep again, knowing what you'd be missing…"

Ponderously, longingly, Harper watched with worry as tears welled up in her grandma's eyes. She felt silence was her best option but wanted so badly to be able to return the favor of healing words to Gran's aching heart. But she knew no stories. No rhymes. No songs. She had no memories of gentle sunsets or friendly beasts or happy adventures. Only metal walls and artificial lighting and dehydrated foods and blackness. Suddenly she realized she hadn't lived all that much. No one in Sewer City had.

Drawn from her own brooding cloud by the horrified screams of her townsfolk, Harper snapped back into reality. She found herself and Gran being jostled side to side by their neighbors as they hustled past. They wound in-between and over each other, shouting cries of surprise and fright, all the while pointing and gawking at the ceiling.

"Gran, what is that?" Harper gaped skyward, eyes set wide in childlike joy.

Gran stared very seriously up at the glass being pummeled with heavy beads of liquid, some solid enough to drum out an ominous, powerful beat against the dome's top.

"Rain...and hail."

"Wow!" Harper drew in a sharp breath, a bubbling sensation welling up inside of her. "It's so much more beautiful to see it for myself! I can't believe—Gran, it's just like your stories! This is so exciting!" A bright streak tore across the sky, ripping open the deep gray of the clouds that rolled above, closely followed by an earth-shaking clap of—"Gran! What was—!"

"Thunder. And lightning, dear," her voice came slow and heavy, so fragile Gran appeared to regret uttering it at all. Harper opened her mouth to cheer again, but Gran cut her off with, "Nothing to celebrate today, Harper." Gran spat on the ground once and tapped a bony fist to her chest thrice.

Harper gawked at Gran in disbelief. The only time anyone made that gesture was in the face of dauntingly hopeless situations. Or death.

"G-Gran...wh-what's...what's wrong?"

"Nature sends storms like this when She's angry. And anyone caught out there—" Gran sealed her eyes slowly and imagined the rain hitting her face to alleviate the pain of knowing—

"Daphne's out there!"

* * *

Harper, Gran, and Mother were rushed and crammed into Town Hall's main meeting room, locked away in soundproof walls that helped to hide the ensuing sounds of chaos breaking from outside their very doors. Sewer City was in a tizzy, to say the least. Everything was turned onto its head. Walls shook, and rock crumbled from above, peppering Ms. Beeter's precious yard with rubble. She was among the frantic shriekers in the front vestibule of the Hall, proclaiming sheer cataclysm at the loss of her fiberglass rosebushes. Moments later, the doors burst open, letting in the pandemic of shouts as well as two armored guards escorting the trembling family group of the young man who went on the Run with Daphne. Melba Johnston and her young daughter, Shelbah, clung to each other while their protector, Pedro, wrapped his arms around his wife's shoulders. His stern face was betrayed by the shattered sheen in his dark eyes. There was no calm, inside or out. Only storm.

From behind the triangular desk in the room stood Sewer City's primary, North Weston of the Grand Oligarchy, one of nine across the sparse continent of North America. She was accompanied by three other stoic-faced, formally dressed agents of her cabinet, all complementing one another in shades of gray. Her square and lanky face was framed by angular glasses, strict collar, and a tautly drawn bun. The stress-induced wrinkles lining her mouth and furrowed brow gave years to her otherwise youthful body.

"Greys—Johnstons," North spoke with rehearsed precision, her austere expression unflinching as some of her companions herded the terrified families closer to her. "As you may be very well aware, we have been hit by a devastatingly brutal storm. It swelled up so suddenly, I'm afraid our radar tower was knocked out before we could even translate the signal. That's why we were in the dark about it this morning when we sent Daphne Grey and Paolo Johnston out on what we presumed would be a standard expedition."

Harper cringed and silenced a yelp as her mother's nails dug mercilessly into her shoulder.

"We have received no correspondence from the helicopter sent from Roote, our partner city, since three this morning. Currently we are unable to pinpoint their location, let alone receive any transmissions of distress from either the Roote couriers or one of our Runners."

"Wh-wh-what's going on, then? Where are our children?" demanded Mrs. Johnston.

"This freak storm has quite literally left us blind to all goings-on above," Weston explained, "and no search and rescue team can even risk going out under these circumstances—as you all can understand." Harper felt something wet and warm fall upon her cotton T-shirt—the first of Mother's tears. "I have never been a believer in sewing false hope—" North's face scrunched up in an expression that Harper believed was a stab at commiseration. "So I must be brutally honest with you. The conditions in which your loved ones are lost are extremely difficult and dire. All their training and equipment is not made to withstand something such as this." Melba lost it there, falling to her knees in desperate sobs. "Please, don't worry—we will do all we can to retrieve their bodies and give them proper burial—" Gran's tears let themselves cascade down the divots of her pallid skin. Pedro buried his in his hands. Adeline's grip only began to tremor Harper herself, its tense coil unfaltering. Shelbah, the littlest Jonhston, blanched noticeably in her swarthy skin, weeping into her mother's curly hair. "But I wouldn't count on seeing them alive again."

"You bastards!" Adeline snapped. She lunged at Weston, hands out like talons, slashing at the companions who threw themselves in front of their primary. "That's what you're telling us now?! Our children are out there in this—disaster and all you can say is—FORGET ABOUT

THEM?!" Harper was stunned by the frenzied scene unfolding. She didn't recognize the animalistic bellows emitting from her savage-faced mother. Pedro joined in the attack, accompanied by Melba's helpless shrieks. Gran even started whacking at the primary with her prized sequoia walking stick. Finally, every last inch of the city was raging with storms.

Except Harper. Remarkably, she noted that she was the only one keeping herself together. No tears, no fire, no pity. Nothing. She saw before her only one truth: Daphne was still out there.

And Harper was going to find her.

By the time North Weston's frazzled scream for order calmed the room, her bun had already been pulled out into a rat's nest of tangles when one of Adeline's claws struck home. "ENOUGH! WE'RE DOING ALL WE CAN! I'M SORRY FOR YOUR—"

"Harper?" Gran called, noting a coldness at her side where her granddaughter once stood. She swatted one of the agents off of her brusquely, craning her neck around the room, breathless and bewildered.

"Where is my other daughter?" Adeline lunged like a lioness back into the primary's face, causing the henchmen to flinch away from her fury. "Where is my Harper?"

Only Shelbah had an answer, pointing a shaky finger to the door, wheezing out, "G-g—gone."

* * *

Harper was pretty sure she could feel her mother's cry for her reverberating off her bones as she stepped into Daphne's excess pair of battered boots. She stuffed a backpack full of water bottles, skin protectors, misters, antibiotics, and bandages—she was riding on a wave of madness and adrenaline. She was about to embark into the Otherside. The Great Surface. The Only Frontier. The Wild. No training, no mentor, no words of wisdom from Gran to give her comfort or cause her to turn back. Stumbling twice on her steel-tipped boots, Harper zipped her weatherproof jacket shut tight and strode determinedly towards the abandoned backstreet. She and Daphne had unearthed it over the years. Only once had Daphne taken Harper out with her and, even then, with her brave sister to protect her, Harper was too frightened to remain above ground for more than a mere minute.

That was six years ago. Things had changed. In one instant, one flash of sky-breaking light from the vengeful clouds, Harper had changed, too. She was tired of surrendering all she loved to the gluttonous world that showed no remorse, no hint of holding back. She was tired of being too weak to protect and keep the only ones that made life alive. Bumbling down the dark, dirt-coated path, Harper hurled herself and the daunting weight of her supplies up the rusted metal ladder, each echoing footstep down the crumbling well reminding her there was no turning back.

Her choices quite literally sealed her fate. As soon as she squeezed out from beneath the girth of the industrial vault door, the harsh winds snapped it shut and refused to let it budge until the storm would blow itself away. Harper tried not to let that harrow her as she stood, panting, taking in the desolate landscape. She was lucky in two senses—one, the sun that would have reached fever pitch heat by then was hidden by a blanket of thick, growling clouds. Her second blessing—it had stopped raining. The scent of petrichor clung to the air, but at least all this strange water from the sky pinned the dirt and dust down enough to keep it from stinging in Harper's throat and nostrils. Still, just to be cautious, Harper whipped out her goggles and put them over her eyes. Vision was vital in a strange, new world. And this was a world she'd only ever known to exist in story and legend.

The crunch of the earth felt both unfamiliar and surprisingly welcoming as she pulled out her father's compass and pressed northward, the direction Daphne always said the Mountain Maw Peak lay in. If the helicopter made it all, it would also be harbored there. And if Daphne and Paolo had anchored their travel tank anywhere along the route, it'd be north. She had her motivation. Her direction was set. Harper pretended she was Daphne on an adventure right then—a heroine destined for a happy end. And that seems to be enough to get the feeling back in her legs and keep her walking onward.

How long she journeyed before she came across her first stand-out sight, she wasn't sure. Perhaps minutes. Perhaps hours. When all around you looks like flattened brown sugar, and all you hear is a spiteful wind hissing in your ears and tugging at your hair, time stops carrying such sensible value.

But there it was—a graveyard. A resting place for what Gran called cars. All makes and models were strewn about like skeletons picked clean by decades of erosion. Gran said the disposal of such machines was humankind's first last ditch effort to restore balance to the way of the world, to make amends with the poison they'd pumped into Mother Earth's belly. But by then it was too late. No one ever cares until it's far too late. It wasn't long after the disposal of their vehicles that the people began to give up the Earth itself by hiding within Her skin. Anyone left behind upon the surface seeking peace or a chance to fight back with gritted teeth were dried up long ago. If the searing sun didn't slay you out here, the bitter cold of the night would. Nature had turned its back on mankind, but mankind had turned its back first.

Harper shuddered, crossing her arms. She then saw a strange flying creature with a long, naked neck and an oddly bedecked beak sweep its black wings over the wreckage. It was Harper's first encounter with a real beast. A smile flickered on her lips as it cawed down at her. She thought it was the most beautiful, wretched thing she'd ever seen.

"Wait!" She called out to it, reaching for its receding figure. Even just sensing the spirit of another living thing nearby was a much needed bolstering to her own morale. But the bird vanished beyond the hazy horizon just moments later. Harper turned around and realized why.

A massive cyclone wall of dust, rock, and sand was making its steady way toward her. Harper gasped and stumbled backwards. Oh. That. If only she'd listened when Daphne tried to tell her about weather patterns and changes of the seasons, perhaps she could've read the signs and hunkered down into some of the automobile ruins in time to void being blown away. Instead, she tumbled down into the ditch. Reverse somersaulting along the steep incline, Harper's clunky body seared in sharp pains with each smack into the ground. The compass slipped from her grip, and a few odds and ends broke out of her backpack and raced down with her, adding more obstacles to make for some interesting bruises. Her vision shattered first. She screamed as her eyes split into shards, and it took her the whole tumble down to realize it was just her goggles that were broken. She was throttled with intense shock as her back went crashing into the windshield of a truck. Her shoulder stung bitterly, eliciting a yelp from her mouth. Warmth oozed down her left arm. Her instincts buzzed with only one word: impaled. Dazed, she summoned up what little medical training Daphne had tried to impart to her and wrenched out a dagger she'd brought from home. Oh. That. She almost wanted to laugh. Till the adrenaline began to die down. Then she registered the throbbing in her right thigh, undoubtedly caused by the rusted metal rod sticking through it. Oh...that... No laughing now. Horror-stricken, she put quivering hands on her quickly reddening pants. Harper loosed terse wailings that sounded more animal than anything. Not that—!

But she'd unwittingly challenged the desert when she took those first steps into its barbaric clutches. And that meant war, in Nature's eyes. Harper felt herself losing consciousness as her heartbeats and the wind in her ears pounded on all the harder. This is it, she convinced herself, letting the life leak from her as it pleased. There's no coming back—and Daphne's still out there...

At least she knew she'd see her soon, in one sense or another. Death was a doorway. One in which her father stood waiting for her. Dying couldn't be so bad. And that thought comforted her, even caused a dry laugh to take off from her lips. She closed her eyes softly, forgetting the gritty terror swirling about her. She imagined her father reaching out to take hold of her till she actually swore she could feel a pair of hands swooping her up in its everlasting arms.

"Death," she murmured, opening her eyes to find the face of her rescuer huffing as he carried her hurriedly amongst the wreckage, out and away. Harper blinked hard at him. Death looked a lot like Jonas Bolt. The boy's bright eyes cast down at her as he tossed off her broken goggles, his wavy hair silhouetted by a sudden flash of light. Harper fearfully stroked his face, her cognizance fading all the faster. "Impossible—!" she whispered to this new protector as he lifted her into a sling and began to lower her down a deep, dark hole.

"It's alright." He smiled, his strangely familiar voice echoing as she found herself slumping into belief of him. Maybe dying, if that's what this was, wasn't so bad at all. She felt a dozy sleep trying to claim her.

"You'll be safe now. I've got you..."

As the sunlight faded, Harper held fast to these last few things: his calloused hands that told of seed-sown soil, cracked lips that smirked of seeing stars, and brave eyes that knew of an everlasting golden light.

Hot Clams, Charlene D'Avanzo

Gordy Maloy, fisherman, paced the perimeter of my laboratory. It was his third lap.

"For the love o' God, Karen, what'd you mean the numbers're off! January you said I'd set clam this spring. I got fifty cages for this hot-lovin' creation o' yours. Now, you're sayin' I can't?"

"Gordy, I said you *might*—"

"Christ on a bike. And you're a Maine lobsterman's daughter? You know winter's—what's left of it now—when we get ready."

"Sure. December through March Dad was hold up in his shack fixing busted traps." Memory wisps—wood stove, hemp, red buoys, canary yellow rope—came and went in an instant.

"If you'd stop walking around and come over here, Gordy, I'll show you the data."

My father's stand-in son did as I asked, then put one hand—nearly twice the size of mine—on the lab bench. With the other, he pushed a ratty Red Sox cap up off his face. I hadn't noticed that wrinkles were overtaking his laugh lines.

"Sorry I lost it there, doc. You know—"

"I *do* know." I turned my computer monitor toward him. "Okay. Here's the graph I showed you in January." I pointed with the eraser end of a pencil. "Average growth of bio-engineered seed clams over two months."

Gordy took the pencil and leaned closer. In the air, he traced an upward sweep that mirrored one of the black lines. "Um … that's the one. Two months, and it's still growin' good. The rest of 'em are doin' nothin' or they're already dead."

"Exactly right. 10-10-30 grew fast in water hotter than you'll ever have at your aquaculture site. And every spat acted the same. That's why I was so excited. Of all the strains I made, it's the only one that did that."

He straightened up. "And it's 10-10-30 for October 10, 2030. I know all that."

With a couple of clicks I brought up a second graph.

Gordy squinted, then groaned and added "pissah". I often joked about his mix of Irish and Maine lingo. Not today.

"Yes," I said. "In the last trials, 10-10 was over the place. No trend at all."

"Christ, doc, I got a whole lot of coin in this clam culture. Permits, license, cages, and I'm payin' through the nose for that spot in Eel Bay. The water there's too hot for clams for, what, ten years now. Still, I gotta pay to use it. I got bills. Lots of bills."

"I can loan you money, Gordy, if—"

He backed away from the lab bench. "I don't need your money, Karen. I need clam spat nobody else has that'll grow like the dickens in seawater warm as your bath."

"Come back in two days. I'll work on this and maybe have something then. Okay?"

On his way out Gordy nearly collided with Hal Wenk, the newest addition to our lab. Hal was an attentive worker who was, more times than not, in his own world. Without apology, Hal slipped past Gordy and disappeared into one of our growth chambers.

I looked back at the computer screen. If shaking the blasted thing would help, I'd do it.

"Karen, you all right?" Rachel Butler, my research assistant, slid on to the stool next to mine and put her hand on my shoulder.

"Damn it, Rachel. Gordy's desperate to grow out 10-10. Save clam culture—"

"'Course you're upset. Gordy's closest you have to family. What can I do?"

I patted her hand. "You're a good friend. I'll sit here for a bit and calm down."

Rachel left to join Hal in our walk-in growth chamber, home to over a thousand tiny clams.

I returned to the computer to see, once more, if I could make sense of the 10-10 data. A year ago, I used recombinant DNA techniques to insert genes designed to increase high temperature survival for larvae of the hard shell clam, *Mercenaria mercenaria*. Since hard shells tolerated acidic waters, another outcome of high atmospheric carbon dioxide, I didn't need to worry about that for now. 10-10 showed promise right from the start and for months afterwards. Suddenly, its growth was erratic. In Gordy's words, "It got all wonky."

I lined up charts for the errant strain, then tapped my pencil on the February graph when it all went wrong. Why February? What happened then?

The growth chamber door opened. Hal stepped out, got something off the lab bench, and walked back in.

I retreated to my office to look over my paper calendar. Given our power outages, electronic ones were useless. Starting around 2020, so-called fifty-year storms hit New England much more often—just like climate change scientists predicted. And what used to be rare weather events were as common as muck at low tide. The power grid was a mess, and two or three times a year electricity in Maine could be off for a month or more.

I sat at my desk and flipped through the weeks. No electricity for a week in November, but a generator kept the lab going. Rachel took over when I went down to Boston to spend Christmas with a friend. So nothing there. Another power outage in January, this time for two weeks. But again, the generator kicked in just fine.

I turned the page. February. February 12th was Hal's first day. I stared at the date. I'd hired Hal because he was a whiz with tiny marine creatures and willing, eager even, to work all hours. Microscopic clam larvae didn't wait until Monday morning to be fed. He had great references and lived up to them.

Sure, Hal was a little weird. He was spacey sometimes, well a lot. And shy on the border of timid. No crime in that.

I looked up at the knock on my door.

Rachel poked her head in. "Did you want me to order that new microscope lens?"

"Sure. And come in. I need some help here."

Rachel took her usual chair opposite my desk.

"I've been looking at my calendar," I said, "and wondering what might've happened in February when 10-10's growth became irregular. Any ideas?"

Rachel looked away. She was a gentle soul—an animal-loving vegetarian who carried spiders outside. Someone who took in stray dogs and had three as a result.

"What?" I said.

She sighed and twirled strands of waist-length hair. "A month ago I would've said no. But lately, Hal's been acting odd."

"What do you mean, odd?

"Hard to say. Secretive, I guess."

"What does he do?"

Rachel frowned. I guessed that criticizing anyone, especially a co-worker, was difficult for her.

She crossed her legs and bounced a foot. "Um—well—he looks over his shoulder and closes the lab book when I walk into the growth chamber. That kind of thing."

"Huh. Anything else?"

"Ah, I did find a memo on the floor. From that LME group. It must've fallen out of his backpack."

"LME?"

"Love Mother Earth. You remember."

I nodded. Radical environmentalists, Love Mother Earthers wrecked a genetic engineering lab in Boston a few months earlier.

"But why didn't you say anything?"

She bit her lip. "It's Hal, Karen. He's, you know, different. But malicious? I can't imagine."

I nodded. "Sure. I understand. And thanks, Rachel."

After Rachel left, I walked over to my favorite spot—a floor-to-ceiling window that offered an unobstructed view of Chatham Harbor. Half a dozen pleasure boats swung on their moorings in a waterfront crowded with lobster boats only fifteen years earlier. Sooner than predicted, Maine's famous lobster, *Homarus americanus*, migrated to colder waters in Canada and left a string of devastated fishing communities behind.

Dad, who claimed that "God wouldn't let the ocean heat up", died two years after that. With mom gone over twenty years, I was alone. Gordy was divorced by then, so he stepped in as a kind of hybrid father-brother.

I scanned the harbor and fixed on the empty space in the middle. Dad's old lobster boat mooring site.

That afternoon, Hal left early. As usual, he knocked on my office door, told me where he was going and why (doctor's appointment), and said "see you tomorrow, Dr. O'Shea." I said my customary, "See you tomorrow, Hal" as he gently shut the door. It truly was hard to imagine him as a radical anything.

I'd promised Gordy "something" in a few days, but 10-10's odd growth pattern was a sticky problem. Well, as Dad would say, "Start at the beginnin', girl." That meant looking at the first place clam data went—the lab notebook. So when I left the lab at five, the growth chamber notebook was tucked under my arm. Rachel saw me take it and simply nodded.

It's only five miles from University of Northern Maine's fledgling aquaculture lab to my bit of paradise overlooking the sea. But, given my empty frig, the grocery store was a necessary first stop. Finally, I drove the dirt road down to my cottage with my hand on the notebook.

I poured a glass of wine and took it out front to enjoy the sea breeze for a while, then went back in and sat down at the kitchen table with the opened notebook. What was I looking for? I wasn't sure. Maybe numbers that looked erased or otherwise changed.

I'd just begun to decipher Hal's chicken-scratch handwriting when a god-awful siren erupted outside. My car alarm. That was odd, but there was nothing to do but go out and shut it up. Five minutes later, I walked back into the kitchen and stopped dead. I'd left the notebook in the middle of the table. Now it wasn't there. I scanned the room. Nothing on the counters. Down on my knees, I looked under the old pine table. Nada.

I got up, plopped onto the chair, and stared at the tabletop. Was I losing my mind? No, I brought the notebook home and now it was gone.

Gordy picked up on the third ring. I told him what'd happened. "Can you come over now? I need help here."

Thirty minutes later, Gordy was in my kitchen drinking coffee. He'd changed into his spring-summer-fall onshore attire—tan canvas shorts fringed at the hemline, brown ankle-high leather boots with white socks, a sometimes clean T-shirt. And he talked fast and loud, like normal.

Gordy had a mission.

"Tell me everything that happened after I left the lab."

 I expected a reaction when I described what Rachel had said about Hal. But his only comment was "huh."

"So," he asked. "Your car alarm's never gone off before?"

To my "never," he suggested we go out and look around. The station wagon in the garage didn't interest him, but the mix of mud and pebbles in front of the garage did. He walked back and forth, then squatted and called me over.

"Do you ride a bike?"

"Yes, but I haven't been on it since November."

He pointed to the ground. I knelt beside him. A fat bike tire track ran down the edge of the dirt driveway before it disappeared in a leaf-covered shoulder.

We both stood. "Do kids ride bikes down here?" he asked.

"It's too far from the main road."

He toed the mud. "It rained hard yesterday. This here's a fresh print. Looks like somebody set off your car alarm, then snuck into the house and took the notebook while you dealt with the car."

"You've *got* to be kidding." I looked from the garage to the house and back again. "But—"

"There's be just enough time for someone watchin' you. Think about it. You walked out here, then opened the garage door. Right?"

I nodded. I'd pulled down the heavy door after parking the car.

"Then, what, couple of minutes to figure out how to turn off the alarm?"

Another nod. Inside the garage, my eardrums had pulsed with the piercing scream while I searched for the remote. Two or more minutes easily.

"That's be enough time," he said.

"But Gordy. That'd mean somebody waited for me out here—then went into my *home*."

He put his hand on my shoulder and steered me toward the house. "Come on, I'll make you a cup of that herbal tea you like. Then we'll figure out what to do."

Back at the kitchen table, I sipped steaming chamomile and placed my hand where the notebook had been.

"It was right here, Gordy. Right here."

"Let's look at this logical, like you would say."

It was an old joke we shared, and it helped.

"Why would someone steal—what'd you call it—a lab notebook."

I shook my head. "I have no idea. It's where we record measurements like size of clam spat, number dead. That kind of thing. The data are stored in a computer of course. The notebook's kind of backup."

He thought about this for a minute. "So the numbers in the computer might not be the same as the ones in the notebook?"

The very idea of doctoring scientific data was anathema to me. "Theoretically, I suppose so. But *why*?"

"Think about it, Rachel. If 10-10 panned out, we'd give spat free of charge to the fishing community. So Maine growers'd have a chance to get back into it."

"Yes. And?"

"Remember tellin' me 'bout some rich company holdin' the patent on some corn genes? And farmers could only get corn seed from them? And got sued if they grew seed themselves?"

I nodded. For decades, nearly 100 percent of U.S. corn was genetically modified with bacterial genes to protect the crop from insects and offer resistance to herbicides. Additional genes created heat-tolerant strains. One company, GroGen, was among the richest in the world.

What Gordy was getting at finally hit me. "You can't mean that someone would steal my engineered clams and sell them."

"Do you have a patent?"

"I wanted to wait for the last set of experiments before I filed it. So, no."

"And if you thought this 10-10 was no good, you wouldn't bother with a patent. Right?"

"Yes, that's right."

"So, somebody *could* mess with the numbers, take your 10-10, 'n sell it for a ton of money. You'd probably never know."

"Christ, Gordy. Should we go to the police?"

"They won't get too excited about a missin' notebook, Rachel."

"So it's up to us?"

Gordy leaned back in his chair and crossed his arms. "Yeah. This is our deal." After a moment he said, "Tell me 'bout Hal. Looks like a weird one to me."

I explained my reasons for hiring Hal. "He keeps to himself and he's, ah, different. But that doesn't—"

Gordy interrupted. "But you trust Rachel, right? And she's suspicious of the guy."

I sighed. Maybe it was time to be suspicious of Hal myself.

We tossed around a few ideas and settled on the most obvious one. I described where Hal's apartment was in town so Gordy could inspect Hal's bike tires.

"I might even take a look around his apartment for the notebook."

"Not on your life," I said. "That's trespassing. We've no idea if Hal's done anything sneaky."

He shrugged. "Okay. But I'm going to keep an eye on him."

The next morning Hal acted exasperatingly normal. The missing notebook really seemed to throw him—that it was missing and where he should enter data. I watched how he moved and what he did all day, like an animal I was studying. I hadn't noticed before how robotic he was. Was he really like that or was it all for show?

Rachel was also distraught about the notebook. "It was stolen from your house? Who would do that?" She also asked me to be sure to lock my doors, something I assured her I was now doing.

Gordy found Hal's bike leaning against the apartment landing. The tires were fat, like half the bikes' in town. But the dirty tires did show that Hal was riding it around.

At ten that night Gordy called me at home. "There's a light in your lab," he said. "Is that normal?"

"I suppose Hal could be checking on something."

"Meet me on Water Street, a block from the lab. We can walk over and see."

"It'll be a waste of time, Gordy."

"See you in ten minutes."

I parked my car where Gordy asked. It was dark beneath a row of trees, and I nearly screamed when he appeared from behind an old maple. I whispered, "Don't do that," then wondered why I was whispering.

Under a nearly full moon, we easily made our way up the brick path to the lab's front door. It was locked. I thumbed through a half dozen keys on my ring before I found the right one.

Gordy murmured, "I'll be right behind you." I nodded and stepped into the corridor.

Down the dark hallway, light from the top half of the lab door formed a rectangle on the linoleum floor. I made for the wooden door and pulled it open.

Rachel stood not twenty feet away, gas can in hand. At first, she didn't see or hear me. Then she turned and blinked but didn't say a word.

"Rachel, what the *hell* are you doing?"

I stepped toward her.

"Don't," she said and held up what looked like a toy gun.

I pointed at the thing. "What's that?"

"An electric igniter."

I stared at her. This woman—eyes hard, hair in tangles—was not the Rachel I knew.

I tried to speak deliberately. "Rachel. What is going on?"

"*You ... design ... animals!*"

"What?"

"You're god. Is that what you think?"

"You're not making sense. Give me that igniter."

She screamed. "Not one step closer! You've made monsters here. Little clam monsters. And I'm going to burn this evil place down and stop you! Get the hell out of here!"

She lunged at me and shoved me toward the half-open door. I fell me into the hallway. Rachel grabbed the handle, slammed the door shut, and locked it.

Gordy pulled me up off the floor. "I heard all that. This old building. It'll burn up in a minute."

"She locked the door—"

But his foot was already through the glass window. Good leather boots are useful like that.

Gordy reached through broken glass and opened the door. We both scrambled in.

Rachel held the igniter high in the air, turned to look at us, then leaned over and clicked it on. She'd covered the wooden lab bench and floor with gasoline, and the place was afire in an instant. Her exit was obvious. The end of the lab, right by the door, was free of accelerant. She strode through the space toward us. Her deed done, it looked like Rachel didn't care if she was caught.

My lab tech, my friend, was clearly out of her mind.

Gordy scrambled for the fire extinguisher in Rachel's exit zone. Startled, she fell against a lab stool—backwards into a puddle of lit gasoline.

Rachel screamed. I ran to her, peeled off my sweatshirt, threw it over her, and dragged her across the bit not burning. Then I yanked open the growth chamber door, grabbed her arm and pulled her in, and slammed the door behind us. Rachel, still screaming, clutched her back and rolled on the floor. The room smelled of her scorched hair. I looked down. My clothes hadn't burned, and nothing hurt. I stared out the chamber window. You couldn't see much through the smoke.

I didn't ride with Rachel in the ambulance or see her in the emergency room. After the medics said I was okay, Gordy and I went to the police station and waited in chief constable Rich Bradley's office. I gulped hot tea, good for folks who'd had "a hellava bad time."

"I still can't fathom it," Gordy said. "Tryin' to burn down the place 'cause you added genes to clams? I mean, she did that too, didn't she?"

"Actually, I did all the genetic manipulation. Rachel ran the lab and helped Hal with the clam cultures."

"But when you hired her, didn't she know about the gene stuff?"

I thought back. "Rachel's worked for me for about two years. The genetic engineering research is new for me. I just started doing that a year ago."

"She could've quit then."

I put the mug on Bradley's desk and ran my fingers down my face. "Gordy, I don't know."

"But this craziness. You didn't see it comin'?"

"Well, maybe I should have. Rachel joined some activist environmental group in the fall. But I assumed it was about warming. Pushing for more rapid carbon dioxide decline, that kind of thing. But who'd think—"

I leaned back and closed my eyes. Gordy gave me time to chill out.

We'd already talked about Rachel's future. Arson with intent of burning down our lab was a serious crime. Gordy guessed she'd end up in prison. Still stunned by her Jekyll and Hyde, I just didn't know what to think about Rachel.

Rich stuck his head in the door. "Hey Gordy. Be with ya in a minute."

Like half the guys in Chatham Harbor, Rich fished with Gordy. They got black drum and croaker, what Gordy called visitors from down Chesapeake Bay. The historic fish like cod and striped bass were long gone.

"It could've been worse," Gordy said. "The lab's still standing. Inside's a mess, of course."

"That could be a good thing," I said. "Now maybe UNM will build a proper lab. Seawater's been flooding the basement for years."

"Good to know sea level rise's useful for somebody. Hey, since 10-10's still safe and sound in that chamber of yours, you better get movin' on that patent. We've been bad mouthin' the little guys for nothin'."

"Top of tomorrow's list. Guess what I'll call it?"

"What?"

"Mercenaria gordii."

Double Double, Michael Donoghue

The first time I saw myself was at the Tim Horton's near Memorial University. I wasn't sure right away. I mean, who expects to see himself while ordering a large double double and two maple glaze donuts from his secret-crush Ellie? But, I looked over, and there I was. Sitting at my regular table. Older, wider, with less hair and drinking a double double with a single maple glaze on the side. The clincher was the "$M=10^{27} r + 1$" tattoo. On *my* right wrist it was still crisp, fresh from my black hole PhD defense celebration a year ago. On *his*, however, the ink had bled with age making it blurred, but still recognizable—and entirely unique. I wondered in the future I played the role of inventor or just consumer.

As I walked up behind him, the slap of my Birkenstocks on the tile floor seemed to catch his attention. "Hey," I said as he turned to face me, "I didn't expect to see me here."

"Oh, it's me." He took another slow drink of coffee and smiled like he had recalled a favourite memory. His face was tanned, saggy, with heavy lines around the eyes. Crazily, the tan struck me as the oddest thing about the whole situation. I've never been a vain person that; half my shirts were from Canadian Tire.

Then he seemed to return to present day and said, "Yeah..." as he squirmed on the chair. In that look I recognized what my 14 year-old face looked like after Dad caught me 'borrowing' the Toyota pick-up to drive around the block. I'd never disappointed them after that.

"Look," he said, as if he'd just solved a problem. "I'm here to warn you, Logan." It sounded weird for him to use our name. "Don't ask Ellie out."

"Why not?"

He nodded over to the counter. "You'll just mess it up when you meet her cousin. Then you'll end up alone, broken-hearted. It delays your post-doc by another year. You know what? Go home and work on that application form tonight. Stop putting it off—they'll accept you in a flash—"

"But, what about—"

"Come on." He took another deep sip of coffee. "In your heart you know that's true. It's time for you to grow up and start acting like an adult."

My face went hot. "Don't tell me what to do." This was crazy, I was arguing with myself. Wait, did this make me schizophrenic, I wondered.

"Trust me—you—on this."

"Yeah, well. I don't know how to tell you," I said, leaning down, "but we're not the most courageous person in the world."

"You change."

"I change? You mean, beyond the vain tanning?"

"It's the fucking ozone," he hissed at me in a low voice. "There's none left. Climate change messes everything up. Even wipes out all the decent coffee." He wrapped both hands around the paper cup and held it close. "The spike in temperature was so big it wiped out all the world's Arabica bean. The Robust coffee plants still grow in some really hot places, like Sweden, but it tastes half as good and costs twenty times as much. You know what you need to do? Move to the Northwest Territories or Nunavut as soon as you can. Beat the rush."

Then it hit me—he's acting just like my parents. Our parents. Telling me what to do, ordering me around like he knows better. Making my decisions for me and treating me like a chucklehead. Who is *he* to lecture *me*? I shook my head and went to step away, but the old guy grabbed my arm and pulled me closer.

"That's where everyone lives now, north of 60. As soon as you can—invest in land there. You'll make us a fortune. In the future, all Newfoundland is good for is growing bamboo and bananas. Most of North America is uninhabitable, super storms, super fires— "

I pulled away from him and walked out the door.

* * *

Still, he might have a point. Because of my upbringing, I've always been a bit of a chicken. It took me seven years to finish my physics degree on the properties of black holes, not because I was afraid of hard work, but because my parents had drilled into me a fear of failure. Even though my thesis formula had already been accepted for publication in a respectable astronomical journal, it still took another year before I could work up the courage to submit to my committee. Going home, I clutched the warm cup and brought it up to my nose, inhaling the rich smell before taking my first taste. That first sip. For me, it was like that initial gasp right after you've been holding your breath for a really long time. Coffee makes everything better. And I still didn't have the guts to ask Ellie on a date.

When I started University, I enrolled in a philosophy class as an indulgence. Growing up, I'd been indoctrinated with the scientific method, but I craved to grasp the big questions in life. In the first lesson, while we were all waiting for the prof, I felt a poke in my back. I turned around, and the sight made my stomach lurch like being on a roller coaster.

A girl with brown eyes so big they were almost deer like. A perfect smile that, when it flashed across her face, made me feel like a small child on Christmas morning. But, the best thing? Her freckles. They were scattered over her skin, like random flecks of brown paint on a creamy canvas. It's weird what turns us on, but with Ellie, that's what really did it for me.

"Do you have a spare?" She asked, waving a cheap white Bic in front of her face.

My mouth went dry. I shook my head, unable to form words.

"That's okay." She dropped the pen on the floor and grabbed a bulging pencil case sitting in front of her. "I've got a few extras in here. I'm Ellie, by the way. I chose this seat because I like your face."

At that point, she could have roasted marshmallows from the heat of my face. My brain, which served me well in physics, chess, computer science, decided at that point to fully shut down, terminating any language ability.

Fortunately, the professor arrived.

Next class, Ellie asked, "Do you believe in the philosophic theory of determinism?"

I made a noise similar to a combined hiccup and a burp. But she seemed to understand.

"You know, do you believe in the idea that fate follows a predetermined path?" Her head tilted sideways and she smiled, "Like me sitting here?"

This had to be a test. I always did well on tests, but somehow, with this one, I felt lost. I shrugged, knowing that this had to be the worst possible answer and turned around before I could make things more of a disaster.

By the third class I found the courage to tell Ellie my name. Then my parents found my schedule and made me drop philosophy to take one more calculus course. "Logan, focus on what's important." Their mantra. Their roof I lived under.

Still, Ellie had made those three weeks of philosophy a dream.

I looked for her everywhere, but our schedules weren't fated. Yet, I saw her in the colour of a girl's hair, in the way other girls walked, the freckles on a stranger's face—all made me think of her.

Months later, I found Ellie walking across campus. Some tatted up guy held her hand. I'd blown my chance.

From then on I just longed from afar, but not in a creepy way. She had a couple of boyfriends over the years, but whenever she caught me looking she'd wave and I'd promptly trip over an invisible obstacle or blindly walk into a very visible one.

Then, one year, she wasn't on campus anymore. I guessed some people aren't afraid to leave university.

I avoided real life by doing a master's and then, after that, enrolling in the PhD program. Getting through the course work was a slog, but the thesis turned into a quagmire. I got into a routine where I'd come into Tim's around ten every morning for my coffee and walk to the library where I'd sit for eight hours and do ten minutes of work.

But then, three years ago, I stopped in for my coffee and there was Ellie behind the counter. After that, I pretty much moved in. I wrote, rewrote, and edited the heck out of my thesis there. I swear I'm addicted to their coffee now. For me, home isn't my apartment; it's being surrounded by the familiar smells and sounds of the coffee shop.

Sure, future me had a point, I guess. I should be working on the post-doc application, but who was he to tell me what to do? What if I apply to the best physics lab in Canada, TRIUMF, and they reject me? You can't fail at what you don't try. Besides, there's always next year. What I really wanted, more than anything, was to spend time with Ellie. And to show that jerk face who was in charge.

The next morning I went back and, as I waited in line, I thought about it. I vowed to myself that I wouldn't become him. I also decided I would finally do it. I'd ask her out. When I got to the counter, Ellie took my regular order and then said, "Can I get you anything else?"

"How about a date?"

She tilted her head at me, smiled and said, "A date? Do you mean a date square? Oh, I'm really sorry, we don't have them at this location. You know, Logan, I think the only Tim's that have them are over in Ontario."

"Oh," I said, feeling like I was falling while standing still. I wanted the earth to swallow me and—

"I'm kidding." She laughed. "It's about time you asked."

"So…that's a yes?"

"Don't do it," said my voice behind me.

I could see a look of confusion on Ellie's face as her gaze focused behind me.

"Is that your dad?" she asked, her smile remained, but, somehow, it didn't reach her eyes anymore.

"No, no," I said, as I glanced back. "Never seen him before." I lowered my voice, "Must be, um, you know…care in the community case."

She gave me a look, and it didn't reassure me.

"I would not lie to you. Honest." People always say I'm a terrible liar. I don't think I'm that bad; still, somehow she could tell.

"He can't ask you out, he's got an application to do," the wrinkly version of me said. "If he does go out with you, he'll just mess it all up and end up by falling in love with your cousin Shannon. You know, the one with those huge freckles."

I pivoted around and poked my finger into his chest. "Shut up. I know what I'm doing."

"No, you don't. I know what you're doing. And it won't work."

"You're such an asshole." I couldn't bear to look at that flabby face anymore. I glanced away and automatically found myself checking to see if my regular table was free. That's where I saw two more of me's. They drank coffee, and were dressed the same in tracksuit bottoms and button-down shirts. There seemed to be a correlation between how much their hairlines had receded and their waistlines had expanded.

I turned back to Ellie. She was also looking at my evil twins. She shook her head and just said, "Double double."

"Hey," I said to her, trying to bring her back. "You know that thesis I spent three years writing here?"

"Yeah." Her eyes kept flicking between the four variations of me.

"It was on The Theoretical Creation of a Stable Micro Black Hole in a Controlled Environment. But, here's the thing. With the right tools, like a world-class physics lab, you can turn theory into practice. And if you can build one black hole, you could create two."

"That's right," old-wrinkly me said, edging up to the counter.

"And with two—"

"If they circle each other," he said, twirling his index fingers in the air and giving Ellie a creepy smile. "It creates a spot between them that you can slingshot into and end up being where you were before you started the journey."

"Time travel," said Ellie.

"Yes," said old me. "Now will you take my order? Same as him, but only one donut. They'll give us diabetes, you know. Literally." He pointed at the least-haired, widest-waisted version of me sitting at the table. "And kiss your healthcare system goodbye. Too many people, not enough resources. Canada doesn't even exist as country anymore—the water shortages in the U.S. southwest lead to civil war and then—they invade us. You really don't know how good you have it right now. But you're not going to cut back. Instead, you're going to continue being a chucklehead."

"Can you shut-up?" I told him. "Wait." I grabbed my hair with both hands. "I'm not going to cut back?"

"Not a chance."

"Because—all this is…"

"Predetermined," said Ellie. "Right?"

"No, no…Well, not…Look," he tapped the counter. "Can you just take my order, okay?"

It was like being on the cusp of a discovery, I could tell I was so close to understanding. But it hovered just beyond reach. Mornings before coffee I always suffered fuzzy head. Things were like a fog for me before that first drink of the day. If only I could…then, I got it. "You're *not* coming back to give me life, career advice or investment tips. That's why you looked so guilty when I first saw you. Everything that happens is inevitable. You're using everything I've learned, and that I'm going to learn, so you can time travel back and…" I took a deep breath and balled my fists. "You're coming back for the coffee. Aren't you?"

"No, no," he said, palms up in surrender with beads of sweat breaking out over his ugly forehead. "It's not just about the coffee and air conditioning. I would not lie to you. Honest."

Wow, I really am a lousy liar.

"You have no idea what it's like in the future." His pupils widened. "The equator is a pyrosphere with vast swaths of forest always burning—everything is so hot. People will kill to be able to sit in an air-conditioned place like this. Forget trying to hook up with Ellie. Focus on your post-doc. Too bad you can't listen to me."

"So," I faced Ellie with newfound confidence. "How about tonight? If I'm going to mess this up, then the sooner we start, the more time we'll get to be together."

Ellie shook her head, but said, "Logan, you remember me asking you about the theory of determinism?"

I stopped holding my breath to say, "Yes, about fate following a path."

"Yes. I majored in the opposite. Libertarianism. The original philosophical conviction is that we have free will and we're able to make our own choices. We're not locked into causal laws or events." And she raised one eyebrow towards older me. "Still, you know what?" And she smiled her beautiful smile, "Just to be sure, you're never going to meet Shannon."

It Won't Be Long Now, JoeAnn Hart

At first, Belinda fought against her bedclothes that seemed to be strangling her, then heaved herself upright, alert to the point of fear. "What?" she asked, a variation on the question she usually asked to no avail: "Why?" There had been a prolonged wail, she was sure. Maybe. It was silent now. In the dark, the blinking red light on the monitor told her the unit was on, but not whether her daughter was breathing. She tried to slow her heartbeat to the machine's pulse, and hoped it had been just a fitful dream. Just. But she heard the pained cry again, seeming to come from all directions at once. She could not locate it even as she stumbled across the hall to Rowan's room. At the open door she held her breath and listened without turning on the light. She could hear blood pulse in her temples, but otherwise, nothing. No life-or-death fight for air going on here. Not this time.

She gathered herself together in the doorway, where for so many nights she'd slept on her feet like a horse. It had been a warm September and wet besides. The humid air that made the toilet paper damp and magazines curl encouraged the spores that were her daughter's mortal foes. Single-celled creatures that didn't even know if they were animal or vegetable could take her down like gunshot. Belinda kept a trigger list on the refrigerator, but it might as well say "The World." Not only mold and mildew spores, but pollen from trees, grasses, and weeds, exercise, exposure to cold dry air or hot humid air, industrial emissions, vehicle exhaust, smog, and other air pollutants. Strong emotions. How could she protect her daughter from feelings? It would be easier to hold back the sea with a rope.

A dog bayed from across the mudflats, and Belinda snapped out of herself and crept to Rowan's side. Her breathing was raspy but steady, and Belinda's shoulders eased. Her own breathing was still labored, but that was because of all the lard she carried around her "mid-section" as her doctor called it, like she was a cut of beef. She hated the needy part of herself that made her reach for food when her own strong emotions had her by the throat. The nightlight shone on Rowan, lighting up one

173

side of her buttery, plump face. Ten years old and already "obese," as they said in school. Now there was a word gone awry in the system. It used to be reserved for problem fatties, now it was attached to kids like Rowan who were merely on the pudgy side. Some of that—maybe a lot of that—was because Belinda was afraid exercise would trigger an asthma attack so she kept her out of sports. No lean athletic body for Rowan. Not like her dad, the robust one. Yet he was the one who didn't make it. Jim was a fisherman in a fished-out sea. His captain had been forced to go farther and farther out to catch anything at all, in all weather. On a day the birds were blown inside out like umbrellas, Jim got snagged by a line and swept off the deck. The crew tried, but Jim never came up once. Not once. After a few unfathomable words from the Coast Guard, her future dissolved like salt in water. She buried an empty coffin and called him dead.

Belinda did not want to wake Rowan, but she could not resist a single touch. She let her palm drop on her child's chest, just to feel it rise. Rowan's shoulder was moist beneath her Little Mermaid nightgown, and while Belinda pondered what that might mean, the Banshee wail rose up again and she pulled her hand away as if she'd been stung by a jellyfish. But the unearthly sound hadn't come from her daughter, or even from inside the house. It—a deer? coyote?—was in the backyard. The noise was so alien it could even be a bear. They hadn't been seen in coastal Massachusetts in a hundred years, but then again, neither had coyotes, and yet they'd recently returned as suburban pests. Nothing seemed impossible anymore when it came to nature. But whatever "it" was, it was in trouble. The barks and gasps were like the worst of Rowan's attacks, the ones that sent them to the ER for a few hours on the nebulizer.

Rowan rolled over with a grunt, but did not wake up. Belinda tip-toed out of the room and back to her own. She looked at the clock. Four a.m. The hour of the wolf, as Jim used to say, the time he got up nearly every day of his life. She pulled a sweatshirt over her head and stood at the window, staring out into the gray world of the salt marsh where no artificial light reflected off the water. The moon was long gone. The plaintive moans continued, so there was no use trying to get back to sleep. She held the nylon curtain like a security blanket against her face and waited for the sun to catch up with her. The outbursts continued, less frequently but more disturbing, like something out of a horror movie. "What are you?" she asked. A young animal calling for its mother? An old one pushing hard against the inevitable?

In time, the first yellow glow of the sun began to organize the yard into light and dark. She watched featureless birds shake themselves awake in the branches and fly off. The house cast a long shadow. By the fence, the sunlight fell on the broken swing set with its cracked slide and Rowan's turtle-shaped sandbox, things she'd long outgrown but they had not known how to get rid of. The same with the lobster boat up on a wooden cradle. It was shrouded in a tarp streaked with gull shit, and the keel was hairy with dried green slime. A boat out of water was a sorry thing. Belinda kept putting it on Craigslist, hoping for a nibble, but it was too far gone. Jim had bought it cheap to fix up and start lobstering, since apparently there were still bugs for the catching. Mostly though, he wanted to stay closer to shore for Rowan's sake. So much for that.

She realized that the sound had become silent, and the silence was nothing short of ominous. The sun rose higher, making the house shadow shorter, letting her see farther down where the yard began to morph into tidal marsh. She squinted her eyes. "What the ...?" A black lumpen form. A giant trash bag? It was too far up on the lawn to have come floating in at high tide. Maybe someone got rid of a dog, or even a litter of puppies, tossed like garbage in her yard. It made her sick to her stomach. She was glad it was Saturday so she could take care of it one way or another before Rowan woke up. She didn't want her to know the worst about the world.

She pulled her shell pants on over her pajama bottoms and slipped on Jim's old rubber boots. They were too big, but they worked, and she could not afford to replace anything that still worked. Her job at the diner paid for shit. The little bit of insurance money had run out, and she was wearing out her welcome at the Fisherman's Widows and Orphan Fund. She closed the back door quietly behind her and picked her way down the slope towards the marsh. There had been a mean downpour a few days before. The lawn still squished with the weight of her step. The air had that murky morning stink, and the shadows were so dense she was surprised she could even walk through them.

She stopped at the woodpile to grab a stick of kindling, just in case. There was plenty of it. Their poorly insulated house had been mostly heated by wood, with just a few electric baseboard heaters that she could not afford to turn on. But Rowan's doctor said no more wood stove. "How can she be allergic to wood smoke?" she'd asked him. "Didn't humans evolve with it? Didn't fire jump-start civilization?" He'd shrugged. "Maybe we're devolving," he'd said, with a chuckle. This was the same doctor who told her to get air-conditioning to keep Rowan from coughing up garden slugs, but he did not tell her how to pay for it.

Holding onto her stick, she approached the bag with caution. In the half-hearted light, she saw the bag move. She stopped about twenty feet away. She hadn't thought about how she could safely open the bag. She patted her pants. No phone. That was dumb. As she was wondering if she should just go back and call the police, the pointy end of the bag lifted up and stared at her with mournful eyes.

"A seal? Are you a harbor seal?" She looked around as if the answer were to be found in the reeds. It was far from home, separated from the sea by miles of marsh. She turned back to this baby-faced animal, still not quite believing it. "What are you doing here?" The seal lowered its head, but kept its eyes on her as she inched closer. His dove-gray body was mostly neck and chest, and his head was like a peeled egg with whiskers. As she got closer still, she caught the scent of deep ocean on him, the way Jim used to smell at the end of a long trip.

She stood still, not knowing quite what to do, and as the sun rose, she saw that the seal had deep cuts all over its body and his stomach was raw. "Poor thing," she said. He must have been pulling his blubber on land for some distance. If he was not exactly dying, he was as near to it as to make no matter. She took a step towards it, still clutching her stick, and it lunged towards her with a snap of its yellow teeth.

She jumped back. "Okay! I get it." Because of Rowan, she'd been so used to seeing seals as cute plush toys or cartoon figures, she'd forgotten what they were really like. At the town dock, they lounged on their backs eating live lobsters they'd stolen from traps, holding the struggling crustaceans between two flippers like ice cream cones, crunching through the shells with a bite that could tear off your face.

* * *

A man from the Aquarium, with rimless glasses and a dense beard, looked down towards the estuary. The sky was an even dead white, and the air was warm. It was autumn only by the falling leaves of the swamp maples. "He hauled himself all the way up here?"

Belinda shrugged. "He started making a fuss sometime after I went to bed. I thought it was a human crying or something."

"They can be like that." A woman from the rescue team put down her satchel. "When explorers first landed on Cape Cod, the sailors thought the seals were mermaids, calling to them."

"Want to hear a mermaid joke?" asked Rowan, shyly.

Belinda wished Rowan had stayed up at the house. The yard was lousy with wet leaves, and she could smell the spores blooming at their feet. The "aspirgillosis monster" she and Rowan called the fungus. Besides which, this whole thing might end poorly. But how could she keep her from seeing the seal? Rowan loved animals, yet they could not have a dog, and a cat was out of the question. And here, an animal appears right in her yard. A sick animal, but a real one.

"Shoot." The woman studied the seal with a squint, walking around its six-foot, tapered body. She was almost as tall as the seal was long, but thin as an eel. She wore jeans and a t-shirt and was so tan she had sunburnt eyelids. Belinda was glad she'd made the effort to change out of her dumpy sweats and put on a nice shirt and jeans, even though they were so tight she could barely breathe and her cell phone in her pocket dug into her hips. She even put on her good sneakers, knowing they'd get soaked in the grass. For some reason, she had wanted to make a good impression on these people. Same as Rowan, apparently.

"Okay," said Rowan, squeezing her hands together. "A man and a cat are on a desert island. They see a mermaid on a rock. The man imagines the mermaid as having a pair of legs, and the cat imagines her as all fish." The tanned woman laughed, causing Rowan to squeal with delight. Belinda worried laughing would lead to coughing.

"That's a good one," said the bearded man. "We only see what we need, don't we?"

A man in a hoodie and flip-flops was crouched down near the seal. "Maybe we should just put him out of his misery," he said. "He's in a pretty bad way." Belinda made a face at him and shook her head.

"Misery?" said Rowan, softly.

"Why is it here?" asked Belinda, to switch the subject.

"Look." The woman pointed to its tail. "Fishing filament wrapped around his hindflippers and tail."

"You know what the monkey said when it backed his tail into the lawn mower?" asked Rowan. Everyone stared at her. "It won't be long now."

"That's not funny," said Belinda. The two men made polite ha-ha mutterings and went about their business, but the woman looked concerned, obviously wondering what child would joke in response to a distressed animal. Rowan had developed a sick sense of humor since Jim died. Her counselor at school told Belinda it was her way of distancing herself from pain.

"The seal couldn't use his flippers to swim," the woman explained, as if Rowan's problem was that she hadn't understood the situation. "Looks like he got pretty battered when the tide pulled him in through the marsh channels. It's a wonder he didn't drown."

"He can't drown," said Rowan. "He lives in the water."

"He's a mammal, like us," said the bearded man. "He can hold his breath longer, but he still has to come up for air. If he can't swim, he sinks."

"Probably why he was trying to escape above the tide line," said flip-flop boy. "He's a fighter, I have to give him that."

"Well, let's give him a chance then," said the bearded man, dialing a number on his phone. The tips of his fingers were flat, like a frog's. "I'm going to try to snag a boat and move him that way. He'll be less stressed. Besides, we'll never get the rescue unit out of this muck if we bring it down here."

"Then someone would have to rescue the rescue unit, right?" said the tan woman, making Rowan giggle. "Let's get this line off him first. Jason, go get the halter."

"Will he get better?" asked Rowan.

"We'll see what we can do for him at the Aquarium," said the woman. "He might just need a few stitches and some rest."

Belinda didn't believe a word of it. None of them looked as if they really expected it to live. The seal was watching them, and Belinda thought there was a wordless intelligence behind those big eyes that knew it too.

The bearded man put his phone away. "The harbor master will meet us at the dock. He's got a sweet little inflatable with a lift for us, but he said we might have to wait a bit for the tide to turn to enter the marsh."

Jason came back with a canvas halter, letting it slip over the seal, tightening the straps to keep it still. It did not lunge at them the way it had gone at Belinda, and she was a little put out by that. The woman slipped on rubber gloves that went up to her elbows, protective goggles, and a surgical mask. The kind Rowan had to wear on high pollen days.

"What are you afraid of catching?" Belinda asked, alarmed about a possible new danger for Rowan.

The woman took a pair of curved scissors out of her satchel. "It's not for me. It's to protect the seal from any germs I might have. He's got a lot of open sores." She began to snip away the tangle of line. "What a mess. I think there's a hook imbedded too." The seal twitched, and Jason was having some trouble controlling him.

"This is all we've done for days," said the bearded man, grabbing one of the straps to help Jason. Belinda pulled Rowan back. "A storm out to sea worked up these lines that just float around catching sea mammals like our buddy here. Mostly we've just been counting the dead."

As the aquarium people worked, Belinda was touched that they would go to all this trouble to try to save him. She ought to try as hard to save herself. She looked around at the broken toys and unused boat, the vinyl clapboards peeling off the back of the house. Belinda became painfully aware of how shabby her life must look to them. Since Jim died over a year ago, she had not kept up with the repairs of the house. She had not taken care of so many things, and now it was all falling down around her. Maybe these people were thinking they would have to rescue her as well as the seal.

Rowan coughed and then tried to stifle the next. She took her inhaler out of her pocket and took a hit, then another.

"Come on, you," Belinda said to Rowan. "Grandma's going to be here soon to pick you up."

Her parents both smoked, so Rowan could never go to their house, but they all went on road trips sometimes. Today they would be going to the mall to buy some school things, and knew not to smoke in the car with Rowan. They learned that lesson the hard way. Belinda was going to go along, but now she thought she'd stay and make sure things went smoothly with the seal. Maybe she could be of some help.

"Just stay away from the seal while we're gone," said flip-flop boy. "He wants to rest, and a human presence could send him over the edge."

"Don't worry," said Belinda, once again feeling a little put out. It was her seal after all. It was her yard. "Rowan's off for the day with her grandma and I've got work to do around the house."

"What?" asked Rowan. "What work? I thought you were coming with us."

"Off we go!" said Belinda, patting her daughter on the bum to get her moving. They hiked back up the slope to the house, neither of them breathing pretty.

* * *

In the end, Belinda couldn't help herself. After Rowan and her parents drove off, having explained to her mom, yet again, how to use the emergency call feature on Rowan's phone, she sat at the kitchen table with a coffee mug and looked out the window. The tide was slack, and the seal was quiet. Maybe he was feeling better now that the line had been cut away from his tail. Or maybe he'd just given up.

"You must be hungry," she said out loud. She heaved herself out of the chair and made two tuna sandwiches, one for her, and one for him, stacking them on a paper plate. She found Rowan's unbreakable cereal bowl and covered them with it, then grabbed a plastic water bottle out of the refrigerator and tucked it under her arm. "Okay, then," she said, and carried the picnic down to her salty visitor.

She was still wearing her sneakers, so she slipped a bit on the wet lawn going down to the marsh. The seal seemed to study her progress, wondering how a land animal could be so clumsy on land. She squatted close to him, but not too close. She remembered his pointy teeth. As she bent, she felt the waistband of her jeans slice into her flesh, so she unsnapped her top button and released her breath. "That's better," she said. She threw one of the tuna sandwiches to the seal, half expecting it to catch it mid-air like at Sea World, but it landed in pieces by his clawed flippers. She poured some water into the bowl and pushed it towards him with the piece of kindling, getting it as close as she dared. The seal gave her a look of warning and she backed off, settling herself on the ground well out of reach. She wished she'd brought a folding chair with her. The ground was damp and she was not sure she could stand back up without help. She had to take her phone out of her pocket and put it next to her in order to get comfortable at all.

She dug into her sandwich but the seal did not even look at his. "I know," she said, chewing. "I wish I had chips too. Maybe a pickle." But it wasn't funny. He seemed worse off than before, even without the fishing line. He wasn't moving and didn't blink. Maybe flip-flop boy was right, and he was too far gone after all.

Belinda finished her lunch in a few bites and sighed. It was sad about the seal, but it was nice to be outside doing nothing. She rarely got to just sit. The warmth of the day made her sleepy. Even the wind was drowsy. Nearby was a circle of smooth beach stones with a charred center, all that was left of a few fine summer evenings, where, if Rowan stayed upwind of the smoke, they would sit outside and consider the stars. But the last time they'd had a campfire, Rowan had woken up in the middle of the night in trouble, so they hadn't done it since. It was getting so Rowan could no longer take part in the natural world. Maybe they should do what the doctor suggested and move to Arizona, where the desert air was too dry for spores, and the schools were air-conditioned. But Belinda couldn't imagine leaving this place. It was all she knew.

She looked at the seal. The tuna sandwich sat untouched, attracting flies, some of which began to settle on his wounds. She slowly stretched towards him to wave them away with her paper plate and he bared his teeth at her. His breath smelled like a ship's hold, and she stopped. She wanted to say she was sorry—about the fishing line, about the flies, about everything—but he did not want her sympathy.

"Suit yourself," she said. It's what she got for trying to help. She should just leave him alone and go back to the house, but some instinct would not let her leave his side. He was stranded, just like her. She was a bit seal-shaped herself, with almost the same number of chins. They were both full-blooded mammals, distant cousins, for better or worse. Here was a species who used to live on land but had decided against it. For some reason, the seals had chosen to go back to the sea. She wondered if they regretted that decision, now that the water was getting as dangerous for the seal as the land was for Rowan. In the meantime, the die was cast for them all. If he survived, he would return to his element.

She imagined him healed and healthy, striking out for the sea, pushing himself along the sand with his muscular flippers, then merging with the water as if he and it were one.

Belinda wondered if going back would ever be an option for humans. It had not been an option for Jim. She flashed on his death, as she so often did, his leg caught in the tangle of lines, the frightening change from air to water, him twirling in the green gloom, the panic as he tried to reach for the knife in his belt, then the horrific awareness that it was too late. The vastness of the ocean was nothing compared to the finality of death. She hoped he experienced a moment of beauty before it all went dark, that he felt embraced by the water, swimming in love, as if he were coming home at last.

"Life is a struggle against death, my friend," she said to the seal. The light was dimming. The rescue team had better hurry, what with the days getting shorter. She looked at the marsh, and the water seemed high enough for the boat to enter the channel. "Soon," she said to the seal. "Very soon." Her mind became silent as she stared at him, admiring the perfect arched line of his body, the puppy-dog eyes. He was truly a beautiful being of the sea. When he turned his head away from her, she did what they told her not to do. She shuffled closer to him on her butt, then reached over and touched him.

Who knew such a large animal could move so fast? She felt the bite in slow-motion, the slice through her muscles, teeth against bone, veins and arteries opening wide to the world, coloring it red. The pain was so vivid it did not even register. When she got free, she hugged her arm to her body and would not look at it. The seal was more alert than he'd been all day, arching back like a snake. She felt warmth soak through her shirt and spread across her stomach, and she lay down on her side.

Fear deadened her voice. She could not cry out for help, but she could hear everything with a clarity she hadn't even know existed. Off in the distant harbor, the sound of the sea was a breathing thing. She heard the peals of church bells in town, the brass sound reverberating softer and softer until it was just a whisper. Then she realized that it was not a church bell, but her phone, lying in the weedy grass, vibrating and flashing red. She envisioned her mother in the ER with Rowan, but could not pick it up. She would meet them soon enough. She heard the mechanical hum of the boat as it hydroplaned over the marsh, and the great marsh birds flapping away at its coming. She could almost smell its exhaust. She imagined the blades of the boat's propeller cutting through the water towards her, and the spray rising up to the sky in front of the prow, the vessel leaving a splendid hollow in its wake. "We're saved," she whispered to the seal, even though she didn't believe a word of it. "Saved."

She closed her eyes, and in the darkness the animal heaved itself just that much closer and made a noise that pierced her soul. Her dry mouth formed the question "Why?" as if she did not already know.

Mourning Moon, Janis Hindman

They call it a mourning moon. If you see Vancouver in the fall, you'll know why. Vancouver's a rainy city, always was, but not like this. This was a hard rain, rain that bounced off the pavement then fell again, splashing into an ever-widening stream that coursed to the lowest point, intense rain, rain that meant business.

Jax was heading towards the mountains, the rain had stopped—paused. She crested the hill and looked down towards the North Shore. She smiled. She'd seen this view almost every day of her life, but it still made her toes tingle.

"Bio-interface disconnecting," said the calm, soft voice of the S-cycle, and her smile turned to a scowl.

"Freaking, trucking load of shit!" said Jax, banging the side of the slicker. It whispered to a halt. "You're supposed to warn me when that's about to happen," she said. "And why do you have to wait until the rain's on a break?" She glimpsed something out of the corner of her eye, pushed herself up, and swung her legs out.

"Rats," said Jax. She nudged the small body with the toe of her boot.

"Rats are all around you, underneath your feet, in your roof, in your walls. It doesn't mean anything. They hasten decay, the rats—the rats and the rain," said a voice behind her. Jax didn't turn round. She knew that voice—Bagger, short fem, covered in zits, nose-picker.

"What does that even mean?" asked Jax. "Don't answer, whatever."

"You need rain," said Bagger. "Energy from the rain'll make your slicker work again."

This time Jax turned and glared at her. "I KNOW THAT!"

"Don't be like that, not nice that is, just making convo." Bagger was standing in the road, rocking from heel to ball of one foot. A blader slammed into her then sped off.

"Did you see that? Did you see that?" screamed Bagger.

Jax didn't need this, didn't need this at all. She slipped the scooper from the side of the slicker and scraped the rat off the street. She deposited it in the cropper. She looked around. Surely there must be some dog crap in one of the gutter pits. Yes, there was. That went in too.

"Wanna hang out, Jax?" said Bagger,

"You still there?" said Jax without turning round. She slid back into the slicker.

"Home," she said, and the S-cycle moved silently down Commercial Drive and turned onto a side street. It stopped at a low building, partly hidden by cedars. Jax steered between two trees then up a short ramp that led to a half-green roof. She eased the slicker forward until it nosed against a soft pad that fronted an instrument array. She got out and the rain catcher slid over the vehicle, covering it and closing with a soft tick.

Jax padded across the glass half of the roof until she could see the gardenarium below. She squatted to check the vents. Good, the fix she'd made had worked. Jax grasped the rails at the edge and swung herself down to the front door. She put her hand against the keypad, and the door sighed open. She got inside just as the rain was starting. Again.

She looked in the food cooler: a handful of yesterday's vegetables, some fish protein chunks, and a bit of bread. She threw the vegetables, fish protein, and some de-energised water into a bowl in the cooker for a few seconds with some dried herbs and spices. When she took it out, it was hot and smelt good. She reached into the cleaning unit for a spoon, picked up the bread, and started eating, still standing.

The rain was thumping down now, but Jax realised that the noise wasn't just the rain—someone was hammering on the door. She looked at the security screen. All she could see were boots, but ones she recognised. She was avoiding those boots—Dizzy.

"Open up, Jedi, I know yer in there. I seen the cam blink." *Jedi*. Huh. Dizzy wanted something.

Jax opened the door. A hand grabbed her round the neck and shook her.

"Sure, and I've forgotten the trading units you owe me, never gave it a thought, you needn't have worried," said Dizzy. She lifted a leg behind her, tried to press her heel against the closer pad, but missed. She shook her head like a dog, scattering rain in a wide arc. Each drop sparkled as it hit a surface and was captured.

"You look rough," Jax said. She picked up her food and started eating again. "Slicker's all over the place, bio-interface keeps cutting out. I don't get it."

"I told you countless times what the problem is. Dunno why you take no notice."

"Cos your explanation doesn't allow for any options."

"Sure it does,"

"Naha. Slicker, according to you, cuts without telling me because I have a high metabolism. So if we lived before the bio-interface, you'd be fat and I'd be skinny. And your 'fact' about bio-interface helping to deal with climate change is just your theory,"

"'Tis the truth,"

"And my options?"

"Options for what?"

"For fixing the slicker."

"How do you get through life? Do you NEVER go into the science tanks?"

"Yes, no, a bit; what are my options, Dizzy?"

Dizzy shook her head. She slumped down onto a reclaimer and stretched out. She looked up at the daylight-glass in the ceiling and watched the rain as it hit and was refracted, each drop a transient sparkle of light. She nodded towards it. "How long since you did anything to the array?"

"Every moon, every single moon-cycle I do the updates. I read the stream summaries, and I do the fixes."

Dizzy unzipped a pocket in her sleeve and took out a patch of sheer fabric. She pressed it onto her left hand. She prodded at it with the forefinger of her right hand, pointed it to the left of the glass in the ceiling, then at the two reclaimers. She looked at the display. "Not bad," she said. "Not bad at all. So what I'm wondering is, why can't you do the updates on your slicker? Your solar capture on the roof is working at full capacity, your wind turbine too; your rain velocity extractor's only one upgrade out, and that's only because they just figured out a new tweak that's not even in the stream yet. Your reclaimers are fully aligned, hair, skin cells, movement, sweat and gas, all being absorbed and properly energy extracted,"

"And I do the upgrades on the slicker, every moon, same, but thanks for checking up on me."

"Huh. 'K, so I'm going to give this some thought."

Dizzy got up and went over to the bathroom. She sat on the waster with the door open. Jax put her bowl and spoon in the cleaning unit and followed Dizzy. She stood in the doorway, leaning against the frame.

"Saw that Bagger one trailing you," said Dizzy. "She's doin' Destroyer, got all the signs, skinny as all get out, bad skin, looks like her hair's starting to fall out too,"

Jax shrugged. "Modern life doesn't suit some—easier to buy drugs than spend time solving problems in the tanks."

"Watch it," said Dizzy, "I'm the historian. I pay my community share that way. Don't want you going into the history tanks and outshining me." She smiled and moved her foot to a blue light in the floor to signal that she was done, then waited until the light pulsed to tell her the waste had been recycled and she was germ-free. She stood and pulled up her unders and leggings. "Right. We gotta go," she said.

"Go where?"

"Vintage shop on the Drive. That masc, Fire-angel, said he'd give me a hundred just to play him at Deathstar and five hundred if I win, which clearly he doesn't believe I will, only I have you, my ace-in-the-hole."

"So you want ME to play for you. Why would I do that?"

"Because you owe me,"

"I thought you'd forgotten."

"Oh, c'mon. Anyways, you only owe me a hundred, we can split the rest, fifty-fifty—keep you going for a couple of moons,"

"And if I lose?"

"We just get the one and yer debt's paid,"

"Fire-angel's a dealer."

"Yeah, well, that's his problem."

Jax touched the small screen by the door. The sunglass in the roof darkened, changing from light emitting to energy capture.

Outside, a large bird with glistening black feathers eyed them from a bare cherry tree.

"Bloody huge crow," said Dizzy,

"Raven," said Jax.

The bird's head turned, following them as they went around to the front of the res-unit.

When they reached the shop they went in, moving between the racks of clothing, towards a door at the back. Stairs led down to a half-landing, then further downwards until the only light came from energy recyclers set into the wall. Dizzy pushed a heavy door, inset with leather and metal studs. Behind it was a long, dark room with a bar along one wall and a row of soft screens on another.

The woman behind the bar was dressed in vintage clothing: dress, flesh-coloured leggings, and shoes with heels. A gaunt man was standing by one of the screens, rangy, dark grey hair straggling down to his collar.

"Fire-angel," said Dizzy, "This is Jax. She's gonna match you at Deathstar,"

The man said nothing but slithered into a seat. Jax sat down at the screen next to his. She noticed that Dizzy didn't call her Jedi. Likely she didn't want the man to know how good she was at this.

Jax tapped the screen and waited until Fire-angel had done the same, and then they started. He was quick at navigating the Deathstar, so quick she wondered if he'd taken Vel—he was a dealer, he could get it easily, but it didn't matter, once she was in, she knew she was unbeatable, even against a brain enhanced by a drug like Vel. She found the command room before he did, released the control panel and easily accessed the tools, ejecting and eliminating his avatar. First game over, but the first game was simple.

She felt breath on her leg through the fabric of her leggings. She looked down into two burning eyes and jumped so that her feet were on the seat of her 'claimer.

"What the fra...?!"

"Just a coyote," said Dizzy, and Fire-angel laughed. She didn't know he could laugh. She did now.

"What the frack is it doing down here in this room? How did it get in?"

"You got in," said Fire-angel. He tasered the coyote and it fell back, dead.

190

"Shit!" said Jax. "You can't do that! Coyotes are class-B mammals, you can't just kill them!" She touched it with her foot, just as she had the rat. It was skin and bones,

"Self-defence," said Fire-angel. He turned back to the screen.

"Chill," said Dizzy. "Just chill. You get wound up, and you'll lose level 2."

Jax took a deep breath and tapped the screen again. But she didn't lose. She didn't break a sweat. It was like she knew the Deathstar better than herself. It spoke to her. It was the same with level 3. If Fire-angel had taken Vel, it was no use to him now. Speed was not the issue in level 3—no, you had to think like the Deathstar. You had to BE it, know when you would eat your own insides to better your opponent.

Fire-angel slammed the screen, stood up, and sent the 'claimer scudding across the floor. He pushed his face into Dizzy's,

"You fracking done me, your fem, she cheats."

"I'd like to know how," said Dizzy. "You tell me how you can cheat at Deathstar, well, aside from taking Vel,"

He stared at her, but before he could do anything, someone shouted, "Destroyer!" and there was Bagger right in the middle of a ring of human coyotes. Somebody brought a reclaimer with arms, and she sat back in it, legs apart.

The bartender came out and yelled, "No one's doing Destroyer in here; take it outside."

But nobody moved. Everyone crowded round Bagger who was massaging her cheeks with her hands. She snapped her head back, and the room went silent. Fire-angel was standing up, his attention, like everyone else's, focused on the fem. Bagger's eyes were wide open, and her arms were flung back. A mid-gender came forward and stood behind Bagger, then, very carefully, let a drop of pure white liquid fall into Bagger's eye. She blinked and started shaking, smiling, laughing. She appeared to be swimming, then flying, all the time shouting, but the words made no sense. Finally she became still, and the room itself held its breath, until she snapped her head back once again and growled, "Hit me."

The mid-gen repeated the eye-drop action, and this time Bagger's movements became even more exaggerated her yelling—screaming. It went on and on, and people craned forward until she stilled. And then slumped and then fell off the seat in a crumpled heap, like the dead coyote.

Fire-angel just stood, smiling—but without humour. He turned his head toward Dizzy, a disposable cred-wafer between his first two fingers. "Here, I feel generous," he said, and he walked out of the place.

"Frack," said Jax. "That was harsh. I never liked that snot-nosed fem, but that was..." she shook her head.

"She knew the risk, and she took it," said Dizzy. "She wanted out. Harsh, yes, but simple too. Plus, it saved us trouble from Fire-angel. Hold up your palm-com; I'll transfer 200." As she held the wafer against Jax's hand and moved a finger across it until she reached two hundred, she hooked the coyote's carcass with a foot and pulled it towards them. Jax looked at her and frowned.

"Waste not, want not. It'll go in the Slicker's cropper," said Dizzy.

"You can't put anything higher classification than D into it," said Jax. "And just telling the bio-filter it was self-defence won't fool it."

"Hmm, you may have a point," said Dizzy, and kicked the carcass away.

The mid-gen, who was leaving at the same time as them, turned and said, "Fire-Angel brought that coyote in."

"To distract us?" asked Dizzy.

"Yeah, and to make a point. Dealers and others want to see an end to the new ways. They have money. They don't want to have to reclaim energy and grow or collect their own food. They don't want everyone to have a say in decisions through the think-tanks. They want power, and to get it, they want to resume consumption. They think the new ways brought coyotes back in to where humans live, on account of the greening. But you're the history-fem, Dizzy, you know they were always here."

Outside, the rain had slowed to a drizzle, a fine mist. Dizzy sniffed the air. "I smell trouble," she said. "Don't look now, but that raven from your yard, it's watching us."

"How can you tell it's the same one?" asked Jax.

"The way it's looking at us."

"So why would it be watching us?"

"We'll work it out later, Sherlock," said Dizzy. "I'll come round yours this evening. Let me in this time though."

Jax wondered who or what Sherlock was, but she was damned if she was going to ask. She had the feeling someone was watching her, and when she looked round, there was the bird, just staring. She shivered. It was odd seeing ravens down here. That wasn't the new way, the greening of the city. This was something else.

It was dark when the lights of Dizzy's slicker illuminated Jax standing on the edge of the sphagnum trough.

"Whadya doin'?" Dizzy called.

"Checking that the methane-pocket meters are working properly,"

Dizzy shook her head. "I swear, there's no one quite like you for fine-tuning everything."

"And yet, I still don't understand why my slicker gives up without warning." She peered over Dizzy's shoulder.

"Whassup, Jedi?"

"I can't see it, but I know it's out there. I can feel it watching."

"The raven?"

Jax nodded.

Dizzy pointed her chin towards the res-unit. "Let's get inside, Jax. I know what's wrong with your s-cycle, worked it out meself, I did."

They went inside, and Jax adjusted the ceiling glass from solar to starlight capture.

Dizzy frowned. "Why doesn't it do that on its own?" she said.

"I have it set to manual."

"That don't make any sense, Jedi. The micro-programming works out the optimum moment for switching."

"A human can do it more effectively," said Jax.

"That's out of synch, Jedi. No one can do that." She watched Jax walk to the food cooler, her shoulders hunched, tense. "Right, except someone who can beat anyone at Deathstar."

"What's the fix with the slicker?" asked Jax. She crossed the room and sat in the reclaimer next to Dizzy, turning to face her.

"It's not the bio-interface; it's the trans-capacitor. When the rain stopped, there should've been energy stored. We should take a look at it."

Jax nodded and smiled. "That makes sense. Funny, sometimes I miss the obvious."

"Yeah," said Dizzy. "That's you, Jedi. Do the impossible but miss the obvious."

Dizzy pulled her palm interface out of a pocket and pressed it onto her hand. "Wanna see who's around in the VR room?"

Jax answered by getting her own palm interface out. They leaned back in their reclaimers and touched their screens. The familiarity of the physical contact allowed a seamless slip into the relaxed mental state needed for full connection with cyberspace and their avatars.

Jax's uncurled and opened her wings. Dizzy's jumped into the virtual room.

"Hey, Jedi," said Dizzy.

"Hey, Ban-sidhe," said Jax. The room was full of avatars that stood, sat, bounced, perched, or hung, whatever best suited their form. Most were talking or just sitting and watching.

The Room Op was a blue-bodied elf with dragonfly wings. "Good evening, avatars," she said. A shadow flitted across the room, and all heads turned.

"What was that?" said the Room Op, but everyone shook their head-parts. She turned back to Jedi and Ban-sidhe.

"Enjoy the fray," she said.

But they didn't. The talk was all of the cabal who wanted to resume the old ways and Dizzy, as her Ban-sidhe avatar, spent the evening explaining how the new ways had helped them to stabilise the climate, but they were far from reversal.

Later, when they'd returned to real space, Jax pushed the doorpad of the res unit to let Dizzy out. A flapping of black wings against the darkness startled them both.

"Flaming Nora," said Dizzy. "That's set the old ticker racing." Dizzy stepped out into the night. Jax stood in the open doorway, staring into the trees. She was convinced that the trees were staring back.

After Dizzy had gone, Jax sat on the roof cross-legged and looked towards the mountains. She must have fallen asleep. In her dream, a bird came down and lifted off her raincatcher. She could see the beard of feathers at its throat.

"So, Raven, what are you doing down here?" she asked. She could hear it croaking and clicking, and she could smell the wet earth. She awakened and realised that she was cold. She swung down from the roof, went inside, and showered, still haunted by her dream.

She lay on the sleeping platform and watched the sky through the glass panel above it. She could see the clouds, dark against darker, being pushed by a wind that would be restoring her energy reserves. She could see the stars through a clear patch, and a dark shadow, like a wing, the feathers glistening. Now she could smell the sea. She could smell it all around her, a chalky, salty tang. She was in a giant seashell, and it was closing quietly and slowly. She couldn't escape. As her view of the outside narrowed to a thin strip of starry sky, she saw a single, black, gleaming eye, perfectly round, looking at her, and then gone, as the shell snapped shut.

She awoke once more and lay there, sweating. The sky was beginning to lighten. She got up and went outside. There was no sign of the raven, but she heard the distant haunting 'woo-woo, woo-woo' of an owl. She walked out of the side street and onto the Drive. A pair of skunks ambled down the centre of the road. Jax kept well back.

There was a refreshment lobby just ahead. She had trunies for coffee now—she'd never been successful at growing enough of it in the gardenarium. She knew it was possible, though. She'd watched numerous vidstreams about it. She went in and held her palm to a coffee machine, then moved round to get a pastry. She wandered out onto the street and watched a watery sun come up as she ate her Danish and swilled the coffee.

Jax felt someone watching her, and she looked back over her shoulder. She thought she caught a movement. She scanned the three walled sides of the lobby but could see nothing untoward. She looked back out onto the street and was startled at the flutter of wings, as a large, black bird appeared from behind her, brushing her cheek as it flew out of the open frontage.

"Scared you, did it?" said a voice to her left. Zandra. She looked a bit like a crow herself. She always dressed in black and shared the bird's ungainly walk. In VR, she was delicate and light—her avatar elf-like.

"Yeah, a bit." Jax sipped her coffee. "Got any news?"

196

"Yeah, a bit." Zandra smiled. "Heard you got the attention of Fire-angel."

"Huh. Yeah. So, was that the news, or something else?"

"Else."

A few drops of rain fell on the road in front of them.

Zandra looked at the rain and pursed her lips. "There's been talk of resuming. Full resuming."

Jax shook her head. "Dizzy and I were in a room yesterday," she said. "There was talk. Dizzy says it's way too early. She says resuming can't start until technology's three generations more advanced."

"There's reports of VR rooms going down and worse."

"Worse?" asked Jax.

Zandra looked back at her, "Avatars being trapped inside and their realities not able to detach."

"Frack, that's not possible, is it?"

"Sure it is. You have a psych uplink with your avatar; you'd experience what the avatar did without being able to bail."

"Last night, in the room...."

"What?"

"Dunno, a shadow, just something that was there and not there."

They looked at each other, then out at the rain.

Jax touched her palm fabric with her fourth finger several times, but there was no response. "I can't get hold of Dizzy," she said.

A uni-gender came up the street and jumped into the foyer. "Frack, frack, frack," said the newcomer. "It never stops, just goes on and on, eh?"

"Hi, Kimo," said Jax,

"What you fems chatting about then?" said Kimo. "Anything I should know about?"

"For once, yes," said Zandra. "There's more talk about resuming the old ways—governance instead of discussion rooms, more industrialisation and even some talk of bringing back non-bio-interface vehicles. And there's some weird shit going down in some of the VR rooms."

"I've been hearing about this," said Kimo. "Most distressing, most distressing. So, going old-school, mmmm, old-school. Listen, either of you fems noticed the crows—hey, noticed the crows, have you?"

"Yes, as a matter of fact, I have," said Jax. "Even dreamt about one…except they're ravens."

Zandra looked up at her sharply. "Ravens, you say?"

"Ravens, eh?" said Kimo. "Ravens. Hmmm," and then laughed, a sound that rattled the throat and led to a burst of coughing.

"You alright, Kimo?" asked Jax,

"Sure, sure, just, you know, leftovers from me Crasher days, took far too much of it, messes with your voicebox it does, and your brain, hmmm, shouldn't feed the bad wolf, you know."

"The bad wolf?" asked Jax,

"Yeah, First Nations story. Hmmm, the good wolf, peace and love kinda thing and the bad wolf, fear, anger, the usual suspects—fighting inside the old man, and the grandkiddie, she says, 'Which one will win, Grandpaw? which is good, cos usually they has a tendency to say, 'What big eyes you got,' and so forth. And the grandad do say, '*the one you feed of course.*'"

"Huh," said Jax and turned back to rain-watching. She drank the last mouthful of coffee and aimed the cup at the auto-composter.

"Good shot," said Kimo. "You can ask Dizzy about the rumours after."

198

"After what?" asked Jax.

"She's there, there she is."

Jax held both hands out and shrugged in a quizzical gesture. Kimo started coughing again. "Can't stop myself, mmm, can't stop sometimes. Dizzy, yes, Dizzy. Fem has this theory about the bio-interface tech. Pivotal she said, pivotal. It was developed just at the moment when climate was in the balance. In the balance, I say. Technology was all there for cutting whatdyoumacallit—emissions. Bad stuff. But not enough people were doing it. Bio-interface changed all that." The coughing took over.

"Yes, yes, but we know all this," said Jax. "Bio-interface, according to Dizzy, because it uses a human's own energy directly, allowed everyone to eat as much as they wanted while sitting in the vehicles powered by the calories they'd consumed. But it doesn't explain why people suddenly bought into everything else, cut down on consumption, started growing their own food and paying community share in the VR think tanks."

"People are lazy," said Zandra. "And they rationalise their laziness. With bio-interface, they felt they were doing something big, something good. They went from excusing themselves for what they weren't doing to being proud of what they were, so they took on the whole package."

Kimo had finished coughing. "Fem's there, she's there, is Dizzy, in the VR room. Telling them, she is, telling them we need higher levels of tech to minimise pollution before starting to resume. Stable it is, the climate, but reversal is what's needed."

Jax nodded, then turned to Zandra, "And the ravens, Zan, you know something about them?"

Zandra nodded. "There's a Haida story about a raven releasing the first humans from a clamshell. Found them in there, wriggling about and started pulling them out by the ankles."

Jax felt a chill creep up her body. She became still. "Dizzy, I've got to get to Dizzy. Which VR room is she in, Kimo?"

"Send you the channel I will," said Kimo. "Not moderated, not authorised."

By the time Jax got home, the rain had slowed to a drizzle. She went into the res-unit, sat in a reclaimer and unrolled her palm interface. At first, she couldn't bring her heart rate down enough to make a full connection. She tried to calm herself, listening to the rain and the rustling of the dead leaves as the wind played in them. Finally she relaxed and found herself in cyberspace.

Jedi looked around. She'd seen pictures of Vancouver when it was like this. Tall buildings, cars nose to tail, driven by oil products. Plastic on the streets, cans, bottles. People everywhere, the avatars all took human form.

A single raven flapped down and stood on the ground next to her. It was as big as her. She expected it to speak, but it just stared. Then Dizzy was there. Ban-sidhe. They looked at each other and then at the bird.

"I don't think the raven's an avatar," said Jedi. She swept an arm around, indicating the scene. "Is this what it was like...before?"

Ban-sidhe nodded. "There are still trees," said Jedi. "And the mountains look much the same, but....not as green as now that everyone's responsible for most of their own food and energy. And the cars. It's like I can smell them. Do you think this is how it was before the slickers?"

"I'm pretty sure, yes," said Ban-sidhe.

Jedi smiled. "But no Destroyer or Vel or Crasher, I guess."

"They just had different drugs," said Ban-sidhe. "Different drugs, different problems—same outcomes though."

"What are you doing in here, Ban-sidhe?"

"I have to try to persuade them, Jedi, tell them what we learnt before. We're not ready to go back to that level of consumption, to the power play of centralised government, we're just not. Maybe, with future technology, but we're only just emerging from what our species did before. They can go on playing their games in Virtual Space, but they can't bring it into the real world. Not yet."

The raven dipped its beak down and pushed both of them so that they stumbled back.

"It's right, Ban-sidhe—the raven—we have to get out of here."

"Not until I've convinced them, Jedi. I have to try. I can't just let them do this without giving it everything I've got."

"It's too late," said Jedi. The raven raised both its wings, blocking out everything else in the room. Then, with a sharp movement of its head, the bird knocked them with its beak. They felt themselves falling backwards into darkness, and as they fell, they saw the room close like a clamshell from top and bottom.

In the res-unit, out of cyberspace, a raven was sitting on the back of Jax's reclaimer.

"I wonder how long they'll all be stuck in there," said Jax.

"Until we've reversed some of the damage we've done and our technology's more advanced I should think," said Dizzy.

Dizzy turned to look at the raven, but it was no longer there.

"Alright."

Shelly wanted to bring winter back to Chicago through words. At least autumn was almost happening outside, thought Pam, a late fall, sure, but it was there. She thought of the rowan trees, otherwise known as mountain ash. Their berries could also be used for making vodka and wine.

Just as Pam began typing her story, her neighbor Miss Bronson rang.

"Yes?" Pam answered.

"We're doomed," the old lady said.

"Now, now, Emma," Pam said.

"The rowan berries are out so late. This is craziness for November."

"Honey, I don't like it either. But look on the bright side. You can get a tan this Christmas at Oak Street Beach."

"I don't get tans anymore. I get burn marks between my wrinkles."

"We just have to live with it," Pam reminded her friend.

"Right. Well, I deal with it by getting numb, just like in that ancient Pink Floyd song, *Comfortably Numb*."

"You and your oldies. Get with the times, Emma. You should learn to like the new stuff, the *heat wave boogie-blues*."

"Never mind that noise. Let's get numb tonight. You in the drinking mood?"

"Well, I did have a hot date tonight."

"If you did," Emma said sweetly, "I would tell you to go. Go have fun."

Emma had stuck by her during Chris's death and the aftermath. "I know," Pam said softly.

Because Emma loved wine so much, and sitting on back porches under the moon, getting numb, she agreed to come over later—leaving Pam free to write her column for now.

Pam got on a roll with a winter scene set in a deep, forgotten forest. She loved this anti-block, what her writer colleagues would call a good cleanse. Sometimes when Pam started writing, she remembered the most random things. In summoning the perfect snow, she thought of a madrigal choir trip she had made in high school. Wow, was that like already two decades ago? She and the other small group of students were treated to a weekend in Green Bay, Wisconsin. Hindsight made the memory appear in her memory like a bad photo filter with ultra-vivid colors. She recalled arbitrary moments: her discovery, and subsequent enjoyment, of Petrarch; a cloudless day on the banks of the cold waters of Lake Michigan; goats eating grass on a restaurant roof; and a snow-white sonata being composed in the woods outside the student cabins the second night there, as winter set on.

The memory of that peaceful scene prompted her writing now. So did the music. Led Zeppelin's "The Immigrant Song" came on her playlist, reminding her to summon lands of ice and snow and Norse mythology into her essay. That reminded her of the rowan trees—type, type, type. A legend of Thor said he had almost died in a strong-moving river but was saved by a low-hanging rowan tree branch. The tree was also said to have made the first woman. Its wood had once been used to make staves and runes—and the tree itself was considered magical. It protected wayfarers and showed lost travelers the way home. Not a bad tree. And it was still used for wine, vodka, and her famous chutney. Not a bad tree at all. And that tree had lived for centuries and centuries, coming back every year like planned. Except for the past few years, now that it was confused.

Pam flipped her mind back to snow. Bone moon. Ice stinging the night. Wind that howled with wolves. A bare tree on the edge of a fast river. An ancient forest, the kind that was so ancient and primeval it would be considered impossible now. What else? How to tie this essay together? Pam didn't stop cleansing. She even began to feel chilly from her descriptions. Her sliding office door was open. Earlier, it had been so warm, but now she felt that dreadful scratch in her throat, cueing a cold—ug! She sniffled and shut the window.

By the time Emma joined her that evening, Pam was satisfied with a first draft. The thing wasn't due until Monday morning. Now it was play-time. The women sat out on Pam's deck, on the north side of the city, watching leaves curl into piles. Emma chose to sit in her favorite rattan chair, which had a big seat and a place to put a drink. Emma's body was thin and frail, and she folded into the chair like a bird closing its wings. Her long, silver hair was braided on one side, and her angular features were elf-like, Pam had always thought. Her once blue eyes were now gray, but still keen and sparkly. She looked like an old hippie with her flowered skirt and poncho, her bones and droopy skin filling the deep chair of the autumn night. What a graceful lady, Pam often thought. She was so light and wise, even if her sometimes failing memory buggered up her speech and thoughts at times.

Pam sat on a hammock supported by the sturdy branches of two oaks. Her own long hair stung her face as the wind picked up. She tied a bandana around her brow.

"Are you cold or something, honey?" Emma asked.

"No. Well, maybe a little." Pam tightened a thin shawl around her shoulders and coughed.

Emma grunted.

"Well, maybe I'm going through the change. I can't ever tell if I'm too hot or cold," Pam added.

"You're too young for the change."

"Maybe not," Pam said.

"Fuck the change," the old woman said. "This is good wine. It's that Argentinian Malbec, isn't it? Cheers."

Pam lifted her glass. "Yes, the Malbec. Cheers to you."

206

They talked of life and weather and rowan chutney. It was agreed, like usual, that Emma would come to Thanksgiving, along with Chris's parents (death did not change family relationships) and Pam's relatives. Pam also told Emma about her essay.

"You should call it *Thor's Winter*," said Emma.

Pam liked that idea. The night grew cooler, almost cold, at least to Pam. Emma said it was too hot for November. Felt more like August. At one point, Emma said, in a perceived state of wisdom, "What is new is not old, and what is old is gone."

Pam wasn't sure if her friend was losing her memory right now or if she was just buzzed. Saving grace, Pam said, "How do you pick up the threads of an old life?"

Emma smiled. "How do you go on when in your heart you begin to understand there is no going back? There are some things that time cannot mend."

Their Tolkien quoting game marked the inevitable conversation that showed its somber unwanted face on drunken nights. Pam's mind veered from writing, autumn berries, and forgotten winters. She began to slip into the realm of Chris. It was like falling asleep on Nyquil—a void, a black, a disconcerting silence. They'd been married for almost a decade. He had been her perfect partner—he patient and loving and kind to all, especially her. His solid state subdued her more active matter. He had some faults. He liked to drink Kentucky bourbon, which made him fart a lot and sing old Beatles songs, and very badly at that. He was endearing even in his worst moments. Pam could feel him today as if he'd never left, never gone away in some quirk of terrible fate with 'butt cancer' as he always joked. It had happened so fast and at such a relatively young age. Pam shivered and said, "I miss him."

Emma nodded.

"It feels like he's in the office staring at us through the window. I can see him there in his Bears sweatshirt."

Emma arose and said, "I have to go pee, but when I get back, we'll talk about Chris."

"No. I can't keep talking about him. It has been a year. I ruin all of our drinking nights."

"Bull. No you don't, dear. Resurrecting Chris keeps him alive. We miss him like we miss winters, only worse. But for now my bladder is going to burst." Emma practically ran into the house.

Wine had a way of dulling words and sharpening emotions, so eventually, as always, the spoken memories of Chris faded with drink while the unspoken memories came alive. The full, bright midnight moon was his face. The falling swish of leaves signified his ghost. The dim light streaming onto the back deck was his soul shining upon them. When the night was over, when the first signs of dawn became barely perceptible, when Emma sipped coffee before deciding to retire on the leather sofa in Pam's den rather than making the dark woods journey back to her own house—only then did thoughts of Chris vanish and Pam bid goodnight and crawled into her bed. She shivered again, rose, fumbled around for a comforter in her closet, and nested into the down of sleep.

The next morning, she could barely swallow. When she awoke it was too light and chilly, an anomaly, she hastily recognized when fully awake. Snow. The temperature since early this morning had plummeted unnaturally. From 80 degrees to what felt like far below freezing. *Thor's Winter* had come to life, thought Pam. Would Shelly call to cancel the essay? Pam checked in the den and saw that Emma was softly snoring. She then brewed coffee and thought, *incredible*. It wasn't just a light brushing but a heavy snow that thundered down from the sky and rode the wind like a wild horse, piling drifts into dead leaf corners. Pam shook the cobwebs from her head, drank two sips of coffee, and then realized she needed to turn on the heat. It was also time for the flannel robe, Chris's robe of course.

Emma finally awoke and couldn't believe the weather. "I really should go home," she said.

Pam asked her to stay. "There's some cereal and bananas. The cereal is probably ten years old. I believe that's also the last time I saw snow."

"Pray tell the bananas are not that old."

"I picked them myself from Columbia back in the sixties."

They ate breakfast, watching the oncoming slaughter of winter weather outside the kitchen window.

Pam said, "I don't think the forecasters saw this coming." She tried to switch on a small television near her kitchen table. She hadn't turned that on since Chris died. He used to watch football and hockey games on it. The damn thing stayed dead.

Emma piped up. "There's this thing called new technology, Pam." She logged onto her watch and said, "Unprecedented snowstorm hits the upper Midwest. Warnings of high winds, power outages, and dangerously cold temperatures for the next several days."

Thor's Winter hit with a vengeance that refused to let go. Emma decided to check on things at home, but she returned within an hour with her cat Radagast.

"I'm glad you came back, Emma," said Pam, as she pet the big brown cat who then bounced out of Emma's arms and ran off to hide. "I'm freaked out. It's like we entered the twilight zone."

"Do-do-do-do, do-do-do-do," Emma sang.

They sat again at the kitchen table, trying to clear their hangovers with more coffee.

Emma ran a wrinkled index finger around a coffee ring in the wooden table. "Your kitchen is great," she said. "It's was a centerpiece to so many get-togethers in the past years."

Pam nodded, feeling ill. Winters, kitchen tables, and Chris. Familiar moons.

That afternoon Pam went back to bed. She couldn't get warm and felt feverish. Her throat seemed to be cracking. She dreamt of a rowan tree hanging over a cold, rushing river. Hang on, hang on, she thought in her sleep. At some point she woke up dizzy and watched the snow continue outside. She closed her eyes and felt an icy chill creep through her bones, like the same bleak injection of truth after Chris's death. Nobody lasts forever, said the truth. Maybe she was going through the change. Her body's lifelong ability to control its temperatures was off-kilter. She wrapped more blankets around her thin body, then kicked them off— an endless cycle. Hell, she hadn't gotten that drunk last night, not enough to feel this shitty today.

Meanwhile, the temperature outside dipped, along with a dangerous wind chill. Chicago had once been known for this weather, but those days had ended. At some hazy point that afternoon, Pam arose to make tea. The cinnamon aroma trailed back to the bedroom. She couldn't keep her eyes open.

Emma entered Pam's room later, looking ghostly. "Someone is banging on your door," she said.

Pam sat up quickly. She had been dreaming of ice chunks hitting the roof, but it must have been the heavy knocking of a visitor.

"Could you see who it was?"

"Some guy," explained Emma. "I don't recognize him."

Pam arose, threw on Chris's robe, and went to a curtained window in the front bathroom. She peeked out of the dainty drapes to see a stocky, red-faced man who looked nearly frozen.

"We should see if he needs help," Pam said.

Emma argued. "What if he is here to cause trouble? Your house is too far out of the way. Why didn't this dude stop at Ken's house at the entrance to the cul-de-sac?"

"But he's freezing!"

The impatient man banged on the door again, and despite Emma's protests, Pam answered the door. The poor soul looked like a frozen statue. Ice clung to what strawberry blond hair was left on his head.

Pam asked him if he needed help.

"My car broke down on Saint Mary's Road," he said. "Damn, nobody seems to be home today."

"Well, come in and get warm," Pam said. Perhaps she should have listened to Emma. The guy had a glint in his eyes that was just off. Maybe she was being paranoid. On the other hand, she couldn't not help him.

Emma said, "I am going to get you some coffee," and with that she marched out of the room.

The man stood inside the doorway long enough to begin melting. He reached inside his pocket.

Please let him be reaching for a glove, his watch, anything, thought Pam. Not a gun. But when he pulled out a gun, Pam almost laughed. It was too cliché. She must be dreaming now. As the stranger pointed the gun at her and lifted it to shoot, Pam thought, rather too clinically, she realized, that it wasn't a new, shiny gun but an older one. She knew nothing about guns—only that most people today had one.

"What do you think you're doing?" Pam asked.

"What does it look like? Now, I want you to just give me any cash you have. And some food and warm clothes. Go on. I won't hurt you if you just help me."

"Sure," she said. She should have known, she fumed to herself.

The guy grinned but didn't drop the gun. His face was that of an overgrown boy's, with a hint of madness in his slow, blue eyes.

"My gun's name is Bertha," he said.

"That's nice," said Pam.

"She is dangerous," he reminded her.

Pam's mind told her to go get her purse and give this guy the lousy small amount of cash she had and to fill a thermos of coffee and a box of food and anything else she could find. But her body didn't follow her mind. She felt very dizzy. She began to ask if he wanted a beer while he waited, but her brain gave up. Her body collapsed into the cold marble floor of her foyer.

* * *

Emma came to her bed later with soup. Somehow, the gun guy was gone and Pam had magically been returned to bed. Emma said, "Sorry, the soup is cold. The power's out. I don't know what's going on. The temperatures are still dropping."

Pam lethargically gazed over to her window. It was getting to be dusk. Snow flew by sideways, stinging the shadows of the trees surrounding her house.

"Where's that guy? He had a gun," Pam said. Had she dreamed it?

"Let's just say I took care of him," her friend said. "Then had to get you to bed after you fainted. Way to go, girl."

"How did you take care of him?"

"I gave him some coffee with a heavy dose of sleeping pills that I brought over in case I stayed the night again."

"Emma," Pam wanted to chide her, both for standing up to a man half her age and twice her size—and for her dependence on numbness. But Pam didn't have the energy for lectures. She was sick, feverish, and vulnerable. Times like these she needed Chris. Even a shot of bourbon. It was funny. When someone died you did everything you could to bring them back to you, like wearing their robe. She remembered after Chris's funeral, after everyone had gone home, she had drowned in his bourbon. She farted. She sang Beatles songs, badly. But that had not brought him back. And there was nothing worse, she thought, than a drunken bookworm dancing around an empty house trying to sing "Across the Universe."

"What did you do with that guy after drugging him?" Pam asked.

"I walked over to Ken's house," Emma said, referring to one of their neighbors, "who was able to radio the police, who came to take sleeping fatty away."

"Ug. He was scary."

"Well, he's gone."

Pam nodded. Her toes felt ice-bitten despite layers of blankets.

"We *are* doomed, by the way," Emma said. "The police said that we are hitting all-time record lows tonight. It's dangerous, with no power and heat. Look, I'm going to start a fire when the sun goes down, and we'll get you moved into the hearth room. Do you have any more wood than what's in the garage?"

"Shed," Pam said, feeling breathless and woozy. She wanted to tell Emma that she could bring in the wood, but the words failed to come out. She wanted to say the wood was old. She hadn't built too many fires in the last several years.

Night. A fire. Ken had come over again to help Emma bring in more wood. The fireplace sat centrally on a wall between two facing sofas. Pam laid on one and Emma on the other. Emma had heated up a hot tottie over the fire and given it to her sick friend. Pam kept waking and falling back asleep. Suddenly it was much later, and Emma had finally conked out. Pam awoke to a dwindling fire. She should get up to get more wood. Any moment now she would find the energy. The bay window in her living room was covered with frosted ice except one area that the fire's heat had cleared, and through that part of the window shone a full moon into the black room, transecting shadows with silver shards of faint light.

As Pam drifted off once again, she felt the moon's bone fingers chill her face. The sky swirled with icy debris and appeared to be primordial, as if it were a night in Thor's age. The universe toppled back in time, and bare rowan trees stood like legionnaires on frozen river banks. Cold distant suns and mysterious shadows touched the tallest trees to ever have existed. The climax trees of another era. At their highest boughs were nests of billowy snow. How men had survived back then—heck, how any of us had survived, thought Pam. It was always questionable, but humans had made do for a time.

But the cold, the cold. Pam had never felt anything like it. Emma might prefer this kind of numbness. It entered into the skin, climbed into the bones, pulled up a log to sit and linger. Pam shivered in her sleep. It wasn't supposed to be like this. Just the opposite. The midnight moon burned a hole into a frosty layer of her window. Surrounding the halo were light and ice and hollow things across the universe. The cold settled, hummed, cracked. The night and the moon would not end. Thor was playing a joke on her, on humankind. *I promise to take better care,* Pam thought in delirium. *Give me Chris back. Give me normal winters. I promise I will be good.*

Thor's laughter floated through the night, shaking the moon, his breath the force of a million gales of ice-wind. Buildings and cars turned to blocks of ice, upon which the most magnificent flakes scuttled before springing back into the void. Pam would cease to be. Die. No fires would keep her or anyone else alive. The blankets around her became frigid metal. Blood moved to her core to help her survive. She remembered that from science class. It was called *vasoconstriction.* She would die before her body actually vasoconstricted.

Bitter death came to the Arctic Earth. Pam's spirit fell into a twirl of diamond specs that cavorted amid the Earth's atmosphere. *Fall into something meaningful,* Pam thought. The endless night marked the end of the time of the sun. No longer would the big star rise or sink or guide human and other life cycles on earth or in the sea. Only the white face of the laughing midnight moon ticked by like a mocking clock. Only faraway were twitches of death and light streaking across the universe. She wanted her spirit to die like a star, to offer light to a someday child's hopeful gaze upon the heavens.

Thor shook the moon, shook her. Was that Chris in the sky, waiting for her?

Pam, came the long moan. Pam, Pam.

It was Emma, waking her up.

"Good grief girl, I thought you were a goner,"

"Huh?" Pam shot up from her pillows. An intensely bright sun shone through her windows. The heat of it nearly burned her skin. She had to close her eyes the heat and light were so strong.

"You've been out of it for two days," Emma said. "And you've had the chills. At least your fever finally broke. Doc came over to check you out."

"You mean…what about the snow?

Emma placed the back of her hand against Pam's forehead. "You've been having some major dreams, my dear. You're still a little warm, but I think the worst part is over. You need a cool bath, honey."

Pam was relieved to not have died.

"Today is supposed to be 120," Emma said. "Weird weather we had while you were sick, and the temperatures are climbing. They are saying there will be brownouts, blackouts, water rations. You better get that shower sooner than later."

Pam nodded, weakly making her way to the shower, remembering that she had told Thor she would be good—knowing it was too late in many ways, but there were things she could still do, like cleaning up the woods around the house, like doing with less.

"Emma," she called back to her friend, who now stood next to the bed with an arm full of dirty sheets.

"Yeah?"

"After my shower, I want to pick some rowan berries. Maybe start my chutney tonight."

"That's a weird idea after being so sick. What's gotten into you?"

"Continuity."

"Well, that, my dear, is wonderful," Emma said.

* * *

Note that this story is inspired by the Twilight Zone's "The Midnight Sun" episode.

The Library, Stephan Malone

"Garbage! Just garbage!" Tana yelled, and then threw the ancient book away.

"Now what is it," Cormac said. He sighed as he peered over his glasses. He closed the book that he was reading.

"Hackers."

"So? What about them?"

"That's the third story I read in this dump that has a hacker in it." Tana stood up and snorted. She picked up her coil-gun and shot a round through the rejected relic. A fine tuft of dust poofed around the old book as her bullet shot through with a *thhwwunk*. "Stupid."

Cormac advanced his glasses with his index finger. "Never knew you were so passionate about story clichés."

Tana said, "It's not that. But you can't just throw a keyboard under some random character and have them type type-ity type for thirty seconds." Tara pantomimed typing on invisible keys. "And they magically hack into a secure network or cyber-safe."

"You would know." Cormac resumed his inspection of the dust-borne books that lay everywhere. The abandoned library was unlit, save for their solar torches. Their voices echoed against unseen pillars and shelves with a haunted resound.

"Yeah, I know. Just look how long it took me to break you into this worthless hole." Tana walked toward Cormac and brushed his face with her leather-wrapped hands. "C'mon, I'm bored and horny."

Cormac froze and said, "Maybe you should check on the bikes, Tana."

Tana lay her coil-gun against a pile of books next to Cormac and pushed him back. "Come on, we won't hurt anyone. She'll never know."

"Tana."

"Feel good?" Tana forced a kiss and rubbed herself against him.

Cormac stroked her leather wraps for a few seconds but then regained his senses and pushed her back. "Tana! That's enough! Stop it."

Tana ignored his objection and rubbed her hand on his groin. "C'mon, just fu—"

Cormac shoved her away. Tana's armored leather pants bumped and squeaked as her rear end slid across the five hundred year old stonework floor. "I said stop it! God damn it, Tana! Pull yourself together."

Tana huffed and fluidly sprang herself into a stand. "Whatever, old man."

"Please go check on the bikes."

Tana, a twenty-six year old statue of leather and scars, simply stood there.

"Please, Tana. Just go," Cormac said.

She spun away and disappeared into the darkness, her shadowed mirage following the faint Lumina One markers that led the way outside. In the distance Cormac could hear her faintly repeat, "Old man. Idiot."

Cormac looked around him and exhaled, resigned. They told him that she might be unstable, but he never expected something like this. Tana was about as stable as a vial of nitroglycerin, he decided. He was supposed to simply travel with her into this vacant vault of a city-world lost forever. She could explode at any moment, but he still needed her hacking talents to blow the abandoned library's digital protections clean away.

Perhaps it was really her that carried him here and not the other way around. He didn't know, but it really didn't matter. The endless piles of books waited around him in stacks and heaps that loomed unconquerable. He picked up another book and blew the dust from its cover. The title and author were long gone, the book's surface rendered to ash and rot.

But this one was an easy one. It was written in old world German. Cormac buttered through the pages, at least the ones that were legible. There were pages that had only a handful of words that he could read, the rest randomly blotted into oblivion by mold or water or fire or the mouths of hungry insects. Others were more or less intact, the edges frilled and beaten in, their margins sacrificed to save the precious innermost ink.

He determined that it was a book about the then modern automobile manufacturing process. He couldn't be sure of the publication date but guessed that it was probably printed sometime in the early 21st century based on the phrasing and binding manufacture. The book wafted of mildew, an early specimen, perhaps one of the first books ever printed in someone's own home. The personal bookmaker machines were old 3-D printers that reproduced books anywhere in the world on demand. All that was needed was the digital master file. He wondered what the world would have been like if the do-it-yourself machines and the e-book revolution never happened in the first place. It was stunning, he thought, how fast the world of big-boy publishing changed back then, only to disappear from greatness forever, the years far away. Must have been a crazy time, he supposed.

Tana returned. She sneered at Cormac. "Bikes are fine, old man."

"Stop calling me that."

"How old are you?" Tana aimed her coil-gun at his forehead and pulled the trigger. Cluck.

Cormac shuddered at the sound.

"Hahah! Gotcha, old man!"

"Tana, please stop."

"Stop what?"

"Stop being a nutcase."

"Well, I won't." She pulled her coil-gun and shot a coil-round just to the left of Cormac's head. "Go ahead and tell me how messed up I am, old man."

"Fine. You're not crazy."

"That's better." Tana slinked up to him once more. "So you really don't want to do me, huh?" She twirled around on one foot. "I'm twenty-six," she teased while she extended her words. "I know things." She winked, smiled, and turned around on one foot, like a toybox ballerina.

Cormac wasn't quite sure what got into him, but he decided to play along. He mimicked Tana's taunt and turned around in place. "Forty-six! I know shit too!"

Tana stared at him for a second, speechless. And then she burst out laughing, her voice bellowing against the distant unlit library walls. She laughed so hard she plunked onto her rear, the gel-lined leather armor insulating her from any pain. Dust and webs pillowed into the air. And even then she kept on laughing.

Cormac lowered his arms. "Glad you found that amusing."

"Yeah," Tana managed to speak in between snorts and bubbles. "That was good."

Cormac plopped down next to her. With a whisper he said, "Listen. I'm not gonna lie to you. I'm sure it'd be great, I mean you and me and whatnot. But you know what happen when we go back."

Tana wiggled her right foot. "Yeah, so what? Screw it, let 'em fry me. They can all go to hell! What do I care?"

Cormac looked at the metallic brace wrapped round her ankle. "Besides, I have a wife, you know?"

"Sure, yeah," Tana responded.

"Look, you are very beautiful. There's no question." Cormac brushed her face with his hand, her scars rumpled against his fingertips. Tana lowered her head so he couldn't see her eyes any more. "But we have things to do here. I need to find evidence of what happened. What they were thinking. Why they let it all go. The world. Everything."

Tana nodded her head but kept her face down. "Okay."

Cormac raised her head to meet his with his hand. When she looked at him, her young face reddened and puffed, and they kissed. She pushed herself on top of him and they kissed some more against the silence. The solar torches' low-pitched hums were the solitary sounds amidst their tangle interdict.

A loud rumble echoed throughout the abandoned library. The vibrations were so strong that they knocked one of the solar torches from its small tripod mount. Tana jumped off of Cormac and looked up. Together, they froze in place as if the lights were suddenly turned on and they were discovered by unseen canonical parents. The resonant boom attenuated into a raw, profound silence.

"Second level," Tana said. She grabbed her coil-gun and looked through the scope. "Wake up your girl," she whispered from the side of her mouth.

"Right," Cormac responded. He scuttled over to his roll-along bag and produced a sphere ringed by tiny propellers a foot or so in diameter. "Vana. Seek," Cormac whispered to the balloon. He crawled behind a four foot tall hill of books where Tana lay on her belly.

The probe-sphere floated up and made its way to the second floor balcony. It gently bounced off the balcony's outer rail and then ascended to within two feet of the ceiling arches far overhead. The sphere threw out a visible red laser to highlight the intruders position. Cormac's personal assistant band beeped low three times, a wrist-worn signal from Vana that there were three of them tucked away up there, somewhere beyond the verge of failed and worm-thinned beams.

"Three to two, easy enough," Tana whispered. She looked at Cormac, who presently scanned the balcony above. "Cor," she said with a pressure.

"What?" he said quietly but did not break his focus on the hovering probe.

"Get your rifle, dummy," she said with a hint of irritation.

"Good point," Cormac responded. He briefly smiled, scrambled for his glasses, and pushed them onto his face. He nearly forgot that his coil-gun was even next to him. He had been reading through books and pieces of books for seven hours straight.

"Throw down your weapons and surrender! You are trespassing!" one of the three soldiers announced from above.

Cormac said, "We're only here for the shelter! From the Great Storm! Please leave us alone. We don't mean any harm," he lied.

"This library is sealed! The Council of Emperor has declared it!"

"Yeah, well you should have tacked a damn sign on the front door that said that!" Tana yelled back.

Another voice came down from the dark balcony. "Surrender, or we will shoot!"

Tana yelled up to the shadowed balcony. "Fine! Come down here and get us, you ass!" She turned her head to Cormac, who lay belly down and behind the book pile. She never would have thought in a million years that books could be used as a protective bastion. Then again, they had no sandbags or hescos nearby, so the stacks of ancient books would have to do. "Stay right here. I'll take care of these shitheads," she whispered.

Cormac nodded. His face was red and hot, and his glasses were fogged over from his anxious evaporate. His eyes stung as acidified sweat trickled over them.

Tana rapidly plugged three magnetically propelled coil-rounds into the darkness above her. *Thwwunkk-thwunnk-thwunnk,* she shot up and away, eight times faster than any bullet ever crafted. The large center chandelier, ancient and festered with webs and cocoons, wiggled off a fragile phantom of its shape. The dust vibrated from the crystals and gently cascaded onto the floor below.

Tana spirited from the book pile's safety and cat-walked toward the balcony's stairwell, which was a spun iron skeleton construct. It creaked and groaned with her slightest touch. She knew she could never get up to the balcony unheard. Unseen perhaps, but not with the silent advantage that she needed. No, they would definitely take her down before she could plant so much as a single foot upon the balcony's upper landing.

The soldiers fired blindly at Cormac's position. Tana guessed that they were almost directly over her head. She could just barely see Cormac. He was about thirty meters away, hugging the library's floor even tighter while bullets rained around him and interrupted the gentle sleep of dust and paper. Cormac braved a quick peek-and-shoot as he fired his coil-gun. His shots were poorly aimed as he reached deep against the deadly unprotected air. Simultaneously, the soldiers shot three more times from their covered advantage. Vana, the probe, exploded as it was hit, and its internal hydrogen subsequently ignited. Vana was not a military probe but meant for research and exploration and the occasional critter control if the situation had ever called for it.

Incredibly, one of the Emperor's soldier-men yowled out in pain. "Ahh shit! I'm hit, I'm hit!"

It was sheer luck that Cormac had even shot one of them. The wounded soldier-man yelled out for all to hear, over and over. Tana could hear them scuffling about as the wooden floor-planks overhead whined and squeaked in response to the intrusions of weight and foot. She took advantage of the moment and flew up the spiral stairs of iron. The column growled so strongly under her boots that she was certain they heard her.

But they didn't. The soldiers were too busy trying to keep their fellowman from bleeding out. She heard one of them say, "Hold still, damnit, I can't get at it!" Tana arrived to the spiral stair's upper deck and then stopped. The soldiers had their backs to her as they hunched over their causality, a tactically ridiculous choice. They were probably young and inexperienced, she thought. In all likelihood, this was the first time they had dealt with a wounded friend in actual, real-world combat.

Tana looked around the balcony's sides and wished there were more targets to engage or soldiers to fight, but there were none. They were young, she considered. Oh well. They certainly weren't going to get any older. She looked down to Cormac's position on the ground floor but could not see him anywhere. He was safely pocketed behind the sanctuary provided by the four foot tall pile of books. "Hey!" Tana yelled and then shot her coil-gun straight at the soldier on her left side.

He flung himself away and then slid in his own blood across the ancient wood. Tana had hit his aorta, and the pressured blood gushed in streams of bright red ahead of him. The dark fountain distracted Tana for only a hair of a second, but it was enough time for the remaining live soldier to jump away and scramble toward the balcony's edge. He swung around, leaned against the wooden rail, and managed to shoot two rounds at Tana.

But he was too slow. Tana reacted and strafed to her right, just enough to throw the soldier's aim off. She shot him square in the chest, and he buckled against the oak and maple wooden railing, which was a delicate ghostly crick of its original self. He tried to regain balance to stand, but it was no use. The soldier's self-induced momentum pushed him back even more, and the wooden banister surrendered to the soldier's unbearable weight as if it were fabricated of trick-carved balsa. The soldier-man thudded and collapsed into a heap ten meters below.

Tana slowly walked toward the broken beams but did not lower her guard. She looked down. The soldierman thrashed and screamed, his mouth and face ringed in bubbles and foam and blood. Out of the corner of her eye she could see Cormac stand up, his face painted with relief that the skirmish was so quickly over.

Except that it wasn't. The soldier wielded his battle rifle, aimed at Cormac, and managed to fire off a single shot before Tana peppered him with coil-rounds. The soldier's grip let itself loose against his weapon's drop forged metal as he lost his mortal bound.

For Tana, the exchange was all a blur, a dreamlike smoky wisp beyond real. She flew down the iron spiral staircase and sprinted toward Cormac. He had managed to crawl behind the book pile out of sheer instinct.

She slipped and fell nearly on top of him while he lay there, hyperventilating. His normally red face was now cold and white. "Jesus, why did you do that? Why did you do that?"

Cormac only stared up at the beautiful arches overhead. Their shadow-lines twinkled and danced, animated to life from centuries of burial by the solar torches' light.

"Why did you do that?" she said for a third time.

"I don't," Cormac paused and then coughed while he breathed shallow. "I don't know." He wiggled his head side to side. "Just a damn idiot, I guess," he said and then smiled.

Tana crouched and stared, her facial scars raised and violent. "Shut up, shut up. Don't say that," she said. She was out of breath, not from recent events but because she was reasonably sure that Cormac would not be going home with her. She darted to Cormac's roll-along bag and reached inside. "Okay, what do I need?"

"Metal," Cormac coughed. "...Band," he managed to squeak out.

Tana tossed out clothes and food bricks and water bottles until she produced a steel bracelet. She held it up like a child who had won a new stuffed toy at the county fair.

"Yes," Cormac breathed.

Tana grabbed the roll-along bag and threw it next to him. Cormac held up his right wrist. Without further instructions, she strapped it around his arm. The metal surface changed to black. White characters resolved on its surface fifteen seconds later. It read BP55/27 P174 SO81%.

Cormac rested his head back. This is pretty bad, he thought. Tana had found the stash of auto-gel squares inside the bag. She grabbed one, broke the seal, and slapped it onto his wound. Cormac recoiled at the gel patch's cold slimy texture. "Can you...start an IV?"

"Yeah, sure," Tana responded. She was trained for just about anything that needed to be done in the field in a pinch. She could even operate a gravimetric radio if she had to. It was then that it occurred to her that she should have already known what to do without asking. The short battle must have caused her to lose focus. She cursed herself for being so out of it. It wasn't like her.

Cormac closed his eyes and lay still, in spite of the pain. Tana extracted the instant IV kit from the medical case and lay the guidance prongs alongside of his inner arm. Two jets of antiseptic liquid squirted from the guides' inner surfaces, and then a hair-thin laser beam pointed toward the dead center of his antecubital space. A quick tinny beep signaled that it was in the best angle. She slid the needle past his skin where the laser terminated. Dark blood slowly dripped back. Tana then screwed on the IV solution, a self-contained box with a tube connected to one corner. The IV pack was self-infusing once it detected that it was connected. There was no need for gravity or anything else to push the life-saving fluid in. The device was designed to be plug-and-play and was even armored with a carbon-steel shell. It would work even if it was hit with live fire.

Cormac said, "Tana," and then relaxed to flaccid. The medi-band glowed menacingly red around his wrist. Two over-sized numbers replaced the previous readout: 2 and 6. Tana knew what they meant, but first she had to wrap the thumper around him.

She removed a rolled-up band and unraveled it. She positioned him onto his side, slid one end of the band under his shoulder blades, and then rolled him back. She pulled it taut until both of the ends met. And then she locked the large straps together with three easy-push snaps.

The thumper automatically inflated itself snugly against Cormac's chest until it could expand no more. She pressed the device's only button. After a few seconds and blips the thumper started rapidly pushing on his chest. It made a swooshing sound with each deflate, thump, *shhwwew, thump, shhwwew.*

She inspected the medical case. There were twelve ampules. Each one had a large number emblazoned on their plastic shells, two of each, numbered one to six. She grabbed the number two syringe and pushed it into the IV tubing's only access port. And then she repeated with the number six. She looked at the metal bracelet. It read *wait,* with a countdown in seconds: 105, 104, 103.

She gave him a few rescue breaths. Tana couldn't remember if it was two or four, but she figured two more wouldn't hurt, so she gave all four. The thumper detected her rescue breaths while she couched her mouth against his and briefly stopped its thumping while she desperately tried to revive him.

The band's readout blinked itself into an angered red once more. On its face, the numbers 2 and 4 glowed. Tana used the syringes respectively while the thumper continued working. *Thump, shhwwew, thump, shhwwew.* She gave him a few more breaths.

And then the band changed again. The numbers 1 and 6 were revealed, a dash in the middle. Tana had never seen that before. Did that mean that she was supposed to give all six syringes? She had no more of the number 2s, she had used them all already. So she pushed in the remaining syringes and then gave him some more breaths. The band read out numbers 2 and 6 yet again, but it was no use. Neither vial remained in her arsenal. *Thump, shhwwew, thump, shhwwew.*

Tana tried to stand up when her right foot slipped out from under her. She inspected the auto-gel square adhered to Cormac's left abdomen. Blood rebelliously oozed around the square's edges with each thumper compression. And she realized, at that moment, it was hopeless. The sealing gel was not strong enough to control Cormac's hemorrhage, and he would die right there where he lay.

She pushed the thumper's singular control and then turned it off. For some time Tana stared at the man she once called Cormac, his body wrapped and saturated, his face anemically whitened and sunken in. She stared and then looked around the great library, the thousands of books stacked and piled and tossed about. Tana did not hear anything at all inside that dust-borne tomb save for the IV pack's blip, a three-second signaling that its contents had run dry. It was a shame, she thought, that he had died without knowing what he really meant to her. She threw books onto his body until it could no longer be seen. Not much of a burial she supposed, but maybe it was appropriate. He died doing what he loved, and that was that.

Tana stripped the soldiers of anything valuable that she could find. The first dead soldier, blood-stream guy, had a cinch of Imperial Tens in his left pants pocket, not usable as actual money to her, but they were almost seventy percent silver. Balcony man had a flare, two flash-bangs, and a belt of nines meshed around his waist. She could probably cash in on those somehow. She didn't find a radio among the three of them, which was odd. Perhaps the soldiers were forbidden from entering this lost grave site of books from their very own emperor. Well, they got their wish, Tana thought. Unrestricted admission to the great forbidden library, now and forevermore.

She pulled Cormac's roll-along bag back to the library's entrance. It felt heavier to move than it should have been. Among the food bricks and the water boxes, there were five books that Cormac had selected for salvage. Those would be going home with her, for they were the objective of her assignment. She mounted the bag onto the rear bracket of her solar-bike.

The wind pushed in. It was hot and moist, and the smell suggested deterioration. Tana looked toward the southwest. A super-storm's edge tickled the horizon from one edge to the other. She would probably beat it before making it back home. The storm looked to be a slow mover, and that was a good omen.

She jumped onto her solar-bike and started it up with a smack of her ankle bracelet against its frame. The library's entrance-way reflected in her mirror. She looked and then thought about the time, only hours ago, when the two of them crouched against the twin oversized doors while she worked on breaking the library's electromagnetic seal. She remembered when Cormac said something about being escorted by a twenty-something girl across the new desert and into hostile ground. Tana never knew if he meant it as a compliment or not.

But she guessed that it probably was.

As the great lost library shrank and diminished in the glass, she thought that perhaps she would come back out here again. Not so soon, and not officially, but in the future, yes. Tana raced towards her home and thought about her comfy bed back at the barracks, her floppy pajamas, and maybe, if time allowed, she would find a good little story to fall into.

Panta Rhei, Christopher Rutenber

The book was glossy white with an Irish elk on the cover, its horns spread from edge to edge, and its hooves created ripples on a woodland river. The title read, *Beasts of the Past: Interactive Edition.* Dakota read it eagerly, making lists of the animals inside and mapping where they could be found using his personal, interactive account. Afterward, he would spread out sheets of paper and draw direwolves and primitive horses and mammoths. But his favorite was the mastodon, not as glamorous as the mammoth, or as fierce as the sabre tooth, but more real than them all.

As a citizen of the country, Dakota learned to orient himself to the world from the bigger cities around him—Chicago, Detroit, Grand Rapids— but as he looked through *Beasts of the Past* he saw his county, his town. In the 1920s, several bones of *Mammut americanum* were uncovered where a river had formerly flowed. Now there was only a stone with a bronze cap on it from a forgotten zoological society. Dakota would bike out to see it when he finished feeding the cows and gathering the eggs, when he had finished his daily part in keeping BC Farms alive.

His two older brothers had done their parts for eighteen years apiece; one was in Afghanistan, and one was a dentist in Ypsilanti. They had milked the cows for BC Farms, fed the hens for BC Farms, slaughtered the beef and chicken for BC Farms, and tended to the meager corn crop while Bruce Connell looked forward to subsidies and a better year. The corn was still strong, but so were the insects, and Bruce had no heart to purchase pesticides; the people of the county who came to the little red tent in the park in the middle of the town counted on Connell to be true to the BC Farms legacy of all natural, all local, all family. But the hens wouldn't lay, and the pests were thick in the sky. Bruce didn't know if the world was really getting warmer, but his land was. His farm was smothered. As a child, Bruce had seen the Oakland's farm go to the machines that moved across the fields like glaciers. His father held him and said that Oakland would never really benefit. He would pay and pay and pay for more workers, more tools, and more land, and in the end he'd be no richer than BC Farms. Now Bruce wondered.

But now was the time to push away the bills, the advertisements, and time to mute the arguing voices on the television, because his son was there with his face covered in dust and a smile and Amy was shouting about supper and "clean your damn face up." Now was the time to think of things that endure.

Dakota washed and climbed into his chair. His father did not have a smile. If he had time to walk to see the plaque he would've had a smile; Dakota knew this. While the sun was still high and cool, he left his bike at the top of the hill and crawled through the Black-eyed Susans and the Indiangrass that covered the place where the old private road had been. The county bought the land and turned it into a wildlife sanctuary, and Dakota hardly noted the white signs that warned against hunting. He found a trail and followed it to a clearing and curling, rusted barbed wire, white cockle, jewelweed, bee balm, and thistle. He found the stone, the size of a dog, white and speckled with gray, with a bronze cap and a laminated sign beside it, with a couple black and white photos yellowed with age. The signs said little that interested him; he already knew this land had been under water, which the glaciers moved slowly across it and, like a cat's claws, dug into the world. He knew that the field had been a lake and then a swamp. But seeing the stone incarnated these facts and set in his mind an egg-like idea, incubating in his head on the ride home. And he told his father about the mastodons and the books he had read, and how the mastodons traveled in herds. "There might be a ton more out there. I'm gonna dig around and find them. Where can I dig?"

With a fwisk Amy's fork broke into pot-pie crust. "You got time to dig?" Bruce asked his son. "I don't want you puttin' shit off just 'cause of some bones." But Bruce's reluctance masked his fascination. In the summer of 1979 his father had taken him to Chicago, and he saw the dinosaur bones and how the world was changed. His father said, "Ain't none of this true, but doesn't it make you feel small?" But Bruce could see the future by looking into the past, at the way Damon was satisfied with

232

hunting, but needed to go to war. God bless him for it, but they promised him college when he got back and no one who goes to college comes back. Dan didn't, not when he could sit in an air-conditioned room and clean people's teeth. It's good work, needed work, but so was BC Farms, and in his mind's eye Bruce saw Dakota digging and pulling up rocks, not from his own field, but in South America or China, with a computer that could see into the earth and register if that patch of ground would yield a crop of fossils. How much time was there time to train him, to prevent? Enough, Bruce decided, and there must be time for fun. "You can dig around in the gully where we were gonna put the hogs. I don't have use for it."

In the dark, Dakota's flashlight illuminated the plan he would begin after church. He would take some wooden stakes and twine and make a perimeter like they did in the picture in the book. He would get a shovel and a trowel and—the arguing voices of professional mouths on the television swelled and oozed into his room and interrupted his plotting. "There's no conclusive proof!...Thirty year cycles...Scientists agree....Nah nah, listen to me...No, screw the talking points!...It's peddling, dear, at the expense of honest workers...Well what about..." Eventually it didn't matter who was saying what. The words all held together, congealing into one frustrating, overwhelming mass, and the boy was too tired to try to listen, or the listening was too tiresome. What's bigger, he thought: the men on the TV, the facts his teacher and the internet told him, or was it true when Uncle Matt said, "You don't think this is any surprise to God, do you?" And Dakota wondered.

He sat quietly through the service, and the stories of King David competed with the joy of uncovering a mastodon. David was tempted by God to count the people. Or was it by the Devil? Dakota was having trouble paying attention, and when the prophet gave the king a multiple choice punishment, Dakota wished he was young enough to be back in the little kids' church where God was simple and helped the good people and put the bad people under the water or sent wild hornets on them. With this God, there was no good option. A bunch of people were killed because David wanted to be safe. He couldn't stop it, and then he paid for a field to plead to God to remove the plague David chose.

At least Dad gave him his piece of land. And then his mind was all mastodons and dirt under his fingernails and finding a jawbone or a backbone and scraping it with his old X-Men toothbrush. His mind was on the land, and Dakota didn't hear the pastor's conclusion, which Bruce listened to with care, about the need to sacrifice, about the need to live uncomfortably for God. Bruce wondered if that meant losing his land, or going hungry, or watching his last son become a professor in Lansing, or even out of state. Was that God's will? Were the cool summers, the dry spells, then the gradual increase of heat and the gauntness of his cows part of a call to live without?

Losing sight of his son as soon as the afternoon meal was over, Bruce looked out to the fields and sat on the porch, a beer pinched between his fingers. Up on the hill the dust gathered up and blew over the line of oak trees that hid the west cow pasture. The rain-like sound of Rick Platt's new truck came close and soon the hulking obsidian vehicle stopped in the driveway. The closing of the door silenced the robins and the goldfinches. Rick Platt strode up the cement pathway, and he smiled under his green and blue denim cap and sunglasses. Bruce smiled back, and Amy was already out with a spare beer. Rick Platt, was not the biggest farmer in the township, not compared to the Oaklands, but he'd grown up quick and you'd be a fool to tell him he wasn't. As much money as came in went out to landscaping, new machinery, and most recently a horse stable. The Oaklands looked for land; Rick Platt looked for looks.

"How're the apples coming, Rick?"

"Best crop I had yet," Rick Platt replied, and Bruce could never be quite sure when he was bullshitting or not. His thoughts were hidden somewhere under his shades and his smile, and the habitual way he sat in chairs with his knees and feet pointed out wide, accepting both paths at once as if that was the way of all men.

234

They talked about the summer, and Rick Platt joked about harvesting beets in February. "Since '18 I ain' seen a good snow."

"I know. Ain't none of it true. Yeah, but remember '14?"

Rick Platt laughed and took the spare beer from the white wicker table. "I'm pullin' your leg, Connell. But I'm thinking ah getting them new monitors, the ones you stick in the soil, sends readings to your email. Damned if I'd be able to read it, but Ricky can. He's staying around to handle the north land and all these new technical things. So maybe I'll get those beets after all."

Bruce nodded and let his mind soak in the silence that followed before he said, "You ever been to a dinosaur museum?"

"Nah, I been to the Air Zoo a few times with Ricky when he was a kid," Rick Platt said and rubbed his belly. "We got a kick out of the simulator. They got some fucking huge jets, and you feel fucking huge flying them. Hell, now that you mention it, I think that's what got Ricky into computers and machines, more than anything on the farm, but you keep that to yourself."

Bruce laughed and squinted to make out what was under the newest dust cloud.

Dakota hooked up the trailer to the back of the four-wheeler and was lost to the woods before the shortcake had settled to his stomach. He squinted as the dry air whipped around his face and savored the jolts from every root and rabbit hole. Catbirds cried from up in the canopy, and the red-wing blackbirds joined in with sharp warning cries, louder and louder as he came down to the gully. The view was park-like, with oaks and sedges growing down one side toward the small stream that fed the marshes. On the opposite side, the trees gave way to grasses, chicory, and the last of the milkweed. The canopy of the woods was broken, and all the area was sun-filled. The stream parted as the four-wheeler barreled through it and soaked the boy's calves and ankles. He set to his work at the rise of the meadow-hill, driving the stakes into the earth and running a blue rope into a square around them. The creeping

235

roots of the sedges and the deep roots of the native grasses contested with his shovel. Crickets scattered away while sky-blue dragonflies with ruddy-brown bands upon their wings came to observe, and Dakota remembered that once there had been dragonflies over three feet long when the world was very warm.

He paid close attention to the rocks he found. Anything might be a bone. There was sandstone and little chunks of petrified wood, and these were interesting, and he put them in his backpack, but they were not the goal. The pleasant feeling of the sun on his skin was not the goal, nor the swallowtail that landed on his shovel, neither were the sudden jolt of a locust bursting upward from his foot in a saffron explosion or the heron rising from the stream. These were the unexpected gifts to cling to, though each day proved fruitless, and to think about while he milked the cows by hand because grandfather never believed in milking machines. These joys would not allow him to give up the mastodons.

Dakota was hitting bedrock, and each stroke of the shovel was careful, aimed at the softness. His digging site moved nearer to the stream as the mastodons had moved nearer to the lake that had been there and over most of the township fifteen thousand years ago. The world was getting warmer, and the bright eyes of the pachyderms passed from bull to cow to bull to cow. The glaciers were melting rapidly, and waterfowl gathered around them, and flycatchers and phoebes pecked off the black flies that threatened to draw blood through the hairy hides. This new lake was to be their home, and Dakota looked towards the hill and the house that was beyond it. The sky was tinged with yellow. Food would be on the table soon, so his hands slipped into the water of the stream the way the rocks and silt gave way from the sun-drenched hill above, suddenly, fifteen thousand years ago. His hand felt something smooth and hard; with a hope, he ran to the trailer for his trowel, dug into the shore and, from the mud, withdrew a dappled triangle with a circle in the center, and he knew what it was.

At dinner there was only one subject: the vertebrae laid out as a centerpiece, Amy's Black-eyed Susans set aside. She saw it as a symbol for life and death and thought of her days picking wildflowers from that same place and the things she and Bruce had done there in the stream, as children, as teenagers. "It sure is something. Hell, we had no idea." But she knew it had always been a special place. And if anyone asked to buy some land, as the Oaklands or Richard Platt might, Bruce could never give them that, nothing else either, but not that.

Dakota sent an email that night to the University of Michigan, a picture attached and a promise that he'd look for more. He was not around when the reply was sent. Dakota was widening the stream and finding more backbones. And the spine led to ribs, massive and sharp and just out of sight. These he sent too and with excitement he found that a professor was coming.

A professor was coming. Each day, Bruce was reminded of this and pictured a man with curly dark hair placing his hand on Dakota's shoulders, on his son's shoulders, and telling him that he was needed out there in the world, finding bones. The boy had found so many: a complete backbone, and further upstream a tusk. How many monsters were hiding under his land? The thought shrunk him; he could see them marching in his mind. He could hardly reach them to pat their sides, and they would not regard him. He looked up again and saw only the children swinging in the park, dousing themselves from the stone and mortar drinking fountain, and begging their parents to buy pastries from the Amish. Down he looked to check the totals for a Thursday afternoon's labor, the profits so far. Could be more, could be less, so his father would always say before he'd quote from the Proverbs: *Lord don't make me too small so I steal; don't make me too big so I forget this whole world comes from you.* He looked up again to see a stranger, skinny, with streaks of silver in his thinning blonde hair, and dressed like a man trying too hard to be casual.

He was standing in front of Bruce and the little red tent in the park in the middle of the town with one of Bruce's tomatoes in his hand. "How much for a dozen of these?"

Bruce named his price.

The man bought a dozen and went on to say, "I'm from the University of Michigan and—"

"You're here about my son's mastodons?"

"That's right. We were going to start tomorrow morning if that's all right with you."

That unassuming man with his plaid shirt that fit like a sack came with some college students, frail boys and bright eyed girls who lathered on sun-screen and spoke in quotations, roped off stream and hill and bank. They peeled off the bank like a rind, and moved with a balance of care and efficiency while Bruce watched from the top of the hill. Dakota was there in the midst of it, looking so much stronger and more alive than any of the students unzipping the creek. If they worked as they did with the body of his boy, the farm would always be fruitful. If Dakota became one of them, what discoveries could be had. His pity, and his jealousy, pulled him from the hill down into the valley, and Dr. Jansen led him about the work site for a week as they pulled out new bones and slabs of footprints. And at the end of the week he said, "Mr. Connell, we have found something remarkable. It seems that your son has uncovered a— well, a mastodon graveyard of sorts. We haven't seen one in this area, but it seems—from what we can tell, that there was a landslide here, from that hill into the gully, or the lake, which it was at the time. The mastodons would have been trapped in the sudden rise of the water and the mud. Their size did the rest of the work. What we have here are a lot of old skeletons, bigger skeletons, and calf skeletons. The specimen found in the 1920s, about four and a half kilometers from here, was merely a survivor of this herd, or so we're assuming. This is the real interesting stuff."

Dakota beamed and felt some new stage of life opening as a chrysalis. Bruce thought of the phrase "*merely a survivor*" and continued to think of it while Dr. Jansen suggested an offer for the acreage and *merely a survivor* was mixed with Platt's running jokes about buying a few acres. Then a number was mentioned, and the ever warming sun struck him; the mix was like whisky, burning and dizzying. Bruce was lost in a graveyard he did not know, and he staggered back to his home, Dakota and Dr. Jansen trailing behind.

* * *

The moon was full and hid nothing from the eyes of one walking through the damp grass. Bruce put his flashlight away and gave himself up to the lights God put in the sky, meant to be unchanging, though Dakota said they weren't. In a thousand years there will be a new North Star.

As they moved further into the woods, the voices of cicadas and tree frogs were added to by the faint hiss of the stream, now nearly dry from heat and widening. And, as Bruce stepped out from the woods and saw the water under the harsh moonlight, it looked like the Milky Way itself, with the bones of old gods protruding from the sand and bedrock. Bruce went down to them, under the tape and into the water. He laid there, his head tipped back, his shoulders relaxed, and the shallow frigid water moved over his ears. Why, he thought, was this so hard? It wasn't like selling to Platt. He had no intention of raising pigs. There was no risk but the loss of something loved; offering up this was offering his son on an altar. Bruce closed his eyes and saw the silt falling down around him, trapping him. He would stretch out his trunk to his neighbors, but they were crawling up the lower bank. A little calf was with them. Bruce brayed and struggled. He stomped and scrambled for a footing. The herd was rushing ahead, and the water was brown and thickening and swallowing.

When he opened his eyes he was sitting up straight, looking into the nasal cavity of a half-buried skull with a cracked jaw. It shone bluish-white, and the hole, deep black in the center, looked like a great vast eye filled with secrets. Like the giants in fairy tales, coming from the sky to raid and snatch up, it was something like that, but older and darker, and more real. This was not a giant, not simply a Cyclops incarnate, but a One-Eyed God against change and time, who battled with the water and the earth. Strong.

What would you do? Could you give it up?

The answer was plain. And so was the answer after that. They were loud in the silence.

The One-Eyed God was not merely a survivor.

The Sea Wall at Vancuuver Shoal, Keith Wilkinson

Note that the misspellings in this short story are intentional. From the author: "The story is set 1,000 years in the future...every language has a half-life."

* * *

Shmuul slipped into the ripplesuut, slid into Antrim Bay, and headed out along his usual route—280 degrees to the Shangri La marker, then southwest 224 to a point only he knew, then down. To make it official he'd asked someone from the ShoalSharks to meet him there. The skii was clear, the Westerlies light. Last niite's Southeast storm had left the air fresh.

"Vancuuver Shoal has no monuments," someone from the Midden had told him once, but he'd been skeptical, took it as a challenge, and proved the Midden wrong. It had gained him some brief fame, local respect, and membership in the ShoalSharks. Then he'd faded into the slack backwaters of his city again.

He dropped the ripplesuut out of hyper speed above Kits Point and headed down toward the shoal. Everything was still in place, protected now by the regulations and the surveillance the Midden had set up, as they did for all new archaeological finds. So many things had been found under the water everywhere, but not much was of use, only of interest. The planet was aswim with shoal artists and archeologists.

After he'd discovered the wall, other explorers had surged into the area, looking almost exclusively east, back toward the city centre, to discover more. They'd found very little, but did find what some claimed to be the Kitsilano home of David Suzuuki, one of the early environmentalists who'd warned about the possibilities of oceanrise. They'd identified it by the double-profile sculpture of a Gemini Award with his name etched into it. Critics said corroborating evidence was needed. Most agreed that Suzuuki had lived around there though. Some called the area the

Suzuuki-Barton Shoal, Barton being a skilled watercolourist largely unacknowledged in her time. Some of her paintings of the great northern valleys—Naas, Tatsenshini, Kispiox—were rumoured to be in the mountain villages far to the north, but this was Old Vancuuver and none of her work had survived the rise of the sea. Watercolours.

Few had believed in the science of the waterrise. Climatologists had predicted a maximum five meter rise in sea level after eight decades, but in the end, the oceans had risen sixty meters within two decades and had stayed that way for a thousand years, despite the radical downscaling of carbon emissions and sporadic global geo-engineering efforts to cool the planet, most instigated from China. Antrim had once been one hundred and forty meters above the sea, but now it was less than eighty. Broad shoals existed where once there had been city. Richmound was an underwater atoll known to have once been the location of an international airport graced with public art, including a bronze sculpture titled "The Jade Canoe," depicting an overloaded canuu of mythic animals and wide-eyed people.

A lot more had changed. Whole islands in Oceana had been lost, along with cities from every continent's shore—Miami, Calcutta, Amsterdam, Manila, Honolulu, Shanghai. World population had plummeted. There had been massive migrations inland from the coastal cities. Crops failed, species failed, and interior cultures had either strenuously resisted the flood of climate refugees or dramatically embraced them. Embracing had proved eventually to be not only the best ethical option, but also the most practical one. Immigrants brought high levels of complex skills, plus intense motivation, and these deeply informed what were to become the dominant social structures of the new era, structures that persisted to this day—the culture of science and the culture of the Sangha.

For several centuries after the Great Collapse, regionalism and anarchy reigned around the globe. Then the great huuman cultures of the East—Daoism and Confuucianism—began to take hold, and philosophies of balance—creation, contribution, connection, compassion—became the norm, tempered with varying combinations of pragmatism and science.

Gradually, the melange of anarchy, skilled leadership, goodwill, and engineering brought them to where they were now. And Shmuul, like so many others, was long steeped in gratitude for the wisdom the scientists and elders had brought to the Sanghas during that Great Turning.

The major urban political structure and job provider that had emerged along this particular coastline had been the Uunited Midden Authority, UMA, a vast bureaucratic organization accountable to the Great Uunited Sangha, and responsible to ensure systems for food, housing, practical employment, and social well-being. Shmuul liked to stay on the fringes of the UMA, judging his current capacity to contribute to a productive job-culture as minimal. The alternatives were the local Sanghas or the marginal agricultural communities like the Saturna Ruuminoffs and the Passage Island Solari. Some were generously libertarian, others just idiosyncratic, but collectively they provided creative options to balance the harmonic blandness that prevailed in the Sanghas.

From amongst these options, Shmuul reasoned that the local Sangha was his best bet for a sense of connection, compassion, and contribution. The creative part he could look after himself, or so he thought. Antrim was as good a Sangha as any. So he stayed where he'd been born and where his parents and grandparents had been born. But Sangha life was a bit tight for his Chaructur, like a ripplesuut one size too small. The ShoalSharks were a better psychic fit.

There was never a very long thread to any personal history. Shmuul knew ancestors as far back as grandparents, and then it was just population. He knew that he was as much a product of ingested knowledge as he was of his geenpuul or his social context. His Chaructur, like everyone else's, was pretty much determined by the unpredictable outcome of geen combinations from parents, some of them tailored, plus the ingestion of knowledge through chemical messages sent to the millions of brain receptors through the blood stream. This was an applied science anticipated by Nicholas Negroponte several decades before the great flood, and made commonplace afterward as a tool of species survival. With this strong genetic and psycho-nutrient base structure, each Chaructur was simply allowed to emerge according to its own patterns within the nurturing context of the local Sangha, which was in turn nurtured by the Great Uunited Sangha and, recently, as a result of the intergalactic starprobes, also supported by the Sangha of All Sentients. "GUS" and "SAS," or "Salsa", as they were affectionately known, were like ancient ones serving to foster each Chaructur in the discovery of a unique right way. That was the teaching. That was the ingestion. That was his experience.

The Midden Authority's Old Vancuuver offices were located in mountain retreats a few kilometers inland from Antrim. With Nuutransport and oceanrise, the old ocean ports had become cultural backwaters, but art and archi-tuurism had been encouraged by the Midden, and tuurists, mostly from China, were now coming in large numbers to see the Glittercast.

The Shangri La Glittercast was the long debris field left when the glass towers of Old Vancuuver had come crashing down. The Shangri La had been a hotel named after an earlier mythic place of peace and beauty. Art pieces from a thousand years before had been preserved, along with remnants of the fallen buildings. The Vancuuver Shoal had been unimportant for so long after the Great Turning that when the Glittercast was first explored there was enough good government established regionally and globally to prevent it from being pillaged. The great debris field, along with the art discovered there, had been set aside as a World Heritage Site and Archaeological Study Destination.

Folded in with all the glass that still sparkled beneath the tropical, aqua waters, archaeologists had found many remains of sculptures and murals. The ancient electronic database of the City of Vancouver public art registry told them quite a lot about what to expect—the tile murals of Jordi Bonet, similar to those near L'Anse Aux Meadow in Nuufoundland; the Digital Orca and Infinite Tire sculptures by Douglas Coupland; the Komagata Maru Memorial; Kougioumtzis's Nike, Goddess of Victory, modeled after the even more ancient marble remnant in Paris known as the Winged Victory of Samothrace; hundreds of small details carved in stone from the old Marine Building; and an intact bronze statue of Themis, Goddess of Justice, blindfolded and with scroll rather than sword in hand, found in a deep pool of green glass shards believed to have been the transparent roof of the courthouse of the ancient city.

Nearby, but technically outside the Glittercast, was BeeSee Place, the name generally construed to be a corruption of *busy place*. The consensus was that it had been a large farmuurs' market for the exchange of organic food in the last days before the Great Collapse, a time when frantic efforts were being made to pull back from excessive carbon emissions. A local contrarian group claimed that BeeSee Place had been a coliseum for sporting events, like in the times of Nero. Shmuul thought that the truth about that kind of large, heavily-constructed place would have been retained after the collapse, but it hadn't been. Often, it seemed, it was the smaller remnants that were remembered with least contention—the Dale Chihuuly blown glass bowl, for example, that had survived intact inside its protective case in the middle of the Glittercast. Near it were two boulders, one granite and another, identical in form, cast in bronze—the latter badly eroded—and a fragment of a quotation from Leonardo Da Vinci cut in granite. The glass bowl was unscathed after centuries under salt water. Many other works recorded in the Registry were missing: Douglas Coupland's four metal statues of a local hero, Terry Fox, and further west and deeper down, a large comedic assembly, also in metal, by Yue Minjun.

Shmuul wasn't much interested in the archeology or art of the Glittercast, though. His Chaructur told him to explore the margins, and the ShoalSharks helped him do that with skill and grace—encouraging him, celebrating his successes, ribbing him—and that was all anyone could ask of a community, or so both Confuucian and Sanghan Dharmas taught. The ShoalSharks were looked at with some bemusement by both the conservative Sanghas and the more radical rural communities, but the Sharks liked that marginalization. It was their place, and it was Shmuul's place. Sanghas were communities of comfort, and Gangs were communities of comfort, too.

Despite his somewhat solitary preferences, Shmuul knew he was a social animal as much as any other huuman. He nestled first in one band, then another, and amongst these magnetic fields he explored.

expect yourself
only to connect
the inner fires
—that's what the Sanghan Dharmas taught.

check your pressures
your compasses
your intuitions
—that's what the ShoalSharks taught.

One of the best routes into the main ruins of Old Vancuuver was along the Canada Liine. Its remnants stretched from Richmound all the way to the Glittercast. The middle part, where it dipped beneath the seabed and under Littlemount Atoll, was best, for in this ancient tunnel they had found remnants of old trains and undisturbed skeletons of the city's inhabitants. Some of these artifacts had been preserved as part of the museum: corroded fragments of trains and tracks, tools, and zippers and buttons of the pre-huumans whose stubborn individualism and limited ethics had provoked the collapse. Despite the apparent moral weakness of the time, the balance of evidence suggested that the pre-huumans hadn't been that different from modern huumans. Ethics wasn't studied in the school system then, so the moral weakness was predictable and foreshadowed by cruel wars and exploitation of whole cultures. The earlier civilization also didn't have the benefits of cognitive ingestion, nor very much geen manipulation, but otherwise they ate, drank, made love, made objects, and tried to make sense of the universe they saw, just as modern huumans did.

The tunnels in this small, provincial, coastal city weren't as inspired as those in some places on the planet. The Canada Liine wasn't the Tunnelbana; the murals found under the Glittercast weren't by Keith Haring, Chris Pape, or Diego Rivera; and the tunnels hadn't the solemnity of the New York Freedom Tunnel, now also under water—

but they had a simple integrity, a kind of Zen quality comfortable to the Westcoast Sanghan tradition. Old Vancuuver's tunnels and stations were modest. Cambie City Hall Station wasn't Moscow's Mayakovskaya or Dostoevskaya, Waterfront Station wasn't Stockholm's T-Centralen, Richmond Brighouse wasn't the Universadad de Chile in Santiago, Yaletown Roundhouse wasn't the Kraaiennest in Amsterdam, and certainly Olympic Village wasn't Narcissus Quagliata's Formosa Boulevard Station in Kaohsiung. Shmuul liked the austere, minimalist aesthetics of this tiny Canada Liine. It had a kind of rustic elegance that told about the values and aspirations of its creators. Beyond the Glittercast and the Canada Liine, not much of consequence remained of Old Vancuuver.

Shmuul had found the faded mural wall just by poking around in the shallow Kitsilano Shoals. There was no reason to expect more murals, and not there of all places—a lowland of former dwellings submerged by the Great Collapse. Without the light analysis technology of the annatuul developed for the Higherground Starprobes Program, combined with the particular slant of late afternoon light that day, he wouldn't have seen them at all. What he did find confused him, but the annatuul quickly told him there were layers of paint on a low wall sunk into the mud of the shallow bay. And the annatuul also told him that there were constructed images in each of the several layers. To the naked eye it was just a discoloured wall, badly eroded, but the technology took those few scraps of information, assessed the age and materials used, and reconstructed in vivid colours dozens of separate images that had been layered on the walls in a short span of decades centuries in the past.

Shmuul had taken the images to Tanka—an archeologist and a flutterat—because she was smart, but most of all because he trusted her. She consulted with the Shark leadership, then took the mural data to the Saturna Ruumanoff scholars, her people. At first, Shmuul was annoyed, but then realized that without some scholarly help they wouldn't know what they had. They knew they would have to report it eventually to the Midden Authority and the Antrim Sangha, and also knew the Ruumanoffs would try to claim it and find a way to gain from it, maybe barter it for a star trip. But Shmuul and Tanka were gang-smart and knew how to purge their suits and tools of memories, so despite the satellite tracking only they knew where the murals were.

It was their reveal of this information that gained them their short moment of fame. Short, because the murals, though unexpected, were minor in quality and scope compared to so many found under other waters around the planet. And yet, this place, Old Vancuuver, had long held a special cachet amongst archaeologists and artists.

Their discovery had gained them fame. Their wiliness had gained them respect—from the Sharks, the Ruuminoffs, and the Authority alike.

The murals were a range of painted forms—some in highly stylized text in the old graffiti style. Others had lifelike depictions of fish, notably resembling the contemporary engineered Suukiisamun, and a few whimsical black and white stylized drawings of fantastical animals with long ears.

The Balaclava Tunnel had been Shmuul's discovery, too, and now he was going to show it to Tanka. He had kept it also a secret from the Midden and his Sangha. Technically, it was outside the scope of the Glittercast Authority, but not that of the Midden Authority, and a Sanghan more dutiful than Shmuul would have reported it immediately. He rationalized that he didn't quite know what it was, so he wouldn't know what to report, and he knew that Tanka would know, or figure it out.

He had asked the Sharks to send someone. He knew it would be Tanka, and she was there waiting, early and on coordinates. They didn't need to talk; they synced their gear and went down two meters apart. They were a good team. He found things, and she figured out what they meant. He had found the wall, and she had understood its significance. And now there was the tunnel.

When she saw the opening, Tanka knew immediately what it was and the significance it would have for the archaeological understanding of old Vancuuver. It was an overflow from an underground storm sewer system, at least two meters high, large enough, if it was intact, for huumans to traverse without protection. And it would undoubtedly have all sorts of feeder pipes from streets and buildings in this area. The area had never been explored for this kind of system and barely explored at all for that matter, so there were likely to be ample new artifacts in and near this system of pipes. Tanka also knew that there had once been a uuniversity further west on what was now Grey Atoll. It was possible that this outlet would have connections to the drainage system for that area, too.

All of this had been invisible to Shmuul. He had called it the "Balaclava" tunnel because of an ancient, battered piece of aluuminum embossed with that word that he'd found near the tunnel entrance. Many of these aluuminum slivers had been found throughout Old Vancuuver. "Streetsiines" they'd been called, part of a rudimentary, distributed, way-fiinding system. A crude, boots-on-the-ground method, but redundant and with a high tolerance for error, so with related maps and even oral directions, it had served well for centuries.

Getting release to come down from Saturna Iilund by ripplesuut had been a challenge for Tanka. It was always a challenge. The paternalistic culture of the Saturna Ruuminoff tribes hadn't changed much from that described by Juunes in the 51st Thule Expedition over five centuries earlier, and the current leadership at Ruuminoff was reluctant to see a young woman make a long rippletrip alone. Ruuminoff was male-dominated and constrained all its citizens. Although essentially benevolent, historically the Ruuminoffs had proven to be prone to excessive zeal in applying those constraints. "Followership of the Way" was high on its list of ethical actions. Tanka had managed to get authorization by lying just a little about her purpose, and this time she knew she wasn't going back.

The tunnel stretched straight south, empty and into darkness. It was rectangular, and had it been dry, the ceiling was high enough that they could have walked without stooping. The water that now filled it was relatively clear, undisturbed by tides and winds. According to their instruments it was low in salinity and flowing gently toward their place of entry. Some fresh water was still feeding it. There were the usual inhabitants of dark waters, mostly small fish without eyes or with massive, specialized eyes. Every few meters smaller tunnels entered the main one. A few were large enough to swim up. Some were wet, but void of water, and their instruments showed normal air. Since these tunnels were rising only slightly, it seemed likely that this was trapped air, which meant an impervious earth or rock layer above.

Branching off from the smaller tunnels were pipes too small for them to enter. They sent decimeter waterbots up these and studied the pictures. Most had even smaller pipes entering them. Most of the smaller pipes that the bots explored ended jammed with earth, approximately seabed level or a few meters below according to the instruments. They reasoned that these must have been lines that led to structures— dwellings and public facilities—in the old city.

There had been ruumors that the last residents of Old Vancuuver had suspended containers of valuables in their sewer lines before they left, believing they would be able to return later to retrieve them, even if the buildings were demolished and submerged. But there had been no returning and no interest from the next generations in plumbing the muds of the marshland of Kitshoal. Now, however, there were likely to be treasure hunters.

They progressed almost ten kilometers underground, checking out several side tunnels, but mostly sticking to the main channel. The air producers on the ripplesuuts sounded no alarms, though they realized that this far underground, and with their positioning systems disabled, they would never be found if their systems failed. But there was little sign of collapse anywhere along the way, and in the whole distance they traveled, the tunnel stayed relatively level, even though the landforms above it varied in depth.

At ten kilometers the tunnel began to drop sharply and ended at a two-meter high collapsed concrete pipe. There was little current here. Tanka reasoned that this would be where the pipeline dipped to cross an arm of the Fraser River. They turned back, noting the locations of the most promising tunnels that headed south toward the Grey Atoll Uuniversity ruins.

Back at Kitshoal they headed toward the Glittercast, restoring their locators only when they arrived at the marker.

"I've been asked to go to a place in the Rockies called Ya Ha Tinda Ranch," said Tanka. "It means Mountain Prairie—that's everything this place isn't."

"What would you do there?"

"Figure things out like I do here. The culture there would suit you, too. They encourage exploring."

"But what about your roots, your Ruuminoff community?" Shmuul probed.

"It isn't really a community that suits me anymore—if it ever was. I don't fit in. I need to leave. If I just go to work for the Authority and ask permission to map the new find, the Ruuminoffs won't give their permission. They'll negotiate my return to Saturna and that would eventually do me in. I need to be far away, far from Ruuminoff connections and influuence."

"How did you learn about Ya Ha Tinda?" Shmuul asked.

"Much as I learned about you, Shmuul—by accident." She smiled.

Tanka went on. "I can take refuge there. You've been a kind of refuge for me, but this could be a larger one. It could be my community, my Sangha. I think I could grow there. Maybe you could, too."

"You're suggesting I come along?" Shmuul was a bit startled, but also a bit excited by the idea.

"We'd need rivrips—river ripplesuuts," Tanka said. And besides rivers and lakes there are lots of mountains to explore near the Icefield Parkway. We could go by foot, and we'd need only notebooks and annatuuls and shelters. You could get the gear for us through your

Sangha before you came. There are even old species like horses and grolar bears there."

"I loved making this new find with you, Tanka," Shmuul replied. "And I feel like I won't likely make another one here. The Authority will be mapping all the west part of the Vancuuver Shoal now, and since we seem to have found a sewer line that leads to both the Richmound Atoll and the Grey Atoll Uuniveristy, both of those areas will be up for exploration. With potential artifacts in the tunnels and pipes, they'll secure it, and there won't be anything left for us to do. I think I've explored everything here that's going to be available to me. To us. Everything where we could add value."

"You're an explorer, I'm a connector," Tanka replied. "There's more room for my skills here than for yours. That would be fine if it weren't for the Ruuminoffs."

"I know I need something new," replied Shmuul. "But Ya Ha Tinda? Couldn't we just stay here and be bit players? We could guide visitors through the Glittercast and eventually the Balaclava. You could join Antrim Sangha, and we could keep working together alongside the gardeners and bot designers and other productive discipline practitioners. By example, we'd be affirming exploration as one of the necessary huuman ways. We could explore ideas, ingest all the knowledge we'd need, access the latest engineering, and be part of a caring community without leaving home. I know I'm contradicting myself."

"I know. It sounds reasonable and safe. You may be able to stay, but I can't," Tanka said. "And I think you need to leave, too. Both of us need to be able to do what we do without direct constraints. I certainly need to be free of the control I feel from the Ruuminoffs, so for me there's no choice. Plus, I've already asked the Ya Ha Tinda team, and now I've been invited. We've been invited, because I asked for you too." She smiled again, shy about her own confidence in reading him. "Shmuul, you need to get off this shoal and into the deeper world that you're so well equipped to spot and navigate. You've explored Vancuuver Shoal enough; others will take it over from here. They wouldn't leave room for you to explore, and they'd be very suspicious if they ever found you disabling your locator again. You need to be far away, just like I do."

"Sure, you might find more ancient sewer pipes to plumb," she went on. "But really…think of the truly ancient worlds there are to explore in the mountains, the worlds of rivers and feral animals and terrain scarcely changed in millennia. Not the Anthropocene world but the Pleistocene and the Miocene ones. And you needn't stop at Ya Ha Tinda. You can move any direction from there with the knowledge and skills you'll get in that deep ecology. And I can too."

"What about everything we've learned about this place? Won't that just be wasted?" asked Shmuul.

"The new worlds will travel with us," replied Tanka. "The perspectives we bring from absorbed knowledge and our own exploration won't be lost. And together we'd bring the perspectives of the teachings that both the Antrim Sangha and the Saturna Ruuminoffs have built up in our cultures over the last thousand years, different teachings from what they'll have at Ya Ha Tinda. That will stay with us to the end, and between us there's even a nice level of tension provided by the Ruuminoff-Sangha rift. I think it's time for us to look outward again, Shmuul. It's time for both of us to stop being afraid of destroying our home like our ancestors did. We learned from that, even the Ruuminoffs did. It's time to think again about making star landings and not just crafting this planet."

Shmuul sighed. "You're smarter than I am, Tanka, and I wish I could say you weren't right about this, but I think you are. We can absorb knowledge, but we can't absorb discovery or connection, nor even the desire to discover or connect. Discovery is what my Chaructur does, and connection is what your Chaructur does—so I guess I'm in."

"We don't have to go at once," Tanka said, smiling again. "And we don't have to go together. This time I can go first and do the exploring. That'll be a stretch for me. You can find us the best rivrips and rockbots and swiftwaterbots in the Authority and bring those along after you've said the goodbyes you'll want to say. Your mother especially will need you to say goodbye."

The Chaructur of Hannah, Shmuul's mother, was quite different from his. They both knew this. The whole Antrim Sangha knew this. When he came home at night she knew when his Chaructur had been filled with exploration and discovery and when it had not. Tonight she knew it had been filled, but also, in a new way, opened. She stopped her construction work on the bot and switched to what was going to be required to restore balance for the two of them after his day on the shoals. As she set about to create her part of the right circumstances between them, and between them and the Sangha, she was filled with her own deep sense of warmth from doing this nurturing, which was her most fundamental Chaructur, her Hinduuway. His way was the Explorer's Way and they both knew that they needed this exchange to stay in balance. Exchange across ages, exchange across genders, exchange across professions, exchange across learnings and ingestions. This empathy, this shared understanding, was the central teaching of the Sangha of All Sentients.

Neither of them needed to think about it much. As usual, she set him to work on mundanities while she gathered together some friends and went to the garden to get food for them to prepare together. He knew the value of this and accepted her assignments as part of their shared spiritual discipline as mother, son and village.

> science and chores glow
> embraced by loving kindness
> warm body cool mind

* * *

The Whole Uurth Dharmas

Three weeks later, Shmuul was ready. The sushi was particularly good at the Old Quarry on Littuulmount Atoll that day. He loved the jazz here, the Ryokan poems that graced the menu, and the Hokusai prints on the

254

walls. And now they had added images of what throughout Old Vancuuver would be called The Kitshoal Murals. His murals. His and Tanka's murals. Shmuul Ryder and Tanka Ocean. Who would have thought it? And he was excited. There would be more: first, the findings from the Balaclava and then stories from the Ya Ha Tinda. Maybe someone would riff it all for alto sax one day or even fuse it with the sounds of Buubacar Traoré.

Part 2. Poetry

Poems by Stephen Siperstein

All Along the Pacific Coast

(Originally published in *The Clearing*)

The sea stars are rotting.
Thousands of them, maybe millions
Losing pieces of themselves to a world
Where the invisible flings the visible
Like a small wind shorn craft.

Sometimes beside a dark pool
We kneel, try to count the bodies—
Yellows, purples, greens—before they melt
Into grey chum. Sometimes we turn
Away; sometimes we bargain.

I am told that though most stars die
On occasion the young ones fight back
Against their cells' own wasting. I am told,
And half-believe, that some can grow their limbs
Again and again, and again and again
Watch them crawl off becoming nothing.

Sand Dollars

(Originally published in *Poecology*)

In unquiet water the small grey circles
looked like familiar faces in the light
though strange that they lived upright
swallowing sand to keep themselves

down. We gathered bucketfuls of the dead,
bleached them white on old boards,
glued them to driftwood with limpets,
periwinkles, sprigs of dried heather and
carried them to the fair by the old millpond.

There, travelers handed us dollars
for a chance to decipher those five
pointed instructions on how to live,
how to bury oneself without illusion

of possession, how to make a small protest
against subsidence, and this was ours:
wading through warm water, watching
for the faces of angels rising we covered
those that might still live.

Teaching Climate Change

(Originally published in ISLE, Interdisciplinary Studies in Literature and
the Environment)

It's a lot like searching
for lucky stones after storms
on the beaches of Lake Erie—

"otoliths" my grandma called them—
tiny ear bones of long dead fish,
each one like an ivory scrabble tile

impressed with a letter, "g" or "l"—
that today, arranged on my desk,
I read as an ancient message—

good luck, good luck, good
luck, you're gonna need it.
You are a small man gone

to find balance in miles
of sand and dark water,
then returned to a room, expecting

to feel bigger than before.
My students arrive asking questions—

"How worried should we be?"

Swiftly my voice rolls out "very"—
like a wave breaking over itself,
then pulling back.

"So what should we do?" they ask—
and I try to hear goodness and grace,
a little luck, the sounds of a lake falling

through trees at night, and any words
that might begin an answer.

Drought

Feel the Freon wick drops
from your slick skin.
You sleep at night with dreams
by Ambien and cinematic fears

of apocalypse—
a cyclops storm circling
your childhood home
the waters rising.

Then your friends arrive to help
but they're zombies,
and try to eat your brains.
Funny how you never
read the road signs to find
your way out.

But they say one can learn
to tell whether it's a dream
or not—just notice the words
when they blur—
or when the weather
stops making any sense.

You wake soaked in sweat
crank the AC, eat a banana
from Costa Rica to ease
your shuddering stomach.

Run the tap. They say
this drought is the worst
in 1,200 years. You think

today might be a good day
to go to the movies

and from some place
deep in your gut rises
a ravenous desire

for Raisinets.

Poems by Carolyn Welch

Excerpted from *California Poems* (Moon Willow Press, 2015)

1. Bioluminescence

Big Sur's night glow
Surprises feet in soft whale colors
We linger in blue-green foam,
Thinking it will feel different,
Softer than usual,
But the waves touch us with the same fingers

I saw it once down in San Juan,
The translucent colors crushing water
In their soft jelly mouths.
Up in Big Sur it is rarer, and far below
In the neon sea, blue elves dart
In black water mirages
For a few more years.

2. Wildlife

Ashes are spirits escaping
From the Hades of red Santiago.

They float to my parking lot,
Cling to windshields, suffering.

A deer poses for the camera,
In the arms of a fireman in a yellow suit.

A forest dies in black yawns.

3. Murrelet Song

Marvels in the old growth
Marbles in the pond
He is going down
Down to whiskey town
Where the old men go to die

Biographies

John Atcheson is the author of *A Being Darkly Wise*, an eco-thriller, and Book One of *The Earth Trilogy*, which traces a small group's attempt to deal with global warming over the course of fifty years. His writing has appeared in the *Washington Post, Baltimore Sun, the San Jose Mercury News,* and other major newspapers. He is a frequent and popular contributor to CommonDreams. He has backpacked in some of the most remote areas in North America and is trained in wilderness survival.

Gabriella Brand's short stories, poetry, and essays have appeared in a variety of publications, including *Room Magazine, The Christian Science Monitor, StepAway, Culinate, 3 Elements Review,* and *Switched-On Guggenheim.* She divides her time between the Eastern Townships of Quebec and Connecticut, where she teaches foreign languages. She travels widely, mostly on foot.

Paul Collins lives in Bristol, United Kingdom. After studying chemistry and oceanography, he has spent nearly 20 years as an environmental lawyer. Paul tries to enjoy running and loves gardening.

M.E. Cooper is an undergraduate in English (Creative Writing) and is pursuing a minor in Environmental Science at a local university in Fort Wayne, Indiana. She juggles two part-time jobs: one at a specialized grocery store, the other at LUSH Cosmetics. She shares a house with two of her best friends and a three-legged feline named Kit-Cat. She has also helped conservation efforts for Leatherback sea turtles in Costa Rica. She's had poems and fiction published in the scholarly magazine *The Sullivan* and plans to write herself into a cozy author life.

Conor Corderoy was born in England in 1957. He spent his childhood on Formentera, the smallest of the Balearic Islands. He spent his teens in Cordoba, southern Spain, where he got his first job at age sixteen, breaking in wild horses. He now divides his time between England and Spain. He is an Incorporated Linguist, a barrister, a psychologist and a Master Practitioner of NLP. He has published three novels.

Charlene D'Avanzo is an award-winning environmental educator and marine ecologist who taught at Hampshire College in Amherst, Massachusetts for 35 years. She won the 2015 Mystery Writers of America McCloy prize for new writers. The first book in her *Oceanography Mystery* series, *Cold Blood, Hot Sea*, will be published by Torrey House Press in May 2016. An avid seakayaker, she lives in Yarmouth, Maine.

Michael Donoghue mostly lives in his head, but resides in Vancouver, Canada. His stories have appeared in various anthologies, literary journals, and sci-fi magazines. Michael works in healthcare, where he spends much of his time preoccupied with hand-washing. He can be found on twitter @mpdonoghue.

JoeAnn Hart is the author of the eco-novel *Float*, a dark satire that combines conceptual art, marital woes, and the fishing industry with plastics in the ocean. *Float* was published in 2013 by Ashland Creek, an environmentally aware press in Oregon. Hart lives in Gloucester, Massachusetts, America's oldest seaport, where fishing regulations, the health of the ocean, and the natural beauty of the world are daily topics of conversation. She is also the author of the novel *Addled* (Little, Brown 2007), a social satire that intertwines animal rights with the politics of food. Her essays, articles, and short fiction have appeared in a wide variety of literary journals and national publications, and she is a regular contributor to the *Boston Globe Magazine*. Her work has won a number of awards, including the PEN New England Discovery Award in Fiction.

Janis Hindman is a writer and a teacher of French and English. She has also worked in environmental education. She has lived on three continents and feels that's quite sufficient, although should the opportunity to live in Antarctica arise, she'd give it a thorough pondering. Janis usually writes about Huguenots and Celts, with a sprinkling of Valkyries—quite a heavy sprinkling—so speculative fiction is a glorious meander along a slightly different creative pathway.

Clara Hume's novel *Back to the Garden* was published in the autumn of 2013 and later was discussed at *Dissent Magazine* as part of an emerging genre of climate change novels. She also has a short story series, *Lost*

Ages, which reconciles mythological stories with our modern world. Clara writes under a pen name. Her favorite past-times are hanging out with friends and family in the great outdoors, drinking red wine under the stars, and running.

Stephan Malone works at a local ICU in Cape Coral, Florida. His hobbies include 15-30 mile bicycle rides, night/pre-dawn rides in particular, computer repair, and writing. He is the author of *Polar City Dreaming* (2012, Sunbury Press, futurist eco-non-fiction) and *Lulu and the Manatee* (2014, KDP Publishing, children's story, fiction). He was also awarded "honorable mention" (top ten stories out of over a thousand entries) for a Halo science fiction short story contest back in 2006. His solarpunk story "Windrunner" was published in *The J.J. Outré Review* in 2015.

Rachel May coordinates sustainability education at Syracuse University, running faculty development projects and workshops for students on a wide range of topics. Recently she has been teaching a zine-making class called Climatopia, in which students develop imaginary scenarios for real progress on climate change. This story grew out of that project. Rachel is a grateful member of the Downtown Writers Center at the Syracuse YMCA and of the Armory Square Playhouse, which produced a reading of her first full-length play last year.

JL Morin: Novelist and rooftop farmer, JL wrote her Japan novel *Sazzae* as her thesis at Harvard. It was a Gold medalist in the eLit Book Awards and a Living Now Book Award winner. She is the author of USA Best Book Awards finalist *Travelling Light* and Occupy's first bestselling novel *Trading Dreams*. Her novel *Nature's Confession* is a LitPick 5-Star Review Award winner. Adjunct faculty at Boston University, JL Morin writes for the *Huffington Post* and *Library Journal*, and has published in *The Harvard Advocate, Harvard Yisei, Detroit News, Agence France-Presse, Cyprus Weekly, European Daily, Livonia Observer Eccentric Newspapers, Harvard Crimson*, and more.

Christopher Rutenber is a freelance writer living in rural Michigan. When not writing, he spends his time birding and exploring the nearby trails. Twitter: @CJRTimeTraveler

Robert Sassor combines his twin passions for sustainability and creative writing as a senior director at Metropolitan Group, a social change agency headquartered in Portland, Oregon. Following his years as an English major at Willamette University, Rob conducted research and ghostwrote about a range of social and environmental issues in Washington, D.C., contributing to more than 150 works and two books. Rob's most affecting lessons about conservation occurred in western Tanzania, where he served as the Conservation Action Plan Coordinator for the Jane Goodall Institute. In this role, Rob led a team of eight to develop the conservation plan for the greater Gombe ecosystem and its famous chimpanzees. More recently, Rob assessed the efficacy of negative versus positive messages in communicating and fundraising for nature conservation, which served as the research component for a Masters in Conservation Leadership at the University of Cambridge.

Anneliese Schutlz: A 2014 Pushcart Prize nominee and former Bread Loaf Scholar, Anneliese has an MFA in Creative Writing from UBC. Winner of the 2013 Meringoff Fiction Award and the *Enizagam* Literary Award in Fiction, she has been published in *Enizagam*, the *Toronto Star* and *Literary Imagination*, and recognized by *New York Stories, Glimmer Train, Ruminate, Nowhere*, and the Surrey International Writers' Conference. The first title in her YA climate fiction series, *Distant Dream*, reached the second round in the 2012 Amazon Breakthrough YA Novel Awards, won the 2013 Good Read Novel Competition at A Woman's Write, and is currently under consideration by several agents. Twitter: @anneliesenow

Stephen Siperstein is a poet, cultural scholar, and environmental educator. He is currently a PhD candidate in the Department of English at the University of Oregon and is completing his dissertation on climate change narratives and U.S. environmental literature. He is the editor of *Teaching Climate Change in the Environmental Humanities* (forthcoming from Routledge), with Shane Hall and Stephanie LeMenager, and he also directs the Climate Stories Project, an online forum for individuals and communities to share their everyday personal stories about climate change (http://www.climatestoriesproject.org/). His poetry has appeared most recently in *saltfront*, *Poecology*, and *ISLE*, among other publications. Follow him on Twitter @ssiperstein.

Craig Spence is Executive Director with the Federation of BC Writers. Writing and storytelling in one form or another is his passion. He has pursued his vocation as a novelist, journalist, and communications specialist through various phases of his life. He is now giving himself more time to be a personal narrator (or memoirist) and creative writer.

Carolyn Welch, a native Californian, has written over a decade of poetry that explores the Californian surf, mountains, desert, and people. A technical writer, Carolyn dabbles on the side with creativity that needs an outlet, inspired by her observations of nature. Carolyn's poems are unique, musical, and refreshing, from her anatomizing the city of Los Angeles to revitalizing the San Francisco Renaissance and beat poets. Her poem "Sugar Shack" was previously posted at *Jack Magazine*. Moon Willow Press published her recent collection *California Poems*.

Keith Wilkinson is an educator, editor, and poet and has published work in a number of literary journals and chapbooks and on his blog. *The Sea Wall at Vancuuver Shoal* is the first in a series of stories set in a post-apocalyptic world resulting from dramatic climate change. "Choosing a post-apocalyptic setting", Keith says, "allows me to bypass the depressing and psychologically debilitating reality of our current 21st century climate circumstances and focus instead on hopeful possibilities that could emerge in a future after what eco-spiritualist Joanna Macy has termed "The Great Turning," a time when people continue their struggles toward ethical and personal fulfillment in a radically different physical and social environment." The series of stories begins 1,000 years in the future with the youthful Shmuul and Tanka on the shoals of *Old Vancuuver*, near *Antrim Sangha* (not far from Burnaby's Central Park), and the ruins of the *Shangri La Glittercast*, where the downtown of *Old Vancuuver* used to be.